RESET
TO
NORMAL?

A River Bend Chronicles' Book

Renee Kumor

ABSOLUTELY AMAZING eBOOKS

Habent Sua Fata Libelli

ABSOLUTELY AMAZING eBOOKS

Manhanset House
Shelter Island Hts., New York 11965-0342

bricktower@aol.com
absolutelyamazingebooks.com

Library of Congress Cataloging-in-Publication Data
Kumor, Renee
Reset to Normal?, a river bend chronicles' book
p. cm.

1. FICTION / Romance / Suspense. 2. FICTION / Thrillers / Crime. 3.
FICTION / Mystery & Detective / Private Investigators.
Fiction, I. Title.
ISBN: 978-1-955036-80-1 Trade Paper

January 2025

RESET
TO
NORMAL?

Number 22 in the

River Bend Chronicles' Series

Renee Kumor

We survived a pandemic,
a little crazier,
but with a renewed appreciation of
family and friends.

Books in the *River Bend Chronicles'* Series

PROLOGUE
Fifteen years ago

Jonathan Quinton Templeton watched the young woman moving into the house next door. That's what he loved about living off campus. This student neighborhood of marginal houses offered a great way to meet all sorts of real students. He smirked to himself, this was probably not marginal housing to a lot of other students, he was just wealthier than most. He had been raised with higher standards and higher levels of expendable cash. Life's good, he thought, and went back to watching the young woman struggle with her belongings.

"You need some help?" he finally called from his front porch.

"Yeah, if you think you can get off your fat ass," she called in reply. He laughed and loped down to the curb to help.

When they had everything in her house, Quinn, as he was known to his friends, said, "You owe me a beer." The college version of tall, dark and handsome grinned at the scrawny, disheveled co-ed.

"I'm not old enough to buy beer." Attitude!

"What are you?" he sneered, "a freshman?"

"I'm a sophomore," she replied, matching his attitude. "I couldn't live in off-campus housing as a freshman."

He looked her over—small tits, not much meat on her bones, maybe five- three, mousy brown hair. "Come on over," he tilted his head toward his porch, "I got the beer. You drink don't you?"

"Yeah, I just can't buy." She grinned at him.

He grinned back. "Come on, Mouse, let's get you your first beer of your sophomore year." Turning he hopped up the porch stairs.

"My name's not Mouse." She hopped behind him, plopping on the disreputable glider.

1

"It is now." Two beers, open and cold.

And that's how it began. Because of their schedules and their different social goals, as in he was always looking for sex and she wasn't his type, they usually met on Thursday afternoons sitting on the porch glider to talk about life, share a beer and laugh at the antics of all the other students on the street.

"You date anyone, Mouse?" he asked one afternoon.

"I think it's about time I start looking," she replied, heaving a sigh.

"Looking for what?"

"A serious relationship."

Quinn laughed and gulped his beer. "A serious relationship? This is college. You should just be trying guys out. Here." He threw out his arms in a welcoming manner. "I volunteer. We can fool around and you can see if I'm your type. We can have some fun. No attachments."

She looked at him with a steady gaze. "I think I want more than a meaningless fling."

He laughed again. "You're a virgin! No wonder you sound so idealistic." He sprawled carelessly across the glider, dropping his head onto her shoulder. "I can tell you sex isn't magic. It's a real physical kind of high, but not magic." She continued to stare at him. "So, you're going to tell me you're looking for love." He smirked again.

"Yes." She sounded so positive.

"How do you plan on finding love?"

"First, I'll check you off my list." She was laughing at him!

For a moment he had been concerned that he had hurt her feelings, but there she was—Mouse with her attitude. He asked, "If not me, I have to say your standards are slipping. I'm the best specimen you know." He was. He was the over-the-top example of rich and handsome.

"That's my point," she replied, "I'm enlarging my search area and looking for some better specimen." Zing! She always had an answer.

They sat drinking their beers watching students return from classes as the warm autumn afternoon suggested it would be a great Halloween evening. "How do you plan on enlarging this pool?" Quinn asked. "Are you sending out applications, requests for proposals?"

She studied her beer bottle, then replied, "I thought I'd draw up some standards and start inviting candidates to audition."

"Audition? You crack me up, Mouse." He tousled her hair. "You want to get a practice kiss first, maybe see how they dance, or are you going serious and want to see their GPA?" He drank more beer. "And what are you offering, an opportunity for a date or an opportunity to get laid?" He laughed and dropped his head on her shoulder.

"All of that," she said with a serious nod. "Talking to you is helping me refine my standards and design my audition." She pushed his head off her shoulder and sat up straight on the glider. "I want someone with less experience than you, less attitude."

He frowned at her. "I'm a great guy. What's wrong with me?"

"Nothing. You're a great friend. I think I've told you more of my thoughts than I've ever told anyone. But you're not my choice for a serious relationship." She finished her beer.

Quinn didn't know how he felt about this conversation. He didn't want to take Mouse to bed, but he sort of felt jealous that she was looking for someone to do just that, at least he thought that's what she was looking for. He thought he better get the correct information. "So you want to find some guy who isn't as cool and experienced as me to have sex with? It seems to me you should go for the best." He threw his arms out to offer himself.

She looked him over with that stare that made him want to be his best. Where did that come from? He moved to the far end of the glider, puzzled by his thoughts, and waited for her to answer.

"Here's what I want," she began, "I want someone smart and kind and sweet but a lot less experienced than you." His face fell and she rushed on, "I think you're sweet and kind and smart, but old."

"Old?"

"You know what I mean. You're a senior and a good friend. But I'm younger and naïve and shy –

"No, you're not. You're glib and sarcastic and a smart ass."

"And I want someone who balances me, you know, kind and sweet." She stood because it was time to get back to her house for dinner. "Do you want to help review the applications and do the preliminary interviews?"

"No, thanks, I don't think I want to see some poor schmuck lose his freedom."

That was the last conversation they would have until spring. The weather turned ugly and winter moved onto campus. Mouse seemed to be in a rush with classes and Quinn was making his dash to the graduation finish line.

* * *

It was officially Spring on campus because the club soccer games were on everyone's schedule. Quinn's team, better known as the pre-law team, was scrambling to hold on to its one goal lead against some engineers' team. There were several engineering disciplines but, unless they played each other, the engineering team on the field was just "those damn engineers."

And there was one damn engineer giving Quinn a fit this afternoon. He was a tall, skinny kid with legs that annoyed Quinn at every turn. He dribbled well, and was always one step ahead, the ball in his control.

They were moving down the field. That skinny engineer, with his long legs and mop of unruly brown curls, was about to score, but he tripped, tumbling to the ground taking Quinn with him. They sprawled, Quinn on top. And the engineer was clueless. For all his intense playing, the man had turned into a rag doll. Quinn followed his glassy-eyed, almost lovelorn, stare across the field. And there she was – Mouse! Quinn laughed out loud as he remembered their conversation last fall. Good god, he thought, this must be someone on her audition list. He struggled to his feet and held out a hand to the engineer. The young man got to his feet, shaking those curls from his eyes, and grasped Quinn's arm.

"I think I hurt my ankle."

"Come on, pal, I'll get you settled." Quinn put an arm around the player's waist and helped him to the bench. He left the young man in the care of the team's medic, probably an engineer with no athletic ability, and ambled over to speak with Mouse.

"That's him, isn't it?" Quinn grinned at the young woman. She tried to look puzzled, but he continued, "He won the audition, didn't he?"

She turned her back on him and concentrated on the field.

"Aw, Mouse, you can tell me. We're friends, remember? Have you two done it yet?"

4

She scowled at him.

"What? He turned you down?" Quinn was dancing around, trying to stay in her face. Her cheeks turned red. "Did you or didn't you?" He was delighted. "You know you ruined his game. He fell all over himself when you came by to watch. You must have made an impression." She swatted at him and he fell on the ground laughing. She stalked off to see to the care of her engineer.

Later that afternoon, Quinn called to her from the porch as she started up the walk to her house. "Come over for a beer, Mouse. We have to catch up on things."

She hung her head and gave his request some thought, finally turning in his direction. "Don't ask me about sex," she said as she took the beer and plopped on the glider beside him.

"That's my first question," he replied, "but I've got plenty of others. Why don't you just start at the beginning?" He settled back on the glider to listen. Mouse sat beside him and rested her head on his shoulder.

"He won the audition," she sighed.

"And you don't know if he feels the same?"

She nodded.

"Mouse, that guy's in love. You walked to the field and he turned into jelly. He was this close to scoring a goal." Quinn held his thumb and index finger up for her to see that they were almost touching.

"But, he doesn't say anything." She looked at Quinn with sad, hopeful eyes.

"He's the guy, isn't he?"

She nodded.

"Are you having sex?"

"No. He hasn't said anything about it and I don't want to have sex just to have sex and still have to find someone." She sniffed and swiped at some tears.

He put an arm around her. "Want my help?"

She laughed through her tears. "What can you do?"

"I can have a fatherly talk with him about a woman's needs and how satisfying you should be his only aim in life."

She laughed again, this time with merriment. "Getting out of school and getting a job is his only aim in life. He's on some scholarship and his family struggles to make up the difference. He even works at some campus job – maintenance, I think."

"Give him a break, Mouse. He can't do all those things and focus on you, but I can tell you, if he had the time, he would have you in bed in a second. He's in love – but I guess he's got too many demands. When do you see him again?"

"We have a date to study tonight and we're going to a movie on Sunday night."

"What movie?"

"Whatever's playing at the student center."

Quinn's stomach clenched. He had to tell her the truth. "He doesn't have any money for anything else, Mouse. I meet those guys all the time. They have no money and most choose not to date. At least your guy's making an effort."

"Should I pay for a date?" She didn't have much money either.

"It'll work out, you'll see." He handed her another beer.

* * *

Several days later, Quinn was on the soccer field again. Mouse's engineer was on the sidelines. Quinn trotted over and asked, "How's the ankle?"

The tall, skinny engineer studied him a moment. "You're the guy I took out," he grinned.

"I thought I took you out." Quinn revised the replay.

The young man gave him a shy grin. "I lost my concentration."

"A girl?"

"Didn't you see her? She's beautiful. I thought I saw you talking to her, you know, Sara."

Sara? Quinn had to think quickly. Did he know Mouse's real name? Could it be Sara? "You mean that little, skinny kid with the long hair?"

The engineer turned red and nodded.

"Having a girl and studying is a tough combination," observed Quinn with a knowing nod.

"Yeah." It was a long thoughtful sound.

The sound told Quinn that the engineer was struggling with the combination. "Maybe I can help."

6

"You?" the young man laughed. "I don't have your money and stuff, you know, experience and things, to get me anywhere."

"What do you mean, money and stuff?"

"You're a legend around here, man. Money, women, cars, clothes." He said it all without a trace of envy.

Quinn held out his hand. "I'm Quinn Templeton."

"I know. I'm Josh Margolin." They shook hands.

"I might have cars and money," said Quinn as he let go of Josh's hand, "but you got a girl who cares about you – not your cars and money."

"That's good because I don't have either." Josh stopped and thought a moment. "She cares?"

Quinn smacked him on the back of the head. "It *is* true what they say about you engineers."

"What?" Josh rubbed the back of his head.

"That you guys are clueless about women."

"That's true." Josh nodded his head sadly.

"Don't you kiss her? Hold her hand?"

"I guess."

"What do you mean, guess? Don't you know how to kiss?" Quinn was aghast.

"I kiss her good-night and maybe sort of snuggle with her before I leave her."

Quinn smacked his own forehead. "You need help. Don't you wrap her up in your arms and just, you know, nibble her ear, kind of use your tongue to trace her lobe, or, here's one they really like, take a finger and put some of her hair behind her ear so you can kiss her throat."

"Where did you learn all this stuff, man?" groaned Josh, "I barely know how to kiss and I can't figure out how to put my tongue anywhere."

"What are you? A freshman?"

"I'm a junior," came the huffy reply.

Quinn took Josh by the arm. "Come with me," he looked back at the soccer field, "they don't need us."

"Where are we going?"

"To begin your dating lessons."

"She's not that kind of girl," argued Josh.

Quinn scowled at him. "I'm not going to teach you how to have sex," he explained, "I'm going to help you learn how to at least let her know you're warm-blooded."

Josh scowled right back.

* * *

Quinn sat on his porch and watched street life. He noticed Josh as he rounded the corner and trotted to Mouse's place. Quinn drew back into his thoughts – two weeks to graduation and then another two weeks to his wedding. He was kicking himself. He knew he always used condoms – how did she get pregnant? And his father was pissed, but Madeline, his intended, had made a good impression. Good old Pops was willing to continue his support through law school and see that Madeline got good pre-natal care. Quinn was suspicious that she had orchestrated this event. Sometimes he was tempted to ask for paternity testing, but she was beautiful and sexy and seemed ready to live life as the wife of a very rich law student.

Dad had bought them a small house in Chapel Hill, in a great neighborhood. Madeline had been thrilled to take part in redecorating with Dad's staff. They were even members of the country club now. Law school wasn't going to be an economic struggle. And he'd have live-in sex. The baby would be a challenge, but that would be Madeline's responsibility. She had to work for all the perks she would be getting by becoming a Templeton. He blew out his breath. This wasn't what he had planned. But good old Pops had taken over and smoothed things out.

He came back to the present as he watched Mouse and Josh leave the house. She looked over and he waved. She said something to Josh and they both walked toward the porch. "I want you to meet my friend," she announced as they bounced up the stairs. "Quinn Templeton, this is Josh Margolin." The two men shook hands, both making certain Mouse had no idea that they had met before.

"I've run into you on the soccer field," said Quinn.

Josh gave him a slow, shy grin. "Sara told me that you were her neighbor. She says you're OK."

"I'm a great guy," boasted Quinn. He gave Josh a hard stare and the young man gently placed an arm around Sara's shoulders. She blushed at the gesture and moved into him, resting her head on his chest. Quinn grinned.

"You guys have a date?" he inquired. "Shouldn't you be studying for finals?" Even to himself he sounded like a nagging parent.

"We're taking a study break," said Josh, his arm tightening around Sara. She gave Quinn a shy, happy smile.

"You kids go along then." Quinn gave his best imitation of a doting uncle. "I've got my own tests to study for." Josh and Mouse waved good-by and ran down the stairs, Josh's arm never letting go of her.

Quinn returned to the glider. Young love. He blew out his breath. He'd been having sex with willing women since he was fifteen. Young love wasn't in his history or as far as he could see, in his future. What was in his future was a quick marriage, law school and a guaranteed job in the family firm after he passed the bar. He hoped life with a baby and Madeline would at least be enjoyable—or something that didn't intrude on his pleasure. Maybe he should be grateful for his life. If he were someone else, the future might be a challenge. But he was Quinn Templeton, rich, handsome and . . . soon to be married and a dad.

CHAPTER ONE

"Stop sniffling," Lynn Powers demanded of her sister-in-law, Piper Zubov. "He's old enough." Piper's son Doyle Hanby and Lori Santiago had married a few days ago. After courtship through a pandemic lockdown, they had graduated from college and married.

"That's not why she's weepy," Will Zubov teased his wife. "She thinks she's too young to be a grandmother."

"She's pregnant?" gasped Lynn.

Piper smacked her best friend on the arm. "My son wouldn't get a girl pregnant."

"At least not before he married her," laughed Will, "but the boy was real eager to get on with married life. I was surprised they stayed for the reception." He had great affection for all his stepsons, three boys who were a product of Piper's first marriage.

Piper smacked him. "Both of you stop. He's my son and he's perfect."

"And he and his new wife got the Hilton Head house while we have to go to some mosquito infested cabin on the Outer Banks." Dusty Reid, Lynn's husband, threw the last of the luggage into the rented van. Two eager dogs jumped in behind and settled for the ride to the North Carolina coast.

The newlyweds, Doyle and Lori, were on their honeymoon in Hilton Head. Lynn's neighbor, Emily Jacobs, had given them time at her home in Hilton Head as a wedding gift. Dusty had hoped to claim some time at the resort area for himself. But the kids had been delighted to accept the offer. So it was the Outer Banks as the getaway everyone needed to recover from the weeks leading up to the wedding.

Lynn's son, Jason and Piper's other two sons had already taken off in Will's double cab pickup truck carrying all the camping gear. The rental van had the dogs, parents and all the food. Everyone thought this vacation was just right. The world was coming out of the pandemic, vaccines were hitting arms, masks were no longer required except in hospitals. Bars and restaurants were ramping up for a return to normal. Ah, yes, the world had survived.

Lynn was anticipating the summer of returning to normal. "Sara Margolin is taking her kids to Disneyworld. She's working and the kids can enjoy the park. Nathan invited Sean and Lee to spend some time at his family's lake house."

Dusty laughed. "I'm surprised Sara left town with Janet ready to drop that baby." Sara and Janet were partners in an IT consulting firm with clients throughout the nation, including some very top-secret contracts with the US military. Sara was a widow and Janet, her cousin, had married Lynn's brother-in-law Tim Powers several years ago.

"Sara told me Janet wants her back in town in two weeks because a third child doesn't always wait for its due date." Lynn settled into her seat behind Dusty. "I think Sara was looking forward to some time alone with her kids. They all seem to have adjusted to life since they returned to River Bend. But Sara confided that her kids needed time with just her for a few days."

"Why?"

Lynn shrugged. "She seemed to think that after their father's death and then lockdown, they needed to enjoy normal fun."

"I hope they find it," said Dusty as he raced the van out of the neighborhood aiming for the interstate. "I don't think normal is going to be what we remember it was."

"That's ominous," groused Will. "What will it be?"

"I don't know," said the detective, "but I think we all got crazier and forgot what normal is."

* * *

CJ Kirtley, a wealthy, entitled man-boy, slouched on the sectional sofa in Madeline Templeton's condo. He and Madeline had joined forced years ago as the disaffected in-laws of the Templeton heirs. Madeline had divorced Quinn Templeton after presenting him with a son. She was semi-smug about her alimony settlement negotiated with David Templeton, head of the family and controller of its wealth. CJ, married to the only Templeton daughter, had never joined his sperm with a Templeton ovum and was uncertain about his long-term access to Templeton wealth.

"Quinn took your son to Disneyworld," he announced as Madeline floated into the living room, placed a tray with wine and nibbles on the coffee table, and leaned on the arm of a reading chair.

CJ snorted silently because he was certain Madeline never read anything but fashion magazines, certainly not classic novels or thoughtful non-fiction. But she was beautiful and devoted to spending all the Templeton divorce settlement money in maintaining her beauty and designer wardrobe. What a useless human being, he thought. But she had been lucky enough to donate her DNA to a child destined to be the only Templeton heir. CJ and his wife Margaret Kirtley nee Templeton hadn't scored any such prize. Maybe, if Margaret had been a little more fruitful or he had been a little more faithful something might have happened. Alas, he sighed dramatically to himself.

Madeline smirked, "Two unsupervised boys in a playground." She eased into the reading chair. "Quinn will never grow up. I can't wait for the day Colt takes over from his grandfather. My son is very smart. He'll be generous to his loving mama."

CJ smirked back. "You just better keep him in the dark about his mommy and all her vices."

She preened. "I'm always sweet to him. He's handsome and charming. Once he was born I knew I was set. His grandfather is willing to keep paying me lots of money to let Quinn be the responsible parent." She laughed. "I just spend the money. And Quinn tries to be responsible."

CJ got up and poured them both wine. "While Quinn's gone, I'll be moving more funds to those accounts. We'll close out the foundation grant cycle for the next quarter and by the end of summer I'll move more of our funds offshore." CJ was the executive director of the Lela Templeton Foundation.

Madeline spooned a little dab of caviar on a cracker and sniffed it. "I hate this shit but I like to spend money on it because I can." She ate the cracker, sipped her wine and asked in her sexy, promising voice, "Is this the official quarterly meeting of our little scam?"

"It's not little. We've got over ten million in those accounts." He took a cracker. "But things have gotten more interesting in the other accounts." Years ago CJ had been invited into a secret group of investors who were interested in hiding embezzled funds or laundering illegal funds. His position with the Templeton Foundation allowed him to move their funds secretly among all the financial transactions within the foundation. Through an array of fake nonprofits the scheme had worked very well for over a decade. "One of the members in the other partnership, Kip Mahaffey, has pulled out his share of cash recently."

"Why?"

"The fool got himself into trouble with the FBI." He shrugged. "He was running a drug distribution operation and robbing from client accounts in his law firm."

"A busy boy!" She preened. "Did I ever meet him?"

CJ slouched back on the couch. "I don't think so. He lives in River Bend, a town somewhere in the western part of the state. And you don't want to meet him now with all his legal problems." CJ nodded knowingly. "He'll be doing time for his crimes."

The condo was silent as the two scheming partners spent another boring afternoon together. Madeline was, as always, thinking of herself while CJ thought of all the scams and secrets he managed. His funds shared with Madeline, taken from the Templeton coffers, were only a part of his offshore wealth.

There were many millions more to think about. Most recently, Kip Mahaffey had effectively withdrawn all his funds from the loose financial shelter CJ's other partners had created before dying. CJ had helped orchestrate an investment management group that could accept offshore funds and magically bring those funds back home through a small internet bank that surprisingly had attracted some unrelated customers. The bank was happy to serve those legitimate clients as validation of its integrity. The financial structure was a success as proved by Kip Mahaffey's withdrawals. CJ had looked forward to using the financial pathway to launder other funds. Getting control of those funds proved challenging.

The deaths of the partners, Rothman and Garson, had left several millions in accounts offshore, money that should have been available for CJ to claim without having to share with anyone. But someone had taken a chunk of Rothman's personal account after his death. The action caused CJ to suspect that Rothman had a silent partner who might object to CJ claiming the funds. He guessed Rothman hadn't trusted the others. Who did, he smirked to himself?

CJ's hacker, Theo, hadn't found the thief yet and had recommended that they refrain from relieving those accounts of all the dead men's funds until they established that there were no other prior claims. Rothman and Garson had had a few frightening friends. After all, an airplane doesn't usually blow up on take-off as Garson's had. Caution sounded like a good idea.

On a positive note, Mahaffey's withdrawals had worked seamlessly using fake nonprofits and dubious wealth management and internet-based banking creations as receivers and distributors of online funds. When CJ finally found and reclaimed Rothman's missing funds, he was confident all the money, including the funds he planned to steal from Madeline, would move as seamlessly as the Mahaffey money had for easy accessibility.

"I have two partnership questions," Madeline said raising one finger, suggesting her mind might be on the money, too. "How long until we can claim it?" And the second finger. "How long will you stay with Margaret?"

He thought a moment. His concern was how he could claim all the money from all accounts yet disappear leaving Madeline high and dry. "I can't divorce Margaret. Her father will make certain I get nothing. Staying with her allows me to keep skimming grant funds and using her credit cards." Sip of wine and he refilled the glasses. "We can spend it any time. It will be easier to spend funds out of the country than trying to bring funds back in." He gave her a speculative look. "It would be great if you could get David to give you one big settlement."

"I've tried. He wouldn't go for it. I get my annual money until Colt turns eighteen then a smaller sum as alimony unless and until I remarry." She snorted a not-a-chance sound. "I can usually get David to give me extra if I threaten to skip town with Colt." She scowled. "I don't want to have to drag him with me but David always gives me extra when I whine." She grinned, "A threat to take him to Europe might get me more." She seemed to argue with herself, "But I want to stay close or David might not believe my threats and question my motherly concerns." Her face reflected her mental process of weighing all the pros

14

and cons of her various manipulative scenarios until she seemed to reach a conclusion and frowned at CJ.

He agreed with the scowl on her face. He summed up the discussion. "I guess we're not going anywhere for now."

* * *

For three years Darwin Masterson, IT maven in his family, had watched those offshore accounts of that dead guy, Rothman. The man had paid Yetta Masterson a monthly stipend to keep a safe house available in River Bend. When the fellow died, Darwin, with Granny Masterson's encouragement, had gained access to the account and had increased Yetta's monthly allotment. But Yetta had been murdered a few months later and Rothman's money was just sitting there. Darwin and Granny, closing out Yetta's simple estate, had decided to forego Yetta's monthly stipend and instead claim a chunk of Rothman's funds and place that amount in their own offshore account, deciding to keep it all for a rainy day. As Darwin had explained to Granny, "If someone knows about these accounts, we have to get in and out quickly so they can't find our signature." Granny had nodded as though she understood. After all she and Darwin had established a five-million-dollar offshore account.

Then came the rainy day—the pandemic. Darwin was a partner along with his cousin, Zeke Masterson, in a brewery. River Dog Brewery had needed help to survive during lockdown and Granny had decided to use the rainy-day money to keep the brewery afloat through those months. It had worked, but the emergency funds had a dent. She now urged, "You go back to that there place and get the rest of the dead man's money. You boys might need it again."

Darwin had tried to argue. "Granny, it's too dangerous. Someone can follow me out. Technology has gotten smarter since the first time we took the money." But she wanted the backup funds available for her grandsons' business. Darwin got into Rothman's old account, found only two million remaining in one account, and panicked. Someone had been there since his last visit. There had been two accounts; the other account was empty. He took the remaining two million, washed it through as many loops and alleys as he could manage, always watching his back. Darwin was confident that the final withdrawal of funds had not raised interest from anyone in his transaction. He had been as careful as he knew how. As a result the brewery came out of lockdown in good financial shape and the emergency cushion had been replenished.

* * *

Years ago, the same night of Darwin's original withdrawal another party had checked on the offshore accounts. He had been partners long ago with Stanwood Garson and Rupert Rothman. They had recruited others over the years but Walter Varney, a middle-aged man with gray hair, nondescript looks and an ingrained social country club polish, had been an original silent partner. As Garson had always said he looked too honest to be a politician and too wholesome to be a crook. The later recruits to the scam didn't know he existed. They would also not be familiar with the dead partners' accounts. So Varney was surprised when shortly after Rothman's death someone made a raid on one of the accounts. The thief only took about five million. Who cares, he had thought, the rest of the accounts held six times as much. After the small-time thief had worked diligently to move his funds and hide his tracks, Varney took over the accounts, leaving a tempting sum in the pilfered account and emptying the rest of the accounts. He laughed to himself as he went offline. Someone would be surprised, someday.

It had been almost a year since Varney had checked those accounts. He had left a little in one of them to see who took the cheese. He liked these cat and mouse games. He had been surprised at himself years ago to find he had an aptitude for computers. Hunting and scamming through the internet had become a hobby. Sneaking through the cyber labyrinth tonight, checking his old partners' accounts, he chuckled, "Damn!"

"Yeah, Boss?" Big Fish, a man Varney didn't really trust but tolerated as an emissary of the crime organization, was roused from some app on his phone.

"Nothing, Fish," replied the Boss. Walter Varney went on alert. Fish and, by extension, the crime bosses, didn't know about the offshore accounts from Varney's old partnership. He gave a sigh of fake frustration, "Sometimes I can't figure out this computer shit."

"You want me to get our techie?"

16

"Nah," said the Boss, "I've done enough tonight." Closing his laptop he thought about the mouse who had taken his cheese. Mahaffey had taken only his own funds, thought Varney. He was eliminated as a suspect. There was that Kirtley fellow, not too bright, but he had teamed up with a hacker. Varney knew they were afraid to move on the accounts fearing Rothman's friends. So who was this new hacker? Whoever he was, he was a real clever fellow, thought Varney, he's welcome to the cheese.

CHAPTER TWO

"Mouse?"

The woman turned to discover a tall, dark, handsome man, even handsomer than he had been in their college days, waving at her. "Quinn?" She squealed and rushed into his arms. After a long hug, he pushed her out to arms' length and took an inventory of his old friend. No make-up, hair in a serviceable ponytail, still skinny.

"Mom?" Three skinny youngsters stood behind her. Quinn let her go and looked over the children.

"I know who *they* call Dad," he said as he studied the two long legged, thin boys and one little girl, tiny like Mouse, but with Josh's mop of curls. The kids' faces fell. He noted a deep sadness in their eyes.

Mouse rushed into the conversation. "We lost Josh a few years ago. He had an accident on an oil rig in the gulf." The light left her eyes.

"I'm sorry, Mouse." He turned to the children showing them his sincere concern and compassion. "I'm sorry that you lost your father. He was a friend of mine in college. Do you play soccer like he did? We used to play in the campus league."

"He always played soccer with us," lisped the little girl. One of the boys put an arm around her, much like Quinn remembered Josh protecting Mouse all those years ago.

He took Mouse's hands silently expressing his sympathy. Finally he asked, "What are you doing here?"

She grinned at him. "We're in Disneyworld. What do you think we're doing?"

"Dad?"

They all turned to look at a gangly fourteen-year-old boy, about two inches taller than Mouse, who looked just like his father. Quinn grinned back at Mouse. "I guess you're doing the same thing we are. I want you to meet my son, Colt."

"That's a horse," said the little girl.

"It's a name, too," said one of her brothers. "There's a guy in our class with the same name."

"Yeah," said the other brother, "but he's a jerk."

"Are you a jerk?" asked the little girl.

Quinn held his breath. Lately Colt had been showing a lot of adolescent attitude. "Not today," said Colt as he held out his hand to the other youngsters. One of the boys took it.

"I'm Rob, I'm named after my grandfather—Carter Robert Macauley."

"And I'm Paul." The other boy held out his hand. "I'm named after our other grandfather—Alan Paul Margolin."

"Are you twins?" asked Colt. The boys nodded.

"And I'm Matilda. I'm named after a kangaroo." She held out her hand. Colt took it and soon found himself glued to her sticky fingers. Matilda smiled at him, happy to be holding his hand.

"Matilda was born in Australia," supplied Mouse. "We lived there for a few years with Josh's job. We call her Tilda."

"Or pest," said Rob, or was it Paul?

"You've all met my son, Colt. My name is Quinn." He shook hands with the twins but avoided Tilda's hand still glued to Colt's. "And this is Mouse," he told his son, "We were friends in college."

"Mouse?" Tilda, as usual had something to say. "She's Mom."

"No one's called me Mouse since you graduated." Mouse smiled at her old friend and gave him a quick hug.

"Now that we know each other," said Quinn, "maybe we can enjoy the park together. Colt and I are here on our own." The crowd moved around them and they were pushed to the side of the walkway.

"The boys want to go to Mission: Space but I don't think Tilda should go and I'm in a fix about pleasing everyone," confessed Mouse as she took a nose count, making certain all three of her children had arrived at the edge of the pavement.

"It's settled," said Quinn, "Colt and I will take the guys and you gals can go shopping or something." Colt rolled his eyes at his father and tried to come unglued from the little girl.

"Yes!" sang the twins.

Mouse saw Colt trying to free himself from Tilda. "Let me help," she said as she took a wet-wipe from her enormous mom bag and pulled the two hands apart. She handed the wipe to Colt and took Tilda toward a water fountain. Everyone followed the gals.

"Can we, Mom?" The twins were ready to jump in line for the ride.

"I don't think we should interrupt Colt's time with his dad," she replied.

Colt got a look from his father and said, "I don't mind. Dad's kind of boring."

Quinn hung his head. The boy gives with one hand and takes away with the other. But it was agreed. The guys would ride Mission: Space. The gals would entertain themselves.

When they all met after the ride, Tilda was whining, "I want to go on a ride with Colt." She took his hand as soon as the group reassembled. Colt looked at his father, a plea in his eyes.

"Why don't we all go on a ride together," suggested Quinn, "and you can sit with Colt?" The youngster frowned, but, to his dad's relief, held his comments.

"Which ride?" demanded Tilda. It sounded like she didn't trust Quinn.

"Which rides does you mom think are appropriate for you?" He almost hit himself in the forehead. What little kid understands *appropriate*?

To his amazement Tilda said, "She thinks I should stay on the baby rides, but I think I should go on the Haunted Mansion ride with Colt. I won't be scared."

"How old are you?" Quinn asked the little girl.

"I'm seven and I'm smart."

"And a pest," offered Paul, or was it Rob?

"I'll say," muttered Colt.

"Haunted Mansion it is!" Quinn turned everyone in that direction.

Of course walking there included a few stops for drinks and snacks and a photo op with Goofy. To Quinn's surprise Colt got into the spirit of the day, even smiling for the photo as he stood beside Goofy.

As they climbed into the Haunted Mansion cars, Quinn made certain that he got to ride alone with Mouse. "Do you have plans for dinner?"

he asked as the ride began. There wasn't much time for conversation as they were whipped and twisted through the ride.

Finally, she found an opportunity to reply, "We just hang out with no plans. This is our first outing since lockdown."

"How long has Josh been . . . dead?"

"Two years." They were whipped through darkness. "What about your wife?" she asked, "Is she here with you?"

"Colt's mother and I are divorced."

Spin, jolt. "I'm sorry to hear that," said Mouse, breathless as the car came to a stop and they were hauled out by the ride workers.

When they caught up with the children, Colt was standing there without his shirt. "What?" challenged an angry and embarrassed father.

"She threw up." Colt tossed his shirt into a trash container.

Mouse gasped and began an apology, but Quinn just said to Colt, "Run over to one of those stores and get a new shirt."

"Can I do that, too, Mommy?" asked Tilda as she pulled at her soiled shirt.

"Let's go," said Quinn as he organized a shopping spree. "We all need new shirts. It's just a matter of time before I throw up on someone." Colt rolled his eyes at his father but allowed himself a small smile.

As they wandered through the shop, Quinn noticed a small Cinderella swimsuit. "Why don't you all come to our hotel and have a swim. We can cool off and get on the rides later this afternoon."

"We don't have our suits with us. They're back at our rooms," began Mouse as her children danced up and down, chanting, "Can we, Mom?"

Quinn smiled as he grabbed the Cinderella suit and held it up to Tilda. "I think this will fit. What about your boys?"

Mouse frowned at him.

"My treat," he said as the kids searched through the rack of swim trunks. He leaned in close to Mouse and whispered, "You need one, too. I can't life guard all these kids alone."

"I'll buy my own."

"Mouse, what are you suggesting? That I have ulterior motives?" Quinn looked around them, "With all these kids?"

She laughed. "I'll still buy my own."

Directing everyone back to the hotel was another adventure—herding cats came to Quinn's mind. Even Colt was getting into the fun. He and the boys seemed to have computer gaming in common, and the youngster was heard promising the twins that he would rent some games back at the hotel.

Tilda couldn't decide whether to take Quinn's hand or Colt's. She shared her favors, and sticky hands, with both of them. They got to the room, well, suite, two bedrooms, two bathrooms and a living room. Everyone got into swim clothes. Mouse had a terry cover for herself. Quinn didn't remember her making her purchase. He hoped there was a suit, the skimpier the better, under that cover.

The three boys dove into the water as soon as they could. Tilda ran after them begging for their attention. "Mommy, they won't play with me," she complained as she trotted back to the adults.

"Tilda," sighed Mouse, "they don't have to play with you all the time. You know you'll cry because they're too rough. Play in the small pool."

Tilda began to cry, "I never have any fun. Everyone thinks I'm too little."

Surprising himself, Quinn said, "Come with me, Tilda, we'll show those boys how tough you are." The two of them went off as Mouse staked out a few loungers, doffed her cover and stretched out to enjoy about thirty seconds of peace and quiet.

Her eyes popped open in panic as she heard Tilda scream. Then she settled back once she realized Quinn was tossing her daughter about the water and she was enjoying herself.

Quinn finally found a floatable vest for Tilda to wear and he climbed out of the pool to sit with Mouse. "Those are great kids," he said as he kissed her on the cheek and flopped into the lounger beside her. He managed to give her a quick appreciative scan. She had selected a conservative two-piece suit and filled it out better than he would have expected. She was, after all he reminded himself, older—and a mother. He looked again. She was a lovely woman even if she hadn't learned to handle her hair. Disneyworld was going to be fun.

"They are," she smiled, "You and Colt are making this a really fun business trip."

"Business trip?"

"This is work for me," Mouse explained, "I work most mornings and hire a sitting service for the kids." She shook her head in amazement. "They have every kind of service here."

"Don't tell me. Let me guess." He closed his eyes as though he were searching the ether for her future. "You dress up as Cinderella by morning and become supermom the rest of the day." She laughed. He tried again, "Okay, maybe you're Snow White."

"I'm a computer consultant, helping the business office here migrate to a new system." She continued, "While we had lockdown they upgraded some of their back-office software. I finished up today. We leave for home tomorrow."

"Computers?" She looked more like Cinderella than a computer consultant to Quinn.

She poked his arm. "What do you think I studied in school?"

"How to find a husband?"

She poked him again. "I worked for a big firm for a few years then we had the twins and we figured out that I could work from home and stay current. Then we moved to Australia and Josh was making a lot of money so we had Matilda. Then he was transferred to New Orleans and I reconnected with some old clients and got some work." She stopped as she thought about her story. "Then he died and I went full time into consulting."

"You didn't get anything for his death?" Quinn cleared his throat. "I mean, I'm certain his company had insurance for rig deaths and things."

"They did, they do," replied Mouse, "I could spend all that money or save it for the kids' college. Besides, I make a very comfortable living."

"How do you manage with the kids?" he asked.

"I moved back home, you know, to River Bend," she said, "My parents and random relatives help. In fact, I joined my cousin's consulting firm because she kept having babies. It all worked out." She grinned. "What about you?"

"I'm a trust and investment attorney," he replied, "Dad thought I should watch our money and take care of the family fortunes."

"What about your wife?"

"Ex-wife," he reminded her. "She left right after law school. It took her awhile to figure out how to get a great settlement out of Dad. They sort of negotiated her departure. I think she should have been his daughter, they see the world in the same light. Dad always told me I took after my mother. Too kind for my own good."

Mouse patted his arm then took his hand. "You are kind and sweet. You don't have any killer instincts. So what happened to Colt's mother?"

"She uses Colt to get into Dad's checkbook. Mostly by threatening to take him to live in other states. Colt lives with me most of the time and Dad keeps paying her bills." He frowned. "Dad told me I married a barracuda. But he pays because he also says she has no idea how much money she could really ask for. He says we only have to play this game until Colt is eighteen." Quinn shrugged. "I let them keep playing. Colt and I just watch life go by."

"So you're a single dad."

"Sort of. We live with my father and when I travel Colt is supervised by Dad and his staff. We came here at Colt's request for a few days because he said I'd missed spring break. My ex-wife and father want him to go to boarding school in the fall to begin high school." Quinn gave her a sad and lonely look. "I don't. I went to boarding school. It wasn't fun. Colt's lobbying me to go to bat for him. He wants us to move into a neighborhood where he can have friends drop by and where he can walk to school."

"Where do you live now?" she asked.

"I told you we live with Dad," he blushed, "on a rather large estate outside of Raleigh. Colt went to a private school and the chauffeur drove him every day. My son thinks we should be on our own and find a public school for him to attend. No one thinks I can manage being a single parent for a high school student. Dad says I need to stay on top of the family investments and wouldn't have time to pay attention to Colt's teen activities."

"You can stay on top of your business interests anywhere," argued the techie. "That's what I do; I keep people in touch no matter where they settle."

"Yeah, Dad," Colt said as he materialized to sit on the edge of Quinn's lounger. "I wouldn't be any trouble and I could be normal. Like Mouse's kids."

"You really want to live with me and get away from all the –

"Money," finished Colt. "We have too much. Nothing feels real. All my friends try to show off their wealth. Why? They didn't earn it." Colt was perplexed by such behavior.

Mouse looked at Quinn and raised her eyebrows in a question. He shifted on his seat. As everyone waited for his response, Tilda raced up and dived into his arms throwing him back on the lounger, sputtering.

Mouse was on her feet instantly, pulling the little girl off him saying, "That's enough, Tilda. Quinn has played with you all afternoon. He needs a rest." The twins rushed at their mother and, each grabbing an arm, dragged her to the edge of the pool and dropped her in.

As she came to the surface, one of them called, "You had to get your suit wet. We wanted to help." Colt was laughing and Quinn dove into the pool to rescue Mouse.

All four kids scrambled to the edge of the pool and watched as Mouse and Quinn began a splashing game. Soon four children joined them.

* * *

"What a great vacation!" Lynn had enjoyed the time at the derelict cottage on the Outer Banks. It wasn't really derelict. It had character. That's what she had reminded everyone throughout the week. So what if the wi-fi was iffy, and the shower tepid and the screens well-ventilated, they had all been together. Doyle and Lori had shared the delights of Hilton Head through numerous texts causing Dusty and Will to curse at each message. And all the boys threatened Doyle that his honeymoon would be interrupted if he sent one more bragging text.

"We'll get home this evening," said Jason as the boys packed their things into Will's truck. "I can't wait for a ho-o-o-t shower!" He ducked as his mother took a jab at him. "Getting old, Mom. You used to be faster."

"She's sort of like this old cabin," smirked Dusty, "Seen better days." Lynn threw a towel at him.

She kissed Jason. "Check in with your grandfather. Collect the mail from Emily."

"You boys," Piper called to her sons as they hopped into the truck, "make sure your grandparents are okay."

Then Lynn gave all of them a squinty-eyed look as she intoned, "And no tricks! Leave Doyle's house alone!" Doyle and Lori would be moving into their own home in River Bend when they returned from their honeymoon. The boys frowned, but nodded agreement. Bryce revved the engine and they were on their way.

Will watched the truck disappear. "You realize they left us to clean up this place."

"But we also will have one night of quiet," observed Piper.

"And a chance to eat food before it disappears," Dusty said as his stomach growled.

"What a great vacation!" Lynn was a one-line optimist.

CHAPTER THREE

Finishing an afternoon of swimming everyone dripped their way back to Quinn's Disney- world suite. The boys were ready for food so he called down for room service. As they waited, Mouse organized changing of clothes and hanging out swimsuits to dry. The boys got into the video games hoping they wouldn't starve before the food arrived, and Tilda fell asleep. Quinn carried her into his bed and returned warning the boys to be quiet or she would be back pestering them. They got the message.

"Quinn, do you mind if I take a quick shower?" asked Mouse.

"Go right ahead, I have to check in with the office." He walked over to the desk and turned on his computer.

Mouse wandered out of the shower toweling her hair, behaving like her motherly self, Quinn thought as he watched her check on Tilda, survey the boys and finally stand behind him to study his computer screen.

"What software do you use to manage your funds?" she asked, "I'm familiar with several accounting programs, and what they offer."

"We had something developed, or personalized, for us about ten years ago," he replied, "when I took over this job."

"I bet there's a lot of new and better stuff out there now." She pulled him out of his seat and began typing on the keyboard.

"Wait!" he whispered, not wanting Tilda to awaken and interrupt this time with Mouse. "You've lost my information."

"I didn't lose anything," she replied, "I'm just looking at your operating program." She scrolled through the gibberish on the screen, mumbling, "How old fashioned." And, "This is almost antique." Then she stopped. "Hmmmm."

It wasn't a warm sound, but something cautious and suspicious.

"What?" Quinn gave her his attention.

"Shhhh." She continued to scroll, flipping to other screen configurations. Then she pulled her phone out of her big mom bag. Hitting a number she waited for someone to answer. "Where are you? . . . . I need you to look at this program . . . . Okay."

"What?" Quinn sounded as anxious as any of the kids trying to get her attention while Mouse tapped the keyboard and became engrossed with the screen.

Holding the phone to her ear, she said, "I can't understand some of these actions. It looks like some money just disappears."

"Disappears?" he whispered in a panic. "Like what, I'm stealing money from the trust?"

"No," she shook her head looking up at Quinn, "You're sending it to some account and portions of the money vanish. I can't see where it's going. This is somewhat sophisticated." She turned her attention back to the phone. After a few minutes of listening to the person on the other end and typing on the key board, she asked him, "Who's CJ?"

"My brother-in-law."

"Who's James Randall Templeton?"

"My brother." He gulped. "He lives in a group home for the developmentally delayed. I transfer money from his trust to CJ who takes care of paying his bills. He also manages the account for maintenance on the estate, you know, repairing the roof, and gardening and stuff."

"The Lela Templeton Foundation?"

"Our family foundation," he explained, "We channel all nonprofit funding requests through there and give out grants."

"Like all those big foundations?"

"We're a big foundation!" Quinn was proud of the family's generosity. "PBS likes us. CJ is currently executive director of the foundation and helps the board direct giving."

"Your brother-in-law?"

"There are three of us. I have an older sister, Margaret, then me and then James. We call him Jimmy. CJ is married to Margaret."

"He's taking money and moving it to an offshore account."

"He can't be!" Quinn ran his fingers through his hair. "Margaret controls the money. I transfer funds to her account from her trust." He paced the room. "He doesn't need money, he has some from his own family and he has Margaret's credit cards. My office just pays things as they come in. He has his own resources." Quinn stopped as he had another thought. "Is he paying Jimmy's bills?"

"Yes, it seems that you transfer money, he pays bills, leaves a little in reserve and sends the rest offshore. He does that every month with those two accounts and he's doing something with the foundation but I don't understand what. My cousin is checking things out."

"How can she do that?"

"She's a high security clearance consultant for the military and can get into anything. I don't have those clearances."

Mouse continued a phone conversation with her cousin as Quinn let in room service and invited the boys to eat. He returned to Mouse. "Are you sure this is happening?"

"Yes," she replied, "Give Janet and me some time and we'll explain it all. Don't you have any business risk management plans in place?" He shrugged his shoulders. "Can you stop any fund transfers for a few days while we figure out what to do?"

Quinn found his cell phone in the mess on a coffee table and made a call. "Gilda, I want you to stop all fund transfers until you hear from me. I'm having some computer problems and can't seem to follow my activity . . . . I'll call both of them. . . . Remember, no money goes out."

While Mouse watched he made another call. "Dad, I'm having some computer problems, so I'm holding up all transfers. This is Friday and I should have this straightened out by Monday. . . .He's doing fine. We've been in the park all day. . . You could join us. . . . I know, not while we're having some problems. . . . I'll get on it."

Mouse was typing furiously on the computer, doing mysterious things, as Quinn made a third call. "CJ, this is Quinn, I've got some computer problem so I told Gilda to stop all activity on the accounts. . . . I told Dad . . . . I don't know what my problem is."

By this time the boys had paused their gaming to attack the room service cart and stopped to join Quinn and investigate all the computer activity. Mouse gasped and grabbed a soft drink from Colt. She threw the drink on the keyboard.

Quinn sighed. He returned to his phone conversation, "I guess I can tell you, just between us guys. Colt spilled a soft drink on the keyboard."

"Hey," complained Colt, but Mouse took his hand and gave him a smile.

Quinn continued talking with CJ as Mouse reconnected with her cousin, Janet. "Can you see anything? . . . He's what?"

Mouse signaled Quinn to end the conversation by making a slicing motion across her throat. So he said, "Gotta go kill my kid, CJ. I'll see you Monday morning and we can order a new computer . . . . What? . . .You'll have one ready for me when I get in? Thanks, it'll save us all some time. . . . I don't know what I need. I trust you. You seem to know a lot about our computers. . . . Okay, see you Monday."

He turned to Mouse, his eyes bugging out. "What did you do?"

"Calm down, we've saved everything in your computer to Janet's server. No one can get in." She wiped the dripping soft drink off the desk. "I was finishing up when I saw someone looking around."

"Looking around?"

"Evidently, your brother-in-law keeps a close eye on you and your computer activity. He or someone in his office came to check on you and your sick computer."

"Check on me?"

"There's a hidden program on your computer that allows him to watch all your activity."

"Read my email?"

She nodded.

"What else?"

Mouse thought for a moment. "Whatever you do on this computer he knows. E-mail, letters, solitaire, investment info, all your passwords." She waited for him to grasp that information, then she continued, "While you were telling him about your computer problem, he started to do his own search to verify that you were telling the truth. I had to make it true." She grinned and so did Colt.

"Cool," said the youngster. "Uncle CJ is robbing us?"

"We don't know what's happening," Quinn cautioned his son, but they were distracted as Mouse spoke with her contact.

"Theft?" she asked. Colt grinned in triumph.

"Offshore accounts?"

She turned to Quinn, "Who's MVT?"

"Mom?" Colt gasped.

"Those are my ex-wife's initials," said Quinn trying to keep his voice calm.

"CJ and MVT have offshore accounts together that total about ten million dollars. The accounts are about seven or eight years old but much of the high dollar activity has only been going on in the last five years."

"That's when he became head of the foundation," he gasped.

Mouse repeated that information to Janet. "My cousin says you need to investigate now before they hide their trail. We can only keep the system down for a week. That's all the time the general has given her."

"Keep the system down for a week?" He was puzzled.

"We've taken control of all your technology."

"You can't do that," objected Quinn.

"We just did," Mouse assured him, "To your staff and relatives it'll look like a network slowdown. But they can't send instructions to offshore accounts or take money or stuff. The offshore connection is blocked, and nothing will happen."

"Then what?" he asked. "I get home to a mess and CJ has a new computer."

"It gives you time to organize over the weekend," said Mouse.

"I don't know who to call," Quinn moaned, "I'm here and I want someone at the office taking charge now." He paced the room while Mouse finished speaking with Janet. "You have to come home with us," he announced as he stopped pacing.

"I have clients," Mouse argued.

"I'm now your client. I'll pay triple your rates." He grabbed his phone and spoke with someone, then announced, "Our plane will be at the airport early in the morning. Be ready to leave as soon as they can get here."

"My children?"

"They're coming, too." Quinn rolled his eyes. "What did you think? I'd leave Colt here to babysit?"

Now the twins were jumping up and down. Tilda came out of the bedroom asking, "What airplane?"

"We're going home with Colt," said Rob. Quinn was starting to know the twins pretty well.

"He has his own plane," said Paul.

"Can we, Mom?" sang Mouse's trio.

* * *

Janet Bergman Powers was happy to get a call from her cousin, Sara Margolin, on a lazy summer Friday afternoon. "I'm so glad you called. I think I just ate half a watermelon. The kids are napping and Tim is working in his vegetable garden."

"Vegetable garden?" asked Sara.

"Piper's dad helped him plant it. Tim thinks he's becoming a farmer."

Sara laughed. "I called for a reason, even though listening to stories about Tim gardening would be pretty funny. I ran into a friend here and he has some strange things happening in his office software. Boot up and take a look. He's Quinn Templeton, a guy I knew in college and he calls me Mouse." Sara was charmed to be reminded of the old nickname.

"I like that," replied Janet, "It's much better than nerd. . . I'm in." She clicked on her keypad, muttered to herself, exchanged information with Sara, whom she delighted in thinking of as Mouse, and found the perfect elixir for a lazy summer afternoon, that is, a perfect elixir for a very pregnant computer nerd.

With a promise to Sara that she would continue her search and impose some highly secret, and questionable restraints on all Templeton operations, Janet decided to call for help of a different sort.

"Mars, come over to the house," she requested of her good friend and a River Bend detective. "Sara found some interesting activity when she looked into her friend's software."

"Is it a guy?" he asked, "Do you think she's only looking into his software?" Mars had been encouraging Sara to date some of the many men in River Bend interested in her.

"She's in Disneyworld with her kids and she ran into an old college friend. That's all I know. Do you want to look at this stuff or not?"

"Yeah, with Dusty out of town, we haven't had much going on here. I'll see you in five."

When Mars Healey arrived he was carrying a small container of frozen yogurt. "I thought you might need a snack." Janet was pregnant with her third child and everyone knew how hungry pregnancy made her.

As she spooned yogurt, she explained what she and Sara had found. Mars, a CPA and skilled forensic accountant, as well as a detective, understood immediately what was happening in the accounts. "Embezzlement!"

"More or less," agreed Janet, her spoon on autopilot as she ate the yogurt. "It's all in the family according to Sara. And this guy calls her Mouse."

"The guy who's embezzling?"

"No, the embezzle-ee, her friend." Janet licked her spoon and stared into the empty yogurt container in surprise. "There are two issues— where is the money going? It's going offshore, I just haven't found the account yet. I've asked my Army contact for help since I've found illegal activity. And second, I think there's a problem with the family foundation that is also involved."

"What foundation?"

"Lela Templeton," replied Janet, "Do you know them?" In addition to his detecting and accounting skills Mars was a very wealthy man and knew many of the wealthiest people in the state through his family connections.

"Yes, I didn't know Sara knew them."

"She went to school with some guy named Quinn Templeton."

Mars nodded. "I've met him. His family has a big privately held agribusiness corporation as well as real estate and all sorts of other things. They aren't crooks."

"I think someone in the family is. Someone named CJ."

"There is no C.J. Templeton." Mars was puzzled.

"I think he's an in-law."

"What's he doing?"

"He's in charge of managing some family accounts and he routinely takes money and moves it someplace. The Army is looking into that 'someplace' right now. They're using this as a training exercise in case anyone asks."

"Whatever," said Mars as he shook his head, not interested in knowing about any Army spy operations. "How's he getting money from the foundation?"

"That I can't figure out. Once they secure his accounts offshore, we'll track backward."

"So what do you want me to do?"

"Help me and Sara frame this for prosecution. We understand the computers, but not the accounting."

Sure," replied her friend. And they spent the rest of the afternoon on Janet's computer.

* * *

CJ was puzzled by the call from Quinn. That guy was so computer unconscious. Before he could give it more thought, his cell rang. Sitting in the study at Madeline Templeton's condo, he checked caller ID and swiftly closed the door. "Yeah." He knew who it was.

"That brother-in-law of yours has someone inside his computer," the hacker warned. CJ and Theo, the hacker, had been together for years. It all started when CJ was invited to join in a shady group that offered money laundering. Stanwood Garson and some hood named Rupert Rothman had perfected a fake nonprofit called Starship. To look legit they had invited a few wealthy do-gooders to join the board of the illusionary agency. CJ shivered as he recalled the chaos a year or so ago. First one of the do-gooder board members got too curious and an attempt was made to terminate him. Unfortunately the assassin got killed instead. And then founding member, Stanwood Garson, was murdered and Rothman died in a police chase.

He thought back to years before when he met and partnered with Theo. One day a scruffy looking fellow had stopped CJ in the parking lot and had asked, "You one of those rich guys in that starshit stuff?"

"And what about it?"

"I thought you and me could keep an eye on those guys." Theo had sniffed and coughed. CJ had wished he had had a disinfectant spray. "Those guys are crooks," the hacker had shrugged, "so screwing them is okay by me."

"Why me?" CJ had been puzzled and cautious.

Theo had sneered. "Because they wanted me to get into your accounts and be ready to clean out the funds." He had given CJ an eyebrow wiggle. "In case something happened to you."

"They're going to kill me?"

"Nah." He had dug a finger in his ear and pulled it out wiping wax, or something, on his jacket sleeve. "They said they want to be ready if something happens to you or the other partners. They call it executive replacement insurance."

"Those bastards. Who else knows this?"

"I came to you first, 'cause of all of them, you have access to the largest legitimate funds." He sneered. "You can afford me." He was referring to the Templeton wealth.

"And what does that mean?"

"That means. I'd like to be a partner with someone like you who can move money in all directions. That Templeton Foundation moves money all over and it's easy to trail behind them and get lost in cyber signatures." CJ had understood what he meant. Garson, Rothman and Templeton money could all be blended in some digital manner, creating many virtual transfer opportunities and offering the ability to move secretly.

"What have you got in mind?" And CJ had spent a profitable afternoon listening to a digital plan for looting funds from Templeton accounts as well as being prepared to steal Garson and Rothman funds at the first opportunity.

CJ remembered the day. He also remembered another day when Theo had called and said, "They're dead. But their money ain't. You ready?" For a guy who only spoke binary code that was an attention getter. Theo had been Stanwood Garson's and Rothman's IT connection and had been prepared for this sort of event.

"What do you think we should do?" he had asked CJ.

"I don't know if they had their own silent partners. We should wait to see what happens." They both knew what type of 'silent partner' they might encounter. Better safe than dead.

Theo and CJ had tracked Rothman's account activity even before his death, planning to learn enough to eventually access the offshore accounts and help themselves to Rothman's funds. When Rothman got himself killed, trying to fly off the top of a parking deck in River Bend, they relaxed deciding to bide their time. Together, they decided to let the accounts sit idle for a time but soon realized that someone was moving money out of those accounts. Who was tapping those accounts?

All the time they had been monitoring Rothman, CJ and the hacker were not idle. Theo had developed a working relationship with CJ to loot the Templeton Foundation accounts and to begin infiltrating the company computers. They also took over the paperwork of the defunct nonprofit Starships that Rothman and Garson had created and began using it as the recipient of grants from the Templeton Foundation, calling themselves any number of nonprofits but always operating under the tax ID of the original Starships. No one ever checked. They filed all the paperwork and 990s. One year they might be Starships DBA Autism Innovations and another year Starships DBA Women in Crisis. The money kept coming. CJ made certain that Theo was rewarded. Being careful he stashed his own funds in an offshore account that Theo couldn't access. Theo knew what CJ was doing. He let the man believe in his security. Theo was just prepared to grab CJ's accounts should the partners extinguish CJ himself. Honor and thieves!

Joining forces with Madeline had allowed CJ to begin a new operation away from the prying eyes of Theo. They continued to send funds to the alias Starship agency. But once Madeline understood the game, she followed the model and created several very questionable agencies of her own without a connection to Theo. She was a good criminal thinker even though her only interest was in having enough money to shop and travel and have fun. CJ threw in a little sex and she let him manage everything, not interested in more than the bottom line of the funds deposited off shore.

All these thoughts went through CJ's mind as he returned to Theo's initial remark. "What do you mean someone else is in his computer?"

"Well, we watch everything he does, but I set up a small alarm that just told me someone was looking into his operating system. They'll find my monitors. They can't track back to me, but I thought I better tell you. Something's up."

"He just called me to say his son spilled Coke in the keyboard."

"That may be," allowed Theo, "but someone was getting curious."

"I told him, I'd have a new computer for him on Monday."

"That's good," agreed Theo. "I got one here I'll fix and they'll never find the spyware. I'll get it to you Sunday."

They made plans to meet and ended the call as Madeline breezed into the study. "Hey, lover, secrets?"

"Quinn called because Colt spilled Coke in his computer." He opened his arms to her as a means of distraction. "I called my guy to get a computer prepped with that spyware so we can continue to keep track of Quinn's activity." Nibble, caress. "I pick it up Sunday."

Madeline acted her part. She marveled that CJ never suspected. Money was more important to her than sex. He could rub and hump all he wanted, as long as he kept the money coming. She faked another orgasm, did her part to help him with his release, and excused herself to fix her make-up. As she stared in the mirror, she, once again, decided that she had to work too hard for her money. Why didn't that bastard David Templeton just settle twenty-five million on her and be done with it? One day Colt would be in charge. He would take care of his mother. She couldn't wait.

CHAPTER FOUR

Mouse watched the manicured forest slide by the windows as she and her children sat with Quinn and Colt in a limo that had been waiting for them at a small airport. She had known since meeting him in college that Quinn was wealthy, but she hadn't been prepared for the airplane and limo which was probably taking them to a mansion. She prayed, again, that Tilda would keep her comments to herself. That little girl was, as Mouse's mother liked to say, God's revenge for all the embarrassment Mouse had caused her parents. As she thought about Tilda, the little girl snuggled closer and whispered, "Mom, are they kidnapping us?"

Quinn laughed. "We're going to our house, the place where Colt and I live. You'll like it."

"Do you have horses here?" the little girl asked.

"No," replied Colt, "We keep them at the ranch in Montana."

Mouse looked wide-eyed at Quinn. He just shrugged.

"Do you have a horse?" asked Paul. Colt nodded.

"Do you ride in rodeos?" asked Tilda.

"He's a kid," chided Rob, "he doesn't do that cowboy stuff."

"We sort of do," said Colt, "We have some cows and a ranch house and cowboys who work for us. Dad, can we show them sometime?"

"We'll see about a visit after Mouse helps us solve our computer problem," he replied, then gave Mouse a lame smile.

The chorus began, "Can we, Mom?" And she rolled her eyes at Quinn in disgust, or was it surrender.

The limo made a sharp turn and the trees seemed to move back. A magnificent stone mansion stood ahead of them, reflecting the sun from its many multi-paned windows. "It's lovely," whispered Mouse.

"It's home," said Quinn with a wry smile. "We'll get you settled and then meet with my father. He lives here, too." The kids all stared out the window.

Quinn ushered everyone toward the house as the door seemed to magically open. A very large black man greeted them, "Mr. Quinn, Master Colt."

"Samuel," nodded Quinn as he made certain everyone was accounted for. "We have guests."

Samuel gave a dignified nod to Mouse and the children and stepped aside to welcome everyone into the grand home. He then turned to Quinn, "Do they need special arrangements?"

"Yes, they'll be here a few days." Quinn waited for the question so that Samuel could understand what special arrangements Quinn had in mind without asking what Quinn had in mind, especially for the lovely woman in the group. He had never brought a woman to the family home. And this woman had children!

Finally, Samuel asked, "Will the little miss be frightened to be in a bedroom alone?"

Quinn smiled at the clever question. "I think she should stay with her mother and put the twins close by."

"Very good, sir," nodded Samuel, "I suggest the ladies stay in Aunt Dorothea's suite. It's recently been redecorated."

Quinn nodded. "I'm certain they'll be comfortable in there. And the boys?"

"May I suggest the room Master Colt uses for his friends who come to visit."

"Fine idea," agreed Quinn. He turned to Mouse as a mocha skinned woman in a maid's uniform appeared behind Samuel. "If you need anything, Colt and Gracia," he nodded to the woman, "can help. You can settle the kids and we can meet with Dad in about thirty minutes."

"I need to find a place to wash the kids' clothing," she responded, "and mine. We've been away so long we've used everything. I'd like them to have clean clothes for dinner." She gave him a half smile. She wanted her children to look presentable.

"Gracia will take care of everything," replied Quinn, "She'll show you to your rooms and I'll look for you shortly." He turned to Samuel, "Is Dad in his study?"

Samuel nodded to Quinn then turned his attention to Gracia, gave her some instructions, spoke quietly to the chauffeur standing by the door with the luggage and finally spoke to Colt. "Why don't you bring your friends to the kitchen after they freshen up? Cook will have a snack prepared."

Colt gave the man a warm smile. "Sure." With that Colt and Gracia took the family up the curved, ornate staircase.

At the top of the stairs Mouse turned to look back across the expanse of the high-ceilinged foyer and spotted a man down below in the shadows. She ducked back as he approached Quinn.

"Good lord," he moaned, "a woman with children? She must be some sweet treat if she got you to bring her home."

"Good to see you, too, Dad," replied Quinn. "She's not a sweet treat, but she'll be down in a few minutes to explain." Turning back to the butler he asked, "Samuel, can we have some coffee in Dad's office? Ms. Margolin will be joining us. Please show her in when she's ready." Samuel nodded and disappeared.

As the two men turned toward the study door, Mouse scooted after her children. She had seen the enemy.

* * *

"Where'd you disappear to yesterday afternoon?" Danny Valeri asked his detecting partner, Mars Healey. They had just run their usual Saturday morning circuit and had stopped at the bakery for breakfast.

"Janet and Sara are helping some guy find an embezzler in the family." Mars explained what the women had found as he helped Danny clean the abandoned cafe tables left by the messy Saturday morning coffee crowd.

Danny threw the last of the napkins and cups in the trash and sat down to finish his breakfast. "What'd they find?"

"The usual," said Mars, "Money leaving accounts and disappearing. Janet is using some Army software to hunt down offshore accounts. They also think this guy is stealing from the family foundation but they haven't figured out how yet. They can't prove he's taking money, but the offshore accounts have gotten bigger and not with money they can identify." Mars stared into his coffee thinking through the problem.

"A foundation?"

Mars nodded. "The Lela Templeton Foundation."

"Fake non-profits!" Danny slapped his partner on the back. "We've known Lynn long enough that we've seen all sorts of nonprofit shenanigans. And those big foundations go hand in hand with little nonprofits always looking for money. I bet someone has created fakes and passes money to them."

Mars nodded his head. "Not bad detecting, partner." He chewed on his breakfast muffin. "Janet suggested that, too. You think when they track the money back from offshore they'll run into these fakes?"

"Don't you remember that Rothman guy who was working with that fake agency lending money or something?" Danny sat up in his chair. "If Janet finds some names of agencies, we could ask Lynn how to verify which ones are real."

"She and Dusty come home this afternoon," said Mars. "Let's tell Janet to give us some names of groups receiving money, and we can ask Lynn how to track them down and find the people involved."

It sounded like a plan. Their first stop was a visit to Janet with fresh morning bakery products to hold her attention as they explained their suspicions.

* * *

Stepping across the foyer Quinn moved down a short passage, walked into a room followed by his father who closed the door of a sumptuous study. A man's room with rich woods and substantial furnishings. "I have hired Ms. Margolin as a computer consultant."

His father snorted.

Quinn took a deep breath. "What's wrong with you? I don't bring women here. I keep my personal life out of sight. There's no need to give me this shit."

Mr. Templeton walked over to his desk and waved a paper. "This is what the last fling cost. Where do you find these women? She was happy with a shopping spree."

"What? I didn't even sleep with her." Quinn was outraged as he scanned the papers.

"Apparently, you took up enough time that she missed an opportunity to go after someone else. She was quite perturbed that you only wanted a few dinners even though she interpreted those actions as the beginnings of a romantic exchange."

"Do you believe everything anyone tells you that makes me look bad? I took her out to dinner three times over two weeks. I escorted her to a charity ball because she is a beautiful woman." Quinn shrugged. "But I never did anything else."

"I know you didn't," replied his father with a sigh. "I had her investigated."

"Then why -"

"She threatened to talk to Colt."

"About what?"

"I don't know," the older man shrugged, "but you know he's my weakness."

"Dad, he's not a pawn. His mother has used that card for a decade. He's a sharp kid. He can take care of himself."

"He's our only family heir."

Then Quinn knew. It wasn't a questionable girlfriend. It was protecting Colt, protecting the last Templeton. "I'm sorry, Dad," he said, "I'll be more careful. Just promise that you won't pay off any women until you talk with me. Your quick response is going to bring all sorts of scammers to our door."

"That's why I want him at boarding school this fall." The same old argument.

There was a knock and the door opened. "Ms. Margolin," Samuel announced.

Quinn's eyes widened. She'd managed to turn into a very lovely, very professional looking woman. She had on a pair of soft yellow linen slacks and a short-sleeved white silk blouse cut modestly low with a small collar. Her hair was tied and secured at the nape of her neck in a bun and she wore light traces of make-up. She carried a briefcase over to a small table and put it down. Thumbing the latches she opened it and withdrew her computer. Then she stood and waited.

"Ms. Margolin, this is my father, David Templeton."

Mouse held out her hand, "Mr. Templeton."

He took her hand in a brief shake and nodded. "I'm told you're our computer consultant. We already have someone." He glared at her.

Before Quinn could jump to her defense, Mouse said, "I'm here because I found some spyware on your son's computer as well as some questionable financial transactions. I've had all accounts frozen and I have a colleague looking through your company's IT. So far, I can tell you that all workings of your corporation are in good hands and well managed by your IT staff. However, funds that leave Quinn's office to various accounts seem to go . . . astray."

"How can you tell?" David's eyes bulged and his face grew red. "Are you using illegal methods to scan my operations?"

"Maybe," answered Mouse, in a wary, soft voice. Quinn recognized that his father's outrage was rapidly reaching an eruption and worried that Mouse would be unceremoniously ushered from the house. He hoped that the kids had gotten a snack before they were all tossed out.

Before she could continue, David barked, "We'll see about that and about your methods." He grabbed his desk phone, flipped through his address book and connected with someone. "I've got a problem," he growled into the phone. "I want this person in my office arrested for illegal computer spying . . . . Margolin . . . Huh? . . . er . . . Okay." He handed the receiver to Mouse. "He wants to talk to you."

Mouse took the phone and gave a tentative, "Hello?" Then she smiled. "Kyle, do you know Mr. Templeton? . . . . I'm at his place with my kids . . . . I ran into Quinn at Disneyworld and one thing and another . . . .Yes, yes, later . . . . anyway I noticed strange activity on Quinn's laptop and found some irregularities. So Janet . . . yes, that's who we made that request for. Mr. Templeton's funds from some of his trust accounts are vanishing and Janet says they're going offshore. In addition, someone put some spyware into Quinn's computer so I disabled it and Janet tied up all accounts that we thought were at risk as well as the offshore accounts . . . . . That's our plan." She handed the receiver back to Mr. Templeton who was trying to hide his surprise.

Templeton spoke into the phone. "Yes, Kyle," he said in a subdued voice, "Yes, yes . . . . we'll check back when Ms. Margolin has things under control . . . . Thank you for your time." He ended the call and stared out the windows for a few minutes, watching the children eating a snack on the patio. He finally turned to Mouse. "The General holds you and your friend in high regard."

Mouse nodded. "We've worked with him for years. And he thinks highly of you also." She smiled at the older man.

His sigh was thoughtful. "I need a full explanation. Please be seated." He gestured toward the table where she had placed her briefcase. They each took a seat as Samuel entered with coffee.

"When would you like lunch, sir?"

David checked his watch. "Twelve-thirty."

"Are CJ and Margaret joining us?" asked Quinn.

"Yes, sir," replied Samuel. He nodded and left the room.

Quinn looked at Mouse and smiled. "You better talk fast, our suspect will be here in about an hour." David started up from his chair, but Quinn placed a hand on his shoulder. "My consultant and her team," here Quinn smiled, "her team that seems to include the US Army, have things in hand."

Both men looked at Mouse. She began her story about looking over the operating software for Quinn's office, following the money, calling Janet, and finally throwing Colt's soft drink on the key pad. David laughed at that.

"So CJ and the barracuda are in league together?" he mused, standing to look out the window. "I wonder if Margaret suspects?" He paced his office. "How much money are we talking about?"

"The barracuda is my ex-wife," Quinn offered as an aside.

"The offshore account has ten million," replied Mouse. "We haven't found any other accounts. So I don't know if there are other funds in other places. And I can't tell you how much has already been spent. All that would take an audit."

David slapped his palm on the table. "The audit! They would have found this."

Quinn shook his head. "The trust audit is all that counts and it's clean. We don't look closely at those accounts, house maintenance and Jimmy's funds, that CJ manages because we just assume it's all spent. Although I am wondering about the foundation's audit. We don't look closely at the grants other than that they are given to bona fide nonprofits."

Mouse cleared her throat. "Janet has someone looking into fake nonprofits."

"Fakes?" David roared.

"It's possible to create a nonprofit on paper, receive a foundation grant and file the appropriate forms. The audit isn't of the grantees, but the grantor, your foundation. It probably takes a lot of managing but—

"CJ is clever and he's an attorney," said Quinn. "But I don't think he'd work that hard."

"The barracuda would," commented David with a growl. "That woman —

"I know," said Quinn waving his arm in surrender. "I haven't made that mistake again." He threw himself back in his chair and blew out his breath. "What do we do now?" Both men looked at Mouse.

"For the long term, I suggest that the foundation and trust manager's office contract with your corporate IT to manage their computer operations, including security. They are very good. You get your money's worth." She nodded to David. "In the short term, you have to clean house. May I set up my computer, because Janet will be calling in and Kyle may want to take a peek at our work." David nodded.

Quinn's stomach growled. "I guess we better get ready for lunch."

* * *

"What a great week," Lynn sighed as she stretched out her legs in the seat behind Dusty. They had rented a big van for the drive to the Outer Banks. It was the only way to get Will, Piper, Dusty, herself and two dogs along with all their gear to the vacation rental. The boys had joined them and had returned yesterday, leaving the four parents to clean the rental and have one last night of beach serenity. Dusty was a little sun burned. Piper had more than her share of mosquito bites; Will had lost his sunglasses. But they had enjoyed every minute. And here they were on their way back to River Bend on Saturday afternoon.

"Wasn't it great?" she asked the van passengers. Dusty was driving and sort of nodded. Each dog raised a head, wagged a tail and returned to a sprawl. Will was reading on his iPad while riding shotgun, and Piper was gently snoring, sprawled on the other back seat.

Lynn's phone rang. She jumped. No one had called her for a week.

"Yes? . . . Mars? Is something wrong?" She listened for a long while—enough time to make everyone else in the van very curious. "There's a book in my office listing all the incorporated State nonprofits by county. That's a good place to start if you have names . . . . Herbie and Rory have keys . . . Call if you need something else. We should be home by dinner time." She slipped her phone back into her pocket and put her head back to rest.

"Well?" demanded the three other passengers.

She smiled to herself. They were so predictable. "Mars is helping Janet do some research on some potential fake nonprofits. He mentioned possible embezzlement at a big state foundation."

"He's investigating someone in River Bend?" asked Piper.

"No, he says it's for a job Sara and Janet are doing."

"They aren't investigators," Dusty, the detective, reminded her.

"I'm only telling you what he told me," she said in her you-don't-own-all-crime voice.

CHAPTER FIVE

"Mr. and Mrs. Kirtley have arrived," Samuel announced to the three people in the study.

"Ask them to join us," instructed Quinn, "and keep the children entertained." Samuel nodded.

CJ and Margaret entered the study with a flourish. "Daddy," she crooned, "we're looking forward to the party at the club this evening. It will be the first big event since we threw off those damn masks." She stopped when she noticed Mouse. "We haven't met."

Mouse stood as Quinn said, "Margaret, you and CJ, please take a seat. We have something to talk about."

"Are you threatening to change your will again, Daddy?"

David sat behind his desk and stared at his daughter. She sat. CJ sat beside her on a small bench in front of the windows.

Once they were seated, Quinn stood and began to pace the room. He cleared his throat. "I want you to meet Sara Margolin. We're old college friends. She works as a computer consultant. I've hired her firm to help us with some problems."

CJ sized up Mouse, and with an unctuous nod said, "Your problem is a Coke in your laptop. I'm certain we don't need Ms. Margolin's firm to solve that problem. I already have your new computer ordered. It will be at the office Monday morning."

Mouse looked at Quinn. He gave her a signal to be quiet. "It seems," he continued, "that a fizzing keypad is the least of my computer problems. Ms. Margolin, with the help of her associates, has been able to identify illicit transfer of funds from Jimmy's account and our maintenance accounts. She has her staff looking into the foundation fund transfers as we speak."

"How convenient," snarled CJ, "that you only have suspicions about the funds I manage."

"Are you accusing my husband of being a thief?" demanded Margaret.

"Yes!" roared David rising from the seat behind his desk.

"Really, David," tisked CJ, "Quinn brings home a pretty piece of fluff, obviously trying to get into her pants and we have to be subjected to these insults and innuendo? I thought you were more discerning." He stood and turned his back on the room, entertaining himself with the view of the patio. "Whose children are with Colt?"

"My children," replied Mouse. She stood and walked over to the window. Her five-three willowy frame was in contrast to CJ's six-foot pampered rich boy look. "And I'm here representing my firm to help Mr. Templeton address some spyware issues as well as disappearing funds."

"Daddy, you can't let this woman talk to my husband like that." Margaret was on her feet bracing her hands on David's desk.

He looked at her and asked, "Did you know that he's seeing Madeline? And that they're working together taking our money?"

Margaret screamed, "You'll say anything to hurt me. Lies! You and Quinn have never liked my husband. Now you bring in this woman to spread lies and challenge his good name."

"We have proof that CJ and Madeline have a joint account offshore where they have been stashing our funds—funds taken from Jimmy and other accounts," explained Quinn.

"I don't have to listen to this," growled CJ and he raced for the door. Margaret followed him. In the study they heard the front door slam. Shortly they heard a car's engine roar. The door slammed again and Margaret stomped into the study.

"He told me he's leaving me," she cried, "he says he's tired of being treated in such an insulting manner." She charged at Mouse and slapped her cheek.

"That's enough," thundered David, "He'll be back when he finds out he can't get at his money. Then, my dear, you can take your rage out on the person who deserves it. Now apologize to Ms. Margolin." Margaret fell into a wing back chair and sobbed.

* * *

Mouse left the study. She had no role in this very painful family discussion. She checked in her rooms and found all hers and the children's clothes washed and folded. At least they would leave here clean, she thought to herself as she rubbed her cheek.

Leaving her rooms she went looking for the children and found them in a marvelous playroom—a large room filled with sun. Board games and books were stacked on shelves. A TV stood ready for video games but the four kids were all involved in building some complex Lego facility. Even Tilda was busy, acting as Colt's assistant, retrieving pieces at his request.

As she entered Colt looked up. "Did you talk with Uncle CJ?"

Mouse nodded, deciding to answer all his questions honestly. "It wasn't pleasant. Your aunt is very upset. Your uncle left her here as he drove off."

"Did he admit he sees my mother?" He rose as he asked his question.

"No," replied Mouse, "She may not be involved in this. We only have initials." She studied this youngster, so mature for his age.

"She's involved," stated Colt with a knowledgeable nod. "She likes money too much. It's almost a disease with her. That's why I want to get away from all this money. It makes people who should be loving and kind, well, it makes them crazy and selfish."

Mouse's heart broke. "Your father loves you very much."

"I know," smiled Colt, "but sometimes Grandfather says I'm the adult, not Dad."

"He's not always serious," agreed Mouse, "but he's always been a good friend to me."

"Did you date him?" asked Colt. She tousled his hair and gave him a kiss on the cheek.

"No, we lived off-campus and were neighbors. Every Thursday afternoon we sat on his porch and drank beer and talked about life." She smiled at her memories. "I lost track of him after he graduated, but you can see what a good friend he is. After all that time, he still was so kind and generous when we met at Disneyworld."

"Did Quinn know Daddy?" asked Rob. All the kids joined the conversation.

"He did." Mouse said, "They played soccer. Daddy played for the engineers and Quinn played for the pre-law team. Daddy talked with Quinn on his porch, too. We were all friends." She smiled again at the memory, recalling the night of their third anniversary when Josh admitted that Quinn had taught him how to kiss and as Josh put it, "act warm-blooded." She didn't think she would tell the kids that story.

Quinn and Samuel walked into the playroom. "How about some lunch?" asked Quinn.

Samuel pushed a cart to a round dining table and set out dishes and small trays with fruit and sandwiches. He poured milk for each place. The kids inspected the food and took seats.

"Is there enough for me?" asked Mouse, "I think I'd be more comfortable here."

"So would I," said Quinn. "Samuel, tell Dad where we are and invite him to join us."

It wasn't long before David strolled into the room carrying his own plate and glass. "Margaret is lying down. We're in for some rough times." He pulled up a chair between Tilda and Paul. "I came to meet our house guests." Mouse introduced her children, and David was a gracious host taking time to engage each one in conversation. And in Mouse's opinion, lunch was a far better experience than the meeting in the study.

* * *

"Food," crooned Will as Dusty parked the van in the yard. Lynn's backyard was filled with activity and a smoking grill. "Danny's cooking. I hope it's bratwurst," said Will as he found his shoes under the car seat.

Piper and Lynn let the dogs out so they could be adored by all the children who had come to dinner. Mars', Tee's, and Danny's youngsters scrambled to greet the dogs. Chaos! Mars' wife Trina came out of the house with a large bowl of potato salad. She was followed by Danny's wife, Angie, balancing a tray of condiments. Jason was behind with paper plates and utensils. Piper's sons, Bryce and Jeff, carried out more ice and drinks for the coolers. There were enough cookouts in the yard that everyone knew their task.

The greetings were minimal as Will hurried to be first in line for the food. Soon everyone was eating and Lynn asked, "Did you get that information?"

Danny nodded as he slathered his brawt in mustard. "We got Rory to open your office. He helped us look for the names we had. No luck."

"We think someone created a bunch of fake agencies," offered Mars as he helped his daughter, Holly, attack half a brawt. "Sara has been talking with Janet. We'll know more when she gets back to town."

"Have they found irregularities with a local foundation?" asked Lynn.

"Lela Templeton," replied Mars. "Sara knew one of the Templetons from college. They met at Disneyworld and Sara couldn't resist his computer." He scowled. "She needs a life. She can't just work and take care of those kids."

Piper laughed. "Are you matchmaking?"

He shrugged. "I try to mind my own business." His wife snorted. "I really do. But there're a dozen guys in town interested and she ignores them all."

Lynn put her arm across his shoulders. "Just remember what Dusty told me," she said, "I had to decide when I was finished being a widow."

Mars' wife gave him a hug. "Remember I was a widow until you convinced me to be a wife." She gave him a kiss. "She hasn't met the guy to convince her yet." Everyone nodded agreement. Sara would be a widow until she was ready to be something else.

* * *

"Daddy," called Margaret, as she barged into the study in the lovely mansion in Raleigh. Mouse and Quinn were with David reviewing the information they had received from Janet and planning their strategy for the coming weeks. "We have to attend the dance this evening." Margaret was dressed in a stylish summer gown. Her hair was swept back from her face and she looked every inch a sophisticated, wealthy woman ready to go to war.

David sighed, then he smiled at his daughter. "You've decided to fight back?"

Margaret nodded and turned her attention to Mouse. "I apologize for my behavior this morning. I've known for years that Madeline and CJ fooled around when they had the opportunity."

"You knew?" Quinn was surprised at her acknowledgment.

"It started a few years after you two divorced," said his sister. "Maybe that's why she sought the divorce. I never actually caught them, but there were rumors. You know how one's friends like to spread hurtful gossip and innuendo?"

"They never got serious in their relationship until about five years ago," said David.

"You spied on them?" demanded Margaret.

"I like to know what Madeline is doing so I can be prepared for her next request for funds," he admitted. "Based on what Ms. Margolin has told us, I think CJ was feathering his nest long before Madeline joined him. I suspect she figured it out and that's when the big sums started to disappear." He turned to his daughter. "You can take consolation in the fact that CJ is now in the clutches of the barracuda. He'll be sorry. And you'll have your revenge." He took his daughter's hand and kissed it. "You look lovely. I'll get dressed and we'll meet the gossips head on. Quinn are you interested in joining us?"

"No, thanks," Quinn grinned, "I have house guests to entertain. But I *am* sorry I'll miss Margaret in her stiff upper lip act."

Margaret grinned at him. "I've known my marriage was over for a long time, but I couldn't find the energy to act. CJ gave me just enough attention that I wondered if I was misreading our relationship. Tonight I feel released." David gasped. "Don't worry Daddy, I'll be decorous and charming all evening."

David left the study as he said over his shoulder, "Give me fifteen minutes."

Margaret sat down to wait for him to dress. "I am sorry about the way I treated you," She again told Mouse. "I hope we can get better acquainted during your visit. Stay up late and you can listen to me and Daddy gossip about the dance."

Mouse grinned at her. Margaret was about forty and now that she was relaxing, appeared to be as charming as Quinn. The woman continued, "This dance is a fundraiser for the children's hospital. Our family is usually a generous donor. We're probably a hundred-thousand-dollar donor this evening. I was reading the invitation and noted that the funds came through the office not the foundation. Isn't that interesting?" She turned to Quinn. "Now I understand why the committee went directly to Daddy for money. CJ probably stone-walled them because he was taking the foundation's money."

"I think you're correct," said Mouse. "My colleague has found some suspicious nonprofits that have received grants within recent years. CJ tried to keep a few of the big donations like PBS and Jimmy's group home intact, but he let several other annual, reliable donations lapse."

Margaret leveled her gaze at Mouse. "How did my brother find you so conveniently?"

"We're old college friends," replied Mouse. "Did you ever visit him at his off-campus housing? I lived next door."

"But, you haven't stayed in touch all these years." Margaret was charmed by the notion that her brother had brought a woman to meet the family, no matter what he was using as an excuse. A woman with children, no less. She suspected that there was more here than computer software.

"No," answered Mouse, "we met again yesterday at Disneyworld. I was on a job there but had time in the afternoon to enjoy the park with my kids. We ran into Quinn and Colt."

"And he was carrying his computer and just happened to ask you to check out his software?" Margaret laughed at her double entendre.

"More scandalous than that. We were all in his suite, the boys playing video games and my daughter napping. Quinn checked in online with his office and I got nosy. I can't keep my hands to myself around a key board." Mouse wiggled her fingers at Margaret. "It was easy to see when I went into the operations." She stopped talking because she saw the sorrow trace across Margaret's face. Impulsively Mouse took her hand. "I'm sorry that I've caused you such pain."

"It was going to happen sooner or later," sighed Margaret.

David walked back into the study dressed in his tuxedo. "The car will be out front in twenty minutes. I've asked Samuel to set up something for us in the music room." He turned to Mouse. "Please join us for a cocktail before we leave." He turned to Quinn as they all walked out in search of the promised cocktails. "What do you have planned this evening?"

"I think some movies. I had Colt tell Ray what movies he thought the kids would enjoy."

"We're going to the movies?" asked Mouse.

"No," replied Quinn, "we're watching movies here. We have a media center. Ray is the guy who looks after me and Colt. He's younger than Samuel." As Quinn spoke Samuel cleared his throat and pushed a cart with drinks and light refreshments into the music room.

"Sorry, Samuel," laughed Quinn, "but Ray is younger. He handles the tech stuff, movies video games, things Colt's interested in."

"Yes, sir," growled Samuel. Then he smiled, "He's a good youngster. You know he'll be graduating in another year? My sister is very excited."

"When he's ready, let us know what sort of job he's looking for. Some sort of engineer, right?" said David. "We'll help him find something."

"Thank you, sir." Samuel left the room.

"Colt asked Ray for a pizza party and popcorn for the movies," announced Quinn. "I hope my stomach survives this weekend." He took the drink David offered.

"Breakfast should be more adult," remarked Margaret. "We'll have a brunch —"

"Too late," interrupted David, "Colt has breakfast redesigned. He's requested Belgian waffles with plenty of bacon and sausage. I told Samuel to be sure to include some fresh fruit."

"See how Colt runs this place?" Quinn asked as an aside to Mouse. "He can have anything he wants. Belgian waffles? I haven't seen those in this house since, well, since I don't know when." He almost pouted and Mouse laughed.

"We have to talk about me and my children getting back to River Bend," she said. "I have a job."

"You're working for us." This time Quinn did pout.

"I'm a techie, I can work from anywhere." She sipped from her drink. "The boys are enrolled in soccer camp starting Monday. And Tilda is attending a drama program at the Little Theater starting the following week."

Quinn guffawed. "The drama queen? She'll teach them a thing or two."

David quietly sipped his drink and watched the interplay between his son and the computer consultant and found it very interesting. Margaret had already noticed the same thing. When she turned to her father, he winked and said, "Ms. Margolin, -"

"Call her Mouse," interjected Quinn. She blushed.

"Mouse," David began again, "I would like you to enjoy Sunday with us. My son, Jimmy, comes for a visit and I think he would enjoy your children. Then I would like you to meet with my technical staff on Monday morning. We'll have you and your children home for lunch."

"Thank you."

* * *

Ray had the family theater ready and guided everyone into their seats. He charmed Mouse and her children with his smiles and corny jokes as they selected their seats. "Do you know why lions don't eat clowns?"

Three youngsters shook their heads.

"Because they taste funny."

The twins groaned and Tilda giggled.

Colt got the kids seated in the front row and handed out popcorn, drinks and snacks.

"Where are the other people?" asked Tilda.

"It's just us," Colt explained, "We can make noise and walk around and talk if we want to."

"Can I sit by you?" the little girl asked.

Colt blushed and said, "Sure."

Ray got the kids settled, spoke briefly with Quinn and left the room. Soon the lights dimmed and the movie began. Quinn led Mouse to the back row in the twenty-seat theater. She rolled her eyes as the title of the first movie flashed on the screen. A super hero movie that her sons had been begging to see. She wondered if Tilda would be happy with the choice.

Quinn settled in to watch and took Mouse's hand. He grinned at her when she looked at him in surprise. "I can't watch a movie without holding hands with someone," he explained. She didn't pull her hand away. About halfway through the movie Tilda walked to the back row.

"Mommy, I'm tired." She looked at Mouse and crawled onto Quinn's lap where she made herself comfortable. He let go of Mouse's hand as he adjusted Tilda's head on his shoulder. Mouse squirmed in her seat until she was resting her head on his other shoulder.

"Wow," he whispered, "I've never ended up with all the women at a party. Those guys don't know what they're missing."

Mouse stretched up and kissed his cheek then returned her head to his shoulder.

When the movie ended, Ray came into the room, "Do I run the second feature?" But he smiled as he saw that all the kids seemed to be asleep. He rousted the boys and helped them to their rooms. Quinn carried Tilda and Mouse trailed behind, almost as tired as her children.

"Don't go to bed, yet," Quinn begged Mouse. "We can have a drink and wait for Dad to come home."

Mouse smiled at him. "I did promise Margaret I'd stay up to hear her gossip." She yawned.

They got all the kids into pajamas and tucked in bed then returned to the music room.

"I'd like an herbal tea," said Mouse when Ray asked for her drink order.

"Herbal tea? Bleck!" remarked Quinn hanging out his tongue. "I'll have the same." Mouse laughed.

Ray returned with their drinks and some small cakes and excused himself for the night.

"This is a lovely home and you and your father have been so kind," said Mouse. "It's not even forty-eight hours since we met in Disneyworld and look where we are. Do you always sweep women off their feet like this?"

Quinn sat on the settee beside her and placed his tea cup on a small table. He took her hand. "I don't bring women here. This is the family sanctuary."

"But you do see women?"

"Are you jealous?"

"Curious. I knew your reputation at school. And you're a rich, handsome man. Women must find you irresistible."

She saw a sadness in Quinn's eyes. "I learned that my money is more irresistible than anything else. I rarely date, usually only when I need someone to accompany me to a dinner or other semi-business function. The rest of the time it's me, Dad and Colt."

"Now you sound like all the single moms I know. Dating and kids don't mix."

"It's not even that I have a son," said Quinn, "Some women only seem interested in the kind of life I can offer, not the kind of *family* life I can offer. Does that make sense?"

Mouse massaged his hand. "Colt said something today about people only being interested in money. He wants to find a place where he can be normal and money won't be an issue or one of his defining factors. It sounds like he's learned that from you."

"What about you? Are all the single men in River Bend after you?"

"I am asked out on dates, but no one interests me. My life is busy with the kids and work. It's great that my parents are available to pitch in. I'm too busy to date." As she said that she looked at Quinn and was caught by the pull between them. He started to lean into her when they heard the door in the front hall open.

He reluctantly rose to his feet and called, "Dad, we're in here."

Margaret and David soon joined them. David looked at the tea service. "A night cap?"

"I can mix you something," volunteered Quinn.

"No, we had enough at the club."

"How was it?" Mouse asked Margaret.

"We drew a line in the sand," she gloated. "I told everyone that CJ and I were separated. I said I have hopes that we can save our marriage, because it's important to me, but the ball is in his court." She poured herself some tea. "I was magnificent—just the right amount of sympathy and courage."

"Did you hear any gossip?" Mouse wanted all the news.

"CJ must have talked to someone because my announcement was no surprise," replied Margaret. "I did hear that someone saw him at dinner with Madeline."

"She's in town?" asked David. "I wonder why she hasn't come to me for money."

"She'll be here tomorrow," Quinn prophesied.

CHAPTER SIX

Sunday morning's Belgian waffles were a great success. Mouse didn't want to eat again until Tuesday. Everyone had met Jimmy when he and his attendant arrived. He was polite and spoke sparingly but smiled a lot and seemed to be excited to meet the children. In the swirl of his arrival everyone dispersed, leaving Mouse alone with Quinn.

"We can get some work done," he offered. "Jimmy usually has a late lunch with us and then returns to his home." They walked into the study to refine Monday's presentation to the technical staff.

"Why doesn't he live here?" asked Mouse. She walked to the windows to watch Jimmy, a man of about thirty years of age, sitting on a glider on the patio with David. They were having a quiet, affectionate interlude.

"We tried," Quinn replied, "when Mom was alive. But she died, I was in college, Margaret got married and finding him a place that excited him became our goal. Dad spent a lot of money on research and some nationally known experts. They designed a cluster of homes, funded in part by our foundation, that suited Jimmy and his intelligence level and abilities. And he visits us several times a month. You'll notice that by four o'clock he's eager to return to his place." Quinn came up behind Mouse and placed his hands on her shoulders running them up and down her arms. She stepped back to bring her body against his. He slipped his arms around her waist and pulled her closer. He rested his chin on the top of her head and they watched the activity on the patio. There seemed to be no need to talk.

Mouse abruptly pulled away, startled by what she saw outside. "Tilda has on her swimsuit." Out on the patio they watched Tilda walk by in her Disney World Cinderella suit carrying books under her arm. She walked over to the glider and sat beside David. He had just opened a book to read to Jimmy. They readjusted themselves to make room for Tilda, listened to her say something, then all settled back as David prepared to read a book.

Quinn laughed as he turned Mouse around to face him. He kissed her quickly on the lips then explained, "We have a pool. Jimmy likes to swim. See how wet his hair is? He likes to swim but only for about thirty minutes. His routine is the swim, Dad and he chat, Dad reads him some stories and he plays some more and finally we'll have lunch and he and his orderly will be taken home." He kissed her again as Margaret walked into the study.

"Knock, knock," she called and Quinn almost broke his ankle moving away from Mouse as quickly as possible. "Are you making Mouse work on Sunday?"

"We have to get this work done," said Quinn as he limped to a chair.

Margaret joined Mouse at the windows. "That little girl of yours certainly makes herself at home. She came into my room to help me unpack. One of the security guards and I went to my house so that I could get a few things. Apparently, Mouse, your wardrobe is very bland. Tilda had to try on all my shoes, especially those with high heels, because you don't have any for her to practice with."

"I'm sorry that she's being a nuisance."

But Margaret laughed, "She has a way of showing me how much fun life can be." They watched Tilda on the patio. "Look at her now. She's got Dad reading books to her and Jimmy." Margaret squinted. "I think she's making him read stories for older children—less pictures and more words."

Mouse turned to Quinn. "Security guards? Swimming pool?"

He blew out his breath. Since Mouse and her children had arrived he always seemed to be apologizing for the perks of the estate. "We have an in-door pool and work-out room about fifty feet off the kitchen. You can see it from the play room. We have three security guards on the property at all times. They stay in some rooms attached to the workout room. You don't have to worry about the kids swimming, one of the guards will stay at the pool area as long as the kids are there."

"Why do you need security?"

"It's wise for someone with our resources." He looked at Margaret for help. She shrugged. He continued. "At first we worried that Madeline would snatch Colt. But we've come to understand that she just makes noise so that she gets more money. We've had some angry employees find us and we've had an attempted robbery or two over the last ten years. Today the guards have been advised that CJ is no longer welcome on the estate. And if Madeline comes to call, she'll be escorted by a guard and not be allowed to be alone with Colt."

"She'd take Colt?" Mouse was shocked.

"We've found out about her and CJ's money. I don't know what she might do," he replied. "I'm glad to have the security."

Margaret chuckled as she pulled herself away from the windows. "Tilda has turned Dad into her slave." They watched the little girl carry on an animated conversation with Jimmy as David led them into the house. "So am I interrupting your work?" Margaret asked.

"Yes," said Quinn.

"No," said Mouse.

Margaret tweaked Quinn's nose and left the room, closing the door behind her. He moved quickly to get his arms around Mouse.

"I wanted to -"

"Mom?" Tilda barged into the study, books under her arm, Cinderella swimsuit still damp and her curls bobbing. Quinn dropped his arm from Mouse's shoulder.

"Yes, Tilda?"

"Mr. David needs new books to read. These are baby books. We have to get mine from home." She stood in the middle of the room, barefooted with one swimsuit strap slipping off her shoulder. "I told Jimmy he would like big kid books." She looked at Quinn. "Is he your brother?"

Quinn nodded.

"He likes to play with me. Will you bring him to my house?" asked the youngster.

"That's a fine idea," said David as he followed Tilda into the study. "We'll make arrangements with your mother once we finish this project." He turned to Mouse. "Is that all right with you?"

She nodded.

Jimmy followed his father into the room and ran to his brother. Quinn hugged him and kissed his forehead.

"Do you like Legos?" Tilda asked Jimmy.

"Legos," Jimmy replied.

"Come on," she ordered, "we can build a space ship or a castle."

Jimmy grinned and followed her out of the study.

David flopped in a chair. "That little girl critiqued my reading and my choice of books. I feel like such a failure." Quinn and Mouse laughed. David looked around the room. "I can see that you're working. I need a drink." He left the study closing the door behind him.

Quinn was immediately in front of Mouse again, drawing her into his arms for a kiss as the door opened.

"Mom?" called two damp, swim-suited boys.

Quinn dropped his arms and turned to face the twins.

"Dad?" Colt followed the younger boys into the study. "The guard watching us swim said he would show us some defensive moves in the gym if it's all right with you. He said call him."

Quinn picked up the phone and punched a number. After a quick conversation with the guard, Quinn said to the boys, "He's willing to show you some self-defense moves, but you can't use them on Tilda." The boys frowned. "Those are the rules. Do you understand?"

Three unhappy boys said, "Yes." They ran from the room leaving the door open.

Quinn blew out his breath. "Twenty thousand square feet and they all act like this is the only room in the house." Mouse walked into his arms.

* * *

A buzzer rang as the family sat down for Sunday's light lunch. David took the phone from a side table, listened, and spoke quietly. "Let them in." He turned to Quinn. "You were right, she's here with CJ."

Margaret gasped. "Here comes the showdown."

Two security men came into the dining room. One asked Ray to take the children into the play room as the second assisted the orderly helping Jimmy from his chair. "Sir, do you want me to pat them down?"

"No," replied David, "This will be a civilized meeting."

"Do you want me to leave?" asked Mouse.

"Yes," said Quinn. "You don't need to witness this."

David accompanied by Quinn and Margaret walked to the foyer and waited for the uninvited guests to arrive. CJ pushed open the entry door as he always did, barging in without an invitation. "Well, well, well," he smirked, "a little family gathering. Are we circling the wagons? Where's that fake computer specialist?"

"Fake computer specialist?" taunted Madeline, as usual dressed expensively with her hair and cosmetics setting off her beautiful face.

"Quinn brought home some little snippet, with children, and tried to pass her off as a computer expert," CJ informed her. He then addressed David and Margaret, "You've certainly found out by now that she's a fake and you've accused me with no proof."

Behind CJ and Madeline, Quinn saw Colt then Mouse slip into an alcove in the dim hallway where they could observe the discussion. He caught her eye. She shrugged and moved her eyes to Colt. Quinn understood. His son wanted to be a witness to the family drama and Mouse would be there as his friend.

"I'm afraid that I believe what Quinn's computer expert has to say," said David, "I've verified her credentials with some friends. Of course, you will be given an opportunity to straighten out this confusion. After all, she can only tell us what she finds on the computer, not what your intentions are. Why don't you come to the office tomorrow afternoon and we'll sort this out?"

"That will only give you time to alter the computer records," argued CJ, "I don't trust any of you. You'll use this as an opportunity to drive a wedge further between me and my wife."

"No one can drive it any further," announced Margaret stepping forward. "Our marriage is over. My lawyer will contact you." By the sound of her voice, no one could doubt that Margaret meant what she said.

Madeline said to CJ, "I hope you have better lawyers to help you than I had. David won't give an inch. I even popped out a grandchild and I still got nothing. All those labor pains should have been worth a lot more." She glowered at Quinn. "Maybe I should have gotten more for my great acting, putting up with your lousy love-making."

"It was just as hard on my part," drawled Quinn, "trying to move a cow like you."

"That's enough," ordered David.

"Where is my son?" Madeline asked. "He should hear how his beloved father and grandfather talk to his mother. I can't wait for the day that he controls the family finances. I'll get the money I've always wanted. He'll remember his mother fondly."

"You've worked hard to make certain he only sees your sweetness." Quinn frowned as he acknowledged, "I do see how hard you've worked to deceive him."

He glanced toward Mouse and Colt. She was holding the youngster as he rested his head against hers. Quinn was drawn back into the conversation as CJ asked, "How do you plan on getting the foundation grants out without me?"

"We'll manage," said Quinn, eager to have these people leave so he could get to his son. He walked to the door and opened it. "We'll see you tomorrow afternoon, CJ. Bring a lawyer if you like."

"Why? I've done nothing wrong."

"You're welcome to come too, Madeline," Quinn invited his ex.

"Really, darling, I've probably got shopping to do." She looked at David. "Maybe it's time for another chat about my parental rights and my desire that my son live with me."

David gave her a bored look and said, "Join us tomorrow afternoon." He gestured for them to leave.

As David closed the door, Quinn ran to his son and was surprised to find him surrounded by Mouse and her children.

"She only sees me as a bag of money," said Colt as he swallowed a sob.

"Don't give her a thought," said Mouse as her arm tightened around his waist. The three children gathered closer to Colt and Tilda took his hand. In years to come Quinn would remember that scene as the defining moment when he realized that he needed Mouse and those children in his, and Colt's, life permanently.

* * *

Dusty walked along the stone wall that separated his yard from Emily Jacobs' place. Lynn had spent one summer a year or so ago rescuing the wall from the ivy that had claimed it. It had recently become the meeting place for Dusty and Doug Fiore, Emily's nephew-in-law and the James County acting sheriff. The elected sheriff was currently in the hospital ICU fighting the covid virus. During each visit to Aunt Emily, Doug found time to meander to the stonewall for a quiet discussion with Dusty.

The men hadn't spoken since Dusty's return from the Outer Banks. Doug waved and walked to the wall. "You came back." The man was about ten years younger than Dusty and had recently married Connie, Emily's niece who had two daughters. He brought his son Toby into the marriage. With an exchange of vows, Connie and Doug found themselves the parents of three elementary school aged children. And within months Emily had convinced them to also become the guardians at her death of her three great-grandchildren. Doug had resigned from the highway patrol and taken a job as the community information officer for the James County Sheriff's Department. The job kept him closer to home and offered flexible hours for a family that would one day be six children.

"Were you worried?" Dusty picked at the sunburned skin on the bridge of his nose. Just seeing it was making him cross-eyed. He had not respected the intensity of the sun on the Outer Banks.

Doug nodded. "I didn't realize how much I count on you and your team to have my back." In the short time he had held the communications officer job, Doug had averted many embarrassing moments for the sheriff, explaining incidents clearly while embellishing the sheriff's leadership abilities. After Sheriff Dunwoody had been hospitalized with covid, he had appointed Doug interim sheriff because the hospital stay was anticipated to be lengthy. In Sheriff Dunwoody's mind, Doug would make a good impression as the interim, thereby aiding the Dunwoody reelection efforts.

Dusty's eyes bugged out. "Did someone give you trouble while I was gone?"

"No." The acting sheriff made a calming gesture. "Just the opposite. I got to know several of the folks better. There's some real talent in the department.

"There sure is," Dusty agreed. "Dunwoody keeps stifling them and promoting his favorites." They walked along the wall and listened to the night sounds while the dog chased fireflies.

"Is it true you're going to run against him in the next election?" Doug was curious.

Dusty leaned against the wall. "I've thought about it. It would be great to create opportunities for the talent in the department and maybe help my team advance. And it would be challenging to see if I couldn't get more work out of the dumb ones."

Doug laughed. "I know which ones you mean." They walked some more, reaching the roadway and turning to walk to the back property line. "I think you would do a great job. I also think several of the younger deputies are counting on new leadership soon or they plan to leave."

"It's a while until I have to worry about it." Dusty stared up at the darkness overhead. "My father-in-law is ready to act as my campaign chair and I'm certain the money will be there." I just wish my heart were in it, he thought to himself.

Doug pulled at an overhead branch. "Tell me about this vacation."

"We would have been more comfortable at your place in Hilton Head," Dusty moaned.

Doug laughed. "I'm sure the newlyweds are enjoying themselves."

"They would have enjoyed themselves in a tent someplace."

Doug laughed again. "Next year, I'll owe you."

"Count on it," growled the detective.

CHAPTER SEVEN

Lynn arrived at her office on time Monday morning. Saturday evening, just listening to the detectives talk about how they had helped discover some potential fake grant applicants, she had gotten caught up in the drama of Sara's new client, the Templeton Family. It might become an interesting investigation, she thought, but today she had mail to answer and calls to return after her week's vacation. She would hold on to the Outer Banks afterglow as long as possible.

"You're back," groused Nelda, "that man is crazy." So much for afterglow!

"She means me," called Rory as he breezed into the reception area. Lynn had hired Rory Prentiss after he lost his job with the Arts Council when the agency closed its doors during the pandemic. "Hey, sweetie!" He air-kissed Lynn. "Glad you're back. Remember I'll be out next week working on my Little People Little Theater program. I've got a full class this year. Word is finally getting around." As the former director of the Arts Council he was the driving force behind the Little People Little Theater grant the Philanthropies had funded for several years. The Little Theater ran a summer drama camp for children ages six through ten.

"I'm looking forward to the final show," Lynn teased, thinking the afterglow was still lingering. The theater camp was designed to teach children some stage basics as well as provide some income for the Little Theater. The program ended the session with a stage presentation by the youngsters enrolled in the program. "Who's working with you this year?"

Rory sighed. "Some of my usuals had to leave town to look for work, but Bryce Hanby is helping me every afternoon. Hank agreed to give him the time off with pay." Bryce, Piper's eldest son, worked for Hank

Seymour's industrial waste recycling business, and before the pandemic, had had a blossoming career on Broadway.

"With pay?"

"Everyone told Hank that Bryce works hard and deserves a perk." Rory winked. "I think Dr. Rita had something to do with it. She attended the closing show last year." Dr. Rita was Hank's wife.

"You just make sure my grandson has a good time," ordered Nelda.

"You bet, sweetie," replied Rory. "He'll steal the show if he has your charm."

Nelda rolled her eyes at him and Lynn laughed. "Let us know if we can help with anything," said Lynn as he ran back to his office.

* * *

Monday morning was hectic. Mouse met with the Templeton, Inc. technology staff and explained the problems with the funds. She outlined the management proposal that she had crafted with Quinn and David so that the corporate IT office would be hired to manage all the foundation and trust technology. Everyone thought it was a brilliant solution.

After the meeting Mouse asked Quinn, "Can we go home now?"

"I was going to ask you to stay for that meeting with CJ, but he called and told my assistant that he had to postpone the meeting until he got himself better organized."

"What do you think that means?" asked David.

"It means he hasn't been able to access his offshore money and thinks it's just a system glitch that he can solve with whomever is his computer advisor," replied Mouse. "He must have someone on his payroll who either manages the transfers and other shady actions, or he pays someone whom he has given foundation IT access," she looked at David, "a real breech of your network security. But don't worry he won't get anywhere."

"Take her home," said David as he gave her a hug. "We'll settle up as soon as we've had time to talk with CJ and Madeline."

Quinn took her by the arm as he called Samuel at the house to get the children ready to leave for home.

* * *

The private plane landed at the regional airport in Asheville and Quinn helped everyone off and into a large SUV he had rented. Colt was delighted with the arrangements because he had been invited to attend soccer camp with the twins. They had missed the first day, but Mouse had called ahead and Mars had smoothed things with the program director. It helped that she also enrolled an extra youngster and Quinn had suggested that the Lela Templeton Foundation donate some new equipment.

"Am I missing my camp, too?" pouted Tilda.

"No, dear, your camp is next week." Mouse tried to hide her yawn as everyone climbed into the rental vehicle.

"Where to?" asked Quinn.

"Our house," said Mouse, "and it's much smaller than yours. I hope you can take care of yourself because I have no staff." Colt sat in the seat behind Quinn and grinned into the rearview mirror. Mouse marveled that the youngster seemed to be so happy, even after he heard his mother's rant yesterday.

As the children chattered in the back seats, Quinn leaned over and whispered, "Where will I sleep?"

"At my parents' house. Colt can stay with the boys so I can get them to camp in the morning."

"I want to stay with you. It'll be more fun." Quinn deftly steered around some road kill.

"I don't have room," said Mouse. She directed him onto the highway and they raced to River Bend.

When they arrived at Mouse's place, the kids jumped out and dragged Colt around the yard. It was a comfortable looking older home with a front porch and dormers highlighting the second story. The back yard fell away, sloping to a garage and alleyway. Mouse and Quinn opened the house, raised the windows to let in some fresh air and finally dragged the luggage in.

Quinn inspected the house. "I can sleep here." He pointed the queen size bed in Mouse's room.

"That's my bed."

"We can share."

She ignored the comment and placed some things in the twins' room. "Colt can sleep in here." It was a spacious room with three twin beds. "I've learned that the boys always seem to want a friend to sleep over so I've made a room where they can do that."

"Tilda has an extra bed, too," observed Quinn, "I can sleep in her extra bed."

"No, you can't."

"Can we, Mom?" He imitated the children.

"Tilda can sleep with me and you can sleep in one of her beds. But you have to get permission from her. She's very particular about her things." Mouse walked into her bedroom and closed the door, leaving him alone in the hallway.

Quinn went in search of the little girl. He found her on a swing under a tree in the back yard. "This is a great swing," commented Quinn. "Will you let me use it?"

"You have to push me first," announced the little queen. "I don't have anyone to play with. The boys took the bikes and went to the park." She pointed in a vague direction.

"I'll go with you to the park," offered Quinn. "I can play with you."

Tilda studied him. Quinn could almost see her mind working as she considered what she could gain in this bargain. "I need to have a cookie at the bakery. And you have to carry me if I get tired."

Gotcha, he thought. "I can do all those things, but when we get back home I might be tired. Can I rest in your bedroom?"

"Where will I rest?"

"In your mother's room?"

"You can't play with my toys. They won't like it."

"I won't touch a thing." He held out his hand. "Why don't we go get a cookie?"

* * *

Quinn found sitting in the bakery a lot of fun. He and Tilda sat at the window bar and watched the pedestrian traffic as they ate their cookies. Tilda seemed to know everyone and explained Quinn to everyone who asked.

"This is Quinn," she announced to a smiling, slender woman, "He has a big house with a swimming pool. He calls Mommy a mouse."

"Ah," said the enlightened woman, "You must be Mr. Templeton. I'm Lynn Powers, the executive director of River Bend Philanthropies. I hope we were able to help Sara solve your problem."

"I didn't know you helped," replied a confused Quinn. "I thought her partner or her cousin helped."

"We all did." Lynn thought a moment. "Janet is Sara's partner and cousin. She's the computer consultant and very pregnant. She called in Mars —

"She means Uncle Mars," explained Tilda.

"Uncle Mars is a detective who works with my husband. The detectives helped Janet and Sara investigate some nonprofits." Quinn's eyes grew large as Lynn continued. "Uncle Mars," Lynn knew better than to misspeak in front of Tilda again, "called me for information on nonprofits. We were just returning from the Outer Banks, so he got the key to my office and did some research in my materials. Of course he called a few times and everyone had a party at our house because. . ." Lynn stopped. "This is sounding confusing I'm sure, but they, I mean my husband's staff, had all planned on a picnic with their families when they got this SOS from Janet to help you. So they all, spouses and children, went to my house to research so their children could play in our yard and my son would help entertain them. They were all there when we drove in."

"How many people were involved?" Quinn was even more confused after Lynn's explanation.

"Tee and her husband and three children. Uncle Mars" she glanced at Tilda, "and his wife and three children. Danny and his wife and two children. And, of course, Janet and her husband and two children."

"That's twenty people!"

"And my son and a few friends. If there's food involved, they show up. We call them the college crowd, four or five more."

"Jason always lets us play soccer in his yard." Tilda clarified.

"Jason is my son," said Lynn.

"Was Ricky there?" asked Tilda. "He always helps me score a goal."

Quinn smiled at Lynn. "I see I'm wired into the social life of River Bend just by knowing Tilda." One of the shop workers handed Lynn a cake box.

A woman walked into the bakery and called, "Tilda?"

"Grandma!" The little girl squirmed off the high bar chair and ran to hug the older woman. "I'm with Quinn. He has a big house with a swimming pool. He calls Mommy a mouse."

Oh," said the grandmother. It wasn't the welcoming acknowledgment that Lynn had given him. "You're that man with the big house. Are you expecting my daughter to do all this work for free?"

Quinn's eyes bugged out. "I'm paying triple rates."

"He has a swimming pool and a ranch in Montana," added Tilda. "We're going there when Mommy finishes her work."

"Montana?" Grandmother was not impressed. "Do you always take advantage of single, hard-working mothers?"

Quinn opened his mouth to speak, but Tilda spoke first. "He hugged Mommy."

Lynn laughed. "Really, Charlotte," she teased the other woman, "do you think he came all the way to River Bend to seduce your daughter?"

Quinn frowned because he thought that *was* one of the reasons. In fact, the longer he stayed close to Mouse, the more he was certain that he wanted her and her family as his. He tried to wipe that thought out of his mind because he was certain Charlotte would smell his intentions. She scanned him thoroughly and asked, "Why are you thinking you should stay at her place and not mine? Young, single mothers don't entertain men while their children are at home." She glared at him.

"He took us to his room at Disneyworld," volunteered Tilda. "and bought us swimsuits. He kissed Mommy in the swimming pool."

"I guess I can stay with you now that we've met." Quinn smiled at Charlotte. "I didn't want to impose." Somehow, Quinn's interest in Mouse was like a predatory scent to her mother!

Lynn patted his arm. "Don't worry, Charlotte and Carter are lovely people. Now that you'll be sleeping away from Sara."

"He calls her a mouse," Tilda helped the conversation again.

"I called her Mouse when we were in college," he explained. "Do you want another cookie," he asked the little girl, "so you can't talk anymore?"

Charlotte gave him another sharp glance. "I'll expect you after dinner so Sara and the children can get some rest. What do you eat for breakfast? I'm picking up some of Umberto's cinnamon-raisin bread."

Quinn gulped as though he had been reprimanded. "That will be fine." The woman walked toward the bakery counter.

"I think we should get home," Quinn suggested to Tilda.

"I can drive you two," offered Lynn.

"That would be great. I'm a little turned around." Quinn rubbed his forehead.

"He wants to sleep in my bed," announced Tilda.

Charlotte shot a glance at him from across the store, and Lynn laughed again as she directed Quinn and Tilda to her car.

* * *

Dusty walked into the kitchen. He had only been back to work one full day and was ready to return to the Outer Banks. He placed his phone on the charger, put away his weapon and grabbed a beer. Flopping onto a chair and gulping a long swallow, he placed the bottle on the table and sighed.

"Tough day?" asked Lynn.

He looked around the kitchen. Nothing was happening. "No dinner?"

She nodded. "Tough day." She sat at the table and sighed. They looked at one another and laughed. "It wasn't bad, just mail and calls to return."

Dusty nodded. "The same. My staff took care of everything they could. No murders or robberies, just meetings and paperwork."

Jason came into the kitchen, loosened his necktie, grabbed a beer and sat at the table. "Tough day?" his mother asked.

He nodded. "Gramps had a lot of things for me to do. He says I wasted a week on vacation." Jason was working as a clerk, messenger, and filer in his grandfather's law office. By late August he would be in law school.

Dusty finished his beer and stood. "Come on, I'm buying dinner at River Dog."

"Yeah!" Lynn slipped on her shoes and ran her fingers through her hair.

Jason gulped his beer and dashed into the laundry room coming out within nanoseconds dressed in shorts and an old t-shirt. "I'm ready." They jumped into Dusty's car and headed to the brewery.

"There's a new food truck," announced Jason when they left the car and walked toward the old warehouse. As they approached they waved to friends.

"Business has certainly picked up as masks have disappeared," observed Dusty.

Zeke, one of the owners, came over to greet them. "Look at this place." He threw out his arm. "Everyone is back." The inside and outdoor tables were all filled. Lines formed at the food trucks. Families with children enjoyed the evening in the social hub of Portage.

"Give us an update," said Lynn, "How is everyone?"

"Fine, fine and fine." He smiled. "Eddie's brother fits in real good." Eddie, a partner and brewmaster in the brewery, had succumbed to covid in the early days of lockdown. His brother had come to help the other partners bringing his brewing skills and knowledge to River Dog. Lonnie Erhardt and his wife Dana and their children had been sent to River Dog by Eddie's family, master brewers of a long-time family-owned national beer, to help Eddie's friends.

Zeke's wife came rushing over and almost screamed, "I'm pregnant!" All those within hearing around the brewery applauded. She hugged Lynn.

Dusty shook Zeke's hand. "I guess you kept busy during this down time," he drawled to the happy brewer.

Zeke blushed and shook a puzzled head. "We did stay almost even with income. Granny said we got some money from our cousin Yetta's estate. I don't know anything about it. Darwin handled all the technology."

"Yetta had an estate?" Dusty was puzzled. Yetta Masterson had been a serial quitter, holding a job only long enough to pay rent then moving on. She was murdered by a boyfriend, Heath Dawson. But Dusty didn't know that after her death Darwin Masterson and Granny had found that she was receiving monthly payments from another boyfriend, Rupert Rothman, a man subsequently killed in a police chase. It was clear to everyone that Yetta was not discerning in her lovers. Granny, the brains of the Masterson family, saw the monthly income as a family asset.

Of course, neither she nor Darwin, the family tech savant, told anyone that they had also found and confiscated a few million from the dead boyfriend's offshore account. That was the money that kept River Dog Brewery 'breaking even' all through the initial pandemic lockdown.

As Dusty mulled over the idea that Yetta had an estate, Granny and Darwin were secretly discussing the future of those funds. "What do we do now?" Darwin was asking.

Granny paced the security office of the brewery, a small room above the offices of River Dog and across the alley from the brewery. "You got all that was left?"

Darwin nodded. "I moved two," he couldn't even whisper million, "to our other account and got out as fast as I could. I don't think anyone saw me."

"Saw you?" Granny was sharp, but technology still baffled her.

"Every time I go to that account I leave something like electronic footprints. Someone could be watching and follow me home."

"What about our other account?"

"No one knows about those funds. It's just Rothman's old account, not ours, that could lead folks to us."

"Someone took all the rest but the two million?" she asked. Life in cyberspace was interesting, but all she cared about was keeping her grandsons' business healthy. She'd let some younger, smarter crooks take advantage of virtual criminal opportunities.

"Yeah. I took what was left. I was quick. We're okay, and safe."

Granny seemed satisfied. She turned her attention to the security screens. "Why, Miss Lynn and that lawman come visitin'." With that Granny shuffled from the office in her old work boots, clad in her usual house dress.

Darwin smiled and watched the screen as Lynn and Granny hugged.

CHAPTER EIGHT

Bart Decker had been caught in a drug raid several months ago. The investigation netted Kip Mahaffey, a prominent attorney, and Margaret Eliason, director of the South End Health Clinic as the chief perpetrators in a sophisticated drug delivery system. It caused a big scandal in River Bend, but Bart was a small fry in the operation, just a user caught in the crossfire. The court case today would finalize Bart's negotiated sentence. No one had been eager to pursue a husband and father of three who held down a full-time job. The sentence would be minimal.

Audrey Decker, his wife, had not wanted to attend the court session alone. She had asked her best friend Rory Prentiss to accompany her. He had demurred, suggesting that she ask Lynn, wife of a prominent detective, to go along to the proceedings. Sitting in the courtroom listening to the testimony, Audrey clutched Lynn's hand, immeasurably grateful to have a friend at her side. She knew Lynn had other demands but had graciously accepted the request when Rory had suggested Lynn's presence added more gravitas to the situation than an aging gay guy's.

Lynn leaned over to whisper, "That's Judge Dunn. She doesn't let things get out of hand." Audrey worried about how far out of hand her husband might get.

At the recommendation of his attorney, Bart Decker had pled guilty. Today was the formal hearing. He stood beside his attorney. He had been out on bail after his drug arrest. This was the sentencing hearing as a result of the plea bargain. The crime had been reduced to misdemeanor. According to the attorney, Mr. Grayson, the sentence would be probation and required check-ins with a probation officer. It had been comforting to Audrey when he explained that there had been negotiations with the DA and today's hearing would only be a formality. Bart and the family would not notice any inconvenience as long as he complied with the final orders.

The ADA made his presentation, the judge asked several questions. Mr. Grayson responded. The judge reviewed the papers presented. Audrey was struck that this all seemed to be scripted. She made that comment to Lynn, who replied, "They do this every day."

Judge Dunn cast an evil eye at the two women whispering and they sat up quickly, lips zipped. The judge smirked at her friend, Lynn, then turned to the defendant, "Mr. Decker, I have reviewed the case. And I agree with the sentence as negotiated by the attorneys. I assume this has your approval and you agree to abide by the recommended terms of probation." She stared at the man.

H. Lawrence Grayson, standing beside the man, pinched his client. Decker, startled, replied, "Yes, ma'am, your honor."

The judge smashed her gavel, nodded to the attorneys. "Thank you, gentlemen. Bailiff, call the next case." There was a rustling at the attorneys' desks as they collected papers. In the case of the ADA, he would just close one case file and move to the next. But he had a few minutes to relax while H. Lawrence collected his papers and directed his client to follow the bailiff to wrap up the paperwork.

As the defendant left the courtroom the next defendant entered beside his attorney. H. Lawrence carried his briefcase and went to meet Lynn and Audrey. "It's completed, ladies. All Mr. Decker has to do is behave and report in as directed."

"Where should I meet him?" Audrey asked.

"He's been taken down to the probation office to get himself enrolled in the system. You could probably wait there for him. You might like to meet the officer handling his case, you know, if there are problems."

"Problems?" There was a clear panic in Audrey's voice. Lynn glared at Herbie, silently demanding that he erase the panic.

He fumbled and mumbled and finally said, "You know, if he gets sick or breaks a leg or the kids need some attention, God forbid."

"Oh, you mean in an emergency I could contact this person and explain that Bart might not be checking in?"

"Exactly!" grinned the relieved attorney. He nodded to the women and disappeared in the stream of folks coming and going in the courthouse corridor.

"Thank you, Lynn." Audrey gave her a swift hug. "It was easier than I imagined."

"You're welcome." Lynn hugged her back. "I have to get back to the office and report to Rory. I'm sure he's been worried all morning."

Audrey swiped a tear from her eye. "He's such a good friend."

"I'll tell him that." With one more hug the women parted.

Audrey watched her walk away and thought, bless Lynn. Her friend had listened to Audrey's story of an affair, Bart's discovery of the liaison, and his drug arrest. All in all, a dark chapter of a sad marriage. Even after Audrey had broken down and confessed all, Lynn still had the capacity to offer support and friendship without judgement. The woman had sent Dusty to argue with the board of Exceptional Children to protect Audrey's job. The board had no knowledge of the affair but was concerned about the impact of Bart's arrest on the nonprofit. Dusty had argued that dismissing Audrey from her job for her husband's crimes was not acceptable or ethical.

With a sigh, Audrey told herself that she had to live in the moment—her job, her kids. Once the fallout of this entire incident was behind her, she would examine her life, her options and her children's needs then make some decisions. She read the courthouse directory and went to find the probation office.

Walking into the office she heard her husband screaming as he blamed her infidelity for all of his problems. Everyone in the waiting area heard as he outlined his grievances, damning her for destroying the marriage he thought they had. She listened. He spoke of a marriage that had nothing to do with the recent years she had spent with him. Yes, there had been good times. And certainly there had been children—true gifts in a sham partnership. But the current reality of their marriage was much different than the myth he described.

She listened to what he was saying, "We did everything together. We had a great family. I don't know what happened. This guy —

"You mean the man you accuse of having an affair with your wife?" asked an unseen, professional sounding probation officer.

"Yeah, him," shouted her husband. "I think he got her on drugs or something. He turned her into a stranger. She wouldn't have done this if she was thinking right. Not to the kids."

Thinking right? Audrey didn't know whether to laugh or cry. It was all so confusing. And here they were. Their marriage and family life asunder.

"May I help you?" asked a staffer who walked into the reception area.

"I came to meet my husband's probation officer."

The woman, having heard all of Bart's ranting, grimaced. "I guess you belong to that new guy?" She tilted her head toward the shouting.

"Yes, I'm Mrs. Decker."

The woman turned revealing a side arm at her belt. Audrey's eyes bugged out. The woman smiled, "I'm a probation officer, also. We're armed as part of our job." She looked Audrey over. "Listening to your husband, I don't think I would have been as good a choice as the officer our boss appointed."

Audrey agreed, sadly. "Bart might have a difficult time with a woman. Especially one who carries a gun. He's threatened by strong women. Our relationship takes a little managing."

The woman nodded wisely. "His officer will be Louie Lisella. Just listening tells me the boss made a good choice." The woman then pulled Audrey into another office and closed the door. "I have two things to say. First, will you be safe with him?"

"Yes, he's lost his job and needs my salary. And he's never been violent with me or the children."

The woman smiled. "Second, you've worked magic with my cousin. He lives in one of your group homes. My whole family is grateful. Thank you. Anything you need, let me know." She handed Audrey her card.

Audrey read the card and smiled. "Thank you, Lana." She knew she had a new friend to call on in this new phase of her life.

* * *

"I have to get back to Raleigh," Quinn stated.

His son scowled. "I don't want to go with you." Colt was earnest. "I just met some great guys today. They think I play great soccer. And they want me to ride bikes with them and things."

Quinn was torn. He hated to impose on Mouse, but Colt was so excited living his dream of friends close by and having a normal, non-rich-kid life. "Mouse has work to do and she doesn't need another kid."

"But I could help," offered Colt. "I can babysit and do yard work and wash her car."

This was serious, Colt was willing to babysit Tilda just to stay in River Bend! "I'll talk to Mouse." The youngster grinned. Leaving Colt behind gave Quinn a reason to return quickly! Quinn grinned.

They had just finished dinner, a cookout at Mouse's backyard grill. Quinn picked up the last of the condiments and carried them into the house, already planning his strategy. He found Mouse wrapping up the potato salad and stuffing it into a large refrigerator. When she saw him, she took each jar and found a place in the fridge until his arms were empty. "That must be everything," she said.

"It is." He sat at the window seat overlooking the backyard. "This is a great place. Colt sure likes it."

"And he doesn't want to go home," Mouse stated.

"How did you know?"

She smiled. "He's not been subtle. He's offered to wash my car and rake leaves and even help with Tilda." Quinn opened his mouth in protest or embarrassment, but Mouse waved her hand. "He is so sweet. He's welcome to stay. He can finish soccer camp and get to know his new friends."

Quinn smiled. "He sent me in here to beg you to let him stay."

"You've succeeded and you'll be a hero in his eyes." Her own eyes sparkled.

"That's all any parent could want." Quinn thought about how lonely he was going to be back at the big house. But he knew Colt would enjoy this adventure, so different from the staid, well-organized household in Raleigh. He smiled to himself. Colt would have the opportunity to learn what it meant to have to pick up his clothes, help with chores and not have access to all the perks of the Raleigh mansion.

* * *

Lynn was cleaning up after dinner with Jason's help. She had noted that he was doing more chores around the house. "I appreciate your help."

"And you wonder why I'm so helpful?" He grinned as he swept the kitchen floor.

"That had caught my attention." She was enjoying him as this new young adult.

He leaned on the broom. "Since Gramps gave me a condo for law school." Jim and Marianna had given him the place as a graduation present. "I think I better learn how to care for it." Lynn raised her eyebrows. She had been arguing, teasing and threatening for years to get him to learn some of these life skills.

"I'm delighted. I wouldn't want to visit you at school and have to scrape old food off the kitchen table."

He laughed. "I think I'll eat out a lot. That makes cleaning up easier."

They finished the chores and Lynn suggested, "Let's sit out on the porch." She dried her hands and walked outside. He grabbed a beer and followed. Once they settled on the glider she said, "It won't be long until you pack up. We better start planning what you'll need."

"Need?" There was the teen panic he hadn't quite lost.

"You've got a house to furnish."

"Yikes!" He let her know it hadn't crossed his mind that the condo would be more than a kitchen and a bedroom.

"Don't worry," she said. "Since Bri and Glenda sized down to move into their little apartment and since Doyle and Lori had wedding stuff but needed other things for their house, we've been organizing things."

"*We* have?"

Lynn rolled her eyes to let him know he was behind in the planning process. "I think you will get most of Glenda's kitchen things because Doyle and Lori have all those wedding presents. We'll buy you a new bed and mattress." Then she went on to list the furniture she had collected, the linens and the appliances. "We have a lot of things in the barn." They both looked at the sorry structure listing at the back of the property. Each year Lynn tried to clean it out and each year everyone else in the family added more junk.

"Wow," he moaned, "that sounds so adult."

"That's what you are. You're not my little sweet-pea anymore."

He blushed. "You haven't called me that since we moved here."

She hugged him. "It's not because I didn't think it. But you are growing up."

"I guess." He settled into her hug. They hadn't done that in a long time either. He moved out of her hug, sipped his beer and asked, "What do I have to do?"

She stood, tousled his hair. "Let me get my lists." He groaned.

* * *

"I heard you were in court today," said Dusty as he helped pull down the bedspread.

"I went with Audrey Decker. It was her husband's trial."

Dusty flopped into bed. "I hope they work things out. That guy has the opportunity to straighten up. Or he can keep spiraling down."

"What do you mean?" Lynn perched on the edge of the bed.

"I've seen enough to not make any bets. But middle-class guys with good jobs can pull themselves together and things work out for them and their families." He punched his pillow. "Or the same type of guy doesn't appreciate the clean slate and second chance he's been given and keeps doing the wrong things."

"That sounds depressing."

"What do you think about your friend and her husband?"

Lynn shivered. "I think he's type two. She was having an affair. He found out. I don't know where the drugs fit in, but I don't hold out hope for any reconciliation." She snuggled into Dusty. "I haven't told her that."

"We've learned from our own family. We have to let everyone decide for themselves." It still upset Dusty that his brother, Kent, and wife, Allison, had divorced. But the family had agreed, it was their decision.

Lynn snuggled closer. "Sometimes I think I'd like to live on a mountaintop and not have to worry about friends and family."

"Would you take me with you?"

"Of course." She snuggled closer still. "Mountaintops get cold at night."

CHAPTER NINE

Quinn had only been in River Bend for two days and his father had seemed to phone hourly. It didn't help that he was staying with Mouse's parents. Charlotte Macauley kept an eagle eye on his comings and goings, demanding that he abide by a nine PM curfew. As she said, "Sara and the children need their sleep."

He was sipping coffee in Mouse's kitchen, alone with Tilda, watching her attack a bowl of cereal. The boys had already taken off for soccer camp. "When do you go to camp?" he asked the little girl.

"I go to Mr. Rory's drama school next week." She added another helping of dry flakes to the remaining milk in her bowl. Flakes skittered across the table landing in Quinn's lap. He picked at the random pieces and popped them in his mouth.

His phone rang. "Hey, Dad. . . . . I'm leaving today. Colt wants to stay here." He looked at the kitchen clock. "The plane is picking me up at two." Finishing the call he placed his phone on the table and stared into space.

Tilda finished her cereal and dropped her plastic bowl into the sink, startling Quinn. He had a sly thought. "Are you going out to play?" He was hoping for a quiet moment to say good-by to Mouse. This might be the time.

"No, I'm going to play school in Mommy's office then go swimming when the boys get home." She marched out of the kitchen and he followed her into Mouse's office, a bright sunroom off the living room. They waited at the door while Mouse ended a phone call.

"Mommy, can I play school?"

"Yes, sweetie," Sara said. "But you have to be quiet. I have a Zoom meeting soon." She glanced at Quinn, surprised. "I thought you were leaving."

He nodded. "I came to say good-by and thank you for allowing Colt to visit." He glanced at Tilda already coloring at her small school desk in the corner. "Can I speak with you out here?" He nodded toward the living room. She got up from her work space and followed him. He pulled her into a far corner and wrapped his arms around her. "I just wanted to thank you, again." He brushed his lips across her forehead and moved down her cheek to her lips.

"Mom?" Tilda was standing almost between them. "I can't find yellow."

Burying her face in his shoulder, Sara was shaking with waves of silent laughter. "Maybe it rolled under my desk." The little girl trotted away. Sara put her arms around his neck. "As you were saying?"

He gave her a quick but thorough kiss. "I'll be back next Wednesday." Another kiss. "And we'll finish this conversation." Her laughter followed him out the door.

* * *

Quinn walked into the Philanthropies office. "May I help you?" challenged the efficient looking matron ready to defend the Philanthropies' ramparts against all aggressors.

"I'm looking for the director. Is her name Lynn?" He smiled, but his charm was lost in the mist of her hostility.

The defender scowled. "Maybe."

Quinn thought he should have dressed more professionally, but he hadn't brought many clothes to River Bend anticipating a short stay. "I'm Quinn Templeton and I met Lynn at the bakery the other day."

"Oh, with that little Tilda!" Nelda smiled at the magic words. "Lynn's in her office." She picked up a phone and whispered something. Soon Quinn heard thudding and turned toward the stairs.

"Oh, my God, Quinn Templeton in our offices!" An obviously gay man rushed to grasp Quinn's hand.

"Rory?" Lynn's voice cut through the dramatic greeting. "Behave." She smiled at Quinn. "How nice to see you, Quinn! I told my staff we had met the other day." Nelda and Rory nodded, their grinning faces bobbing. Lynn shook her head at her colleagues. Had they never met a rich man? "Is there something we can help you with?"

He scanned three eager faces. "There is." How much privacy did he need? He had only been in River Bend a few days and he knew how word traveled. He decided to include the entire staff in this discussion. Why not? "Lela Templeton Foundation has just lost its director." He heard a snort and guessed they had all heard about CJ's misdeeds. Mouse's family had been delighting everyone with the Templeton drama. "I need advice about getting the grants out and some help reorganizing the foundation offices." They all nodded.

Lynn said, "Please come into our conference room. Rory and I may have some suggestions." She gave Quinn a curious look. "If that's why you're here?"

He gave her a sheepish grin. "I have to start somewhere." And he had time to kill until the plane picked him up, he thought. He knew he would be grateful for any small hint of his next steps. He remembered CJ laughing at the mess threatening to happen at the foundation.

"I'll get fresh coffee going." Nelda ran ahead of them into the conference room. She didn't want to miss the discussion.

With that as a brief introduction Quinn sat with Lynn and Rory to explain the confusion at the foundation offices as well as his concerns for the future operation. After much discussion, including very thoughtful questions from Rory and Lynn, they finally had a plan of action. And because of the quality of the questions and the insight of both people, Quinn was comfortable in accepting their help.

Lynn began, "I hate it but I think I should loan you Rory for a month or so to be your interim director." She turned to him. "Can you be gone for a month?"

"I have my drama camp," he frowned, "maybe Marianna can help Bryce? But they'll need at least one more."

Lynn made a quick call, chatted with Marianna and ended the call. "She says yes, but," They all looked at her. "You have to get Bertram for the music."

Quinn pulled out a checkbook. "What'll it cost?"

Lynn was thoughtful. "A donation to the Hunger Alliance and the Little Theater summer drama program. Bryce just needs a break from managing trash."

Quinn looked confused. "Whatever you say." He scribbled a check. "What next?"

"Then," Lynn continued, "you have to decide if you're going to prosecute your brother-in-law. Because Mars —

Quinn interrupted, "You mean Uncle Mars?"

Lynn laughed. "Yes, Uncle Mars can put you in touch with his friends in Raleigh and Wake County Law Enforcement."

"Don't forget Beth," offered Nelda who had been in and out as she held the rest of Lynn's appointments at bay.

"I forgot her," said Lynn. "Beth Seymour is a lawyer with the state AG's office working in white collar crime. She'll be helpful in an investigation."

Rory said, "As much as I like taking this leadership responsibility, isn't there an employee positioned as assistant director or someone who can slip into this role?"

Quinn shrugged. "I don't trust the current staff. They may all be innocent. Or they may be working for CJ. I do know that a few of our long-time employees left over the last year, saying they had found other positions."

Lynn raised an eyebrow. "Were they suspicious? Or were they pushed out?"

Quinn nodded. "Something like that." He turned to Rory. "That will be the other part of your job. Get the grants out and then look into staffing. We'll put you up in an executive apartment that we maintain for our managers who have to come to Raleigh from other locations for extended stays."

"I have one more caution," said Lynn. "Let your legal department check every grant applicant to verify IRS standing and certify existence."

"I'm leaving for Raleigh this afternoon. Rory, let's move you in over the weekend and get you in the office Monday morning. Is that enough time?"

"Yes, sir," he held out his hand. "I'll be there, ready to go to work."

Quinn shook his hand and kissed both Nelda and Lynn on the cheek. "This is a great place; you solved all my problems." At least all my foundation problems, he thought as he wondered what more would be on the horizon.

* * *

The interim sheriff walked into Dusty's office. "We need to talk."

Dusty looked at Doug. "I thought you were the one everyone needed to talk to."

Doug laughed. "This is personal."

Dusty's stomach rolled over. He hated personal. "How personal?"

"Aunt Emily needs us to move into her place. We would be neighbors." Emily Jacobs and her three great-grandchildren had moved into the house next door to Lynn and Dusty in The Heights several months ago. Emily was very elderly and had live-in help with Lucia and her son Juan. "She hasn't said anything but my wife and Lucia have been talking. Lucia thinks the children need more supervision."

"They're getting into trouble?" Dusty hadn't noticed any neighborhood disruptions.

Doug shook his head. "Lucia says, and Connie agrees, that Emily can't help with daily things like homework and playdates and other motherly things. Lucia handles cooking and cleaning." Doug squinted at Dusty. "And since your brother hired Juan to be his interpreter and supervisor, Lucia is doing all that work single handed. Connie has to go over most days to drive kids to things. And drive Emily to things." Doug shook his head. "I knew this day would come. Once we agreed to be guardians of those kids when Emily passes, I thought we might need a bigger role in their lives before that day comes."

"What will you have, six kids?" Dusty mentally added kids. Doug and Connie had joined their families making it three children and Emily had three. "That's a house full."

"We might as well start now. It'll be easier than the upheaval when Emily leaves us."

"Makes sense to me." Dusty was thoughtful. "Do you think we'll have a problem?"

"That's what I'm asking. Will we?"

Dusty shook his head. "I'm fine with it."

"That's all I needed to know." Doug morphed back into the interim sheriff. "Did you finish that new travel policy for the county manager?"

"Yeah, yeah," moaned Dusty, "I can't get anything done if you keep bugging me." They both laughed and Doug left the office. Dusty thought about the move. Three more kids running through a neighborhood that already had dogs and Bri Llewellyn and Will with

the vineyard and the agri-cart and the college crowd and Lynn's extended
family cookouts and Piper's wild party ideas. No one would even notice
the extra kids.

* * *

It was another quiet, but tense evening at the Decker home. Bart had
had his day in court and met his probation officer, some big gorilla who,
he thought, could be easily deceived. When he thought about his
predicament he cursed his bad luck. There was no thought that his
choices had been wrong, immature and illegal—just bad luck. And he
would give his right arm for another one of those magic injections.
Whatever they put in the mix made him feel free, successful and above
the day-to-day dreary life of a man trying to support a family and an
unfaithful wife.

Thinking of his wife, he watched as she read a story to the kids and
tried to act as though this was a normal night in their life. She insisted
that she wasn't seeing that man any more. Bart hadn't had time to follow
her. Between looking for a job and being the nanny for the damned kids
he had no idea what Audrey was doing. She said she went to work. She
said she had board meetings. She said she went grocery shopping. Dinner
was on the table each night. And she wasn't running off each weekend
for those meetings that had turned into sex with her lover.

The disgruntled man sat in his recliner, listening to the story his
children enjoyed. He didn't look back on how good their life had been
when they had first married. Nor did he think about the joy at the birth
of each child. He only saw back to that night the FBI arrested him and
the night he got his last high. He was restless. He was unhappy. He
needed that shot!

Audrey finished the story and told the children to kiss their daddy
good night. He accepted the little kisses, knew his wife was watching.
"Good night, little rug rats," he chortled. It was a term that made the
kids giggle as they raced off to bed.

Audrey returned to the den after settling them in for the night. She
picked up her crocheting and settled near the lamp at the end of the
couch, the farthest she could get from him and still be in the same room.

"I gave you three kids," he stated after silently watching her for some time. "What more did you want?" Audrey stared at him. This was the first evening he had spoken in weeks. "We made three children together. We were a family. Until you whored around."

"You're right." She was defeated. How could she explain the emptiness of their relationship and the warmth, not even love, just warmth and friendship, that she found with James Thurman.

"So, why, Audrey?"

"I wanted to be seen, to be loved, to be valued." She looked him in the eye.

"What shit!" He scowled as he sat forward in the recliner. He continued to stare at her. If he had those drugs, he was certain he could ignore her and her lover. He could probably move up in the office to one of those jobs that would keep him on the road. If he had those drugs!

Why had she even answered him, Audrey wondered? He would never understand what she said. She wasn't certain she did either. But her soul was dry. Her children and her job were the pleasures of her life. Her marriage was a void. Her fingers raced over the yarn as she unconsciously created another coverlet for one of the children.

Bart got up from the recliner and went to bed. There was nothing more to say. He wanted to scream at her for causing all his problems. He wanted to run away. But she had the job and they had expenses. He was stuck in his pathetic life until he could figure out something better. And he needed . . . something.

CHAPTER TEN

CJ was pacing in Madeline's condo. "What do you mean nothing works?" he demanded into his phone after listening to the hacker's report.

"I said someone has me locked out. I mean really locked out." Theo's whiney voice annoyed him.

"What about those other accounts?" CJ was not surprised that Templeton had blocked access to the company computers and related funds. But there were other moneys he could use.

"Someone cleaned out all those accounts. I finally caught his tracks." Theo sounded more assured of himself now.

"Who? How?" CJ was stunned. Did Theo mean that all Rothman's and Garson's accounts were empty? "Where's the money?" he demanded.

The hacker sniffed into the phone. "I got it under control," he bragged, "I picked up his signal when he first took funds from Rothman's accounts. I've been looking for him for two years and finally found the signal and tracked him to a town called River Bend. Know anyone there?"

River Bend? CJ had been hearing about that obscure town. That was where Rothman died and where Mahaffey got arrested. He tried to pull up more information from his memory but was distracted by his present problems. "Just get me to my fucking money."

"You don't get it, man, I'm not going to solve this. Someone has locked you out of your accounts. And someone has cleaned out all the other accounts. There's some woman involved, Margolin or something. I don't know how she's involved but her name popped up in one of my searches." CJ heard a keyboard clicking. "Got it!" commented Theo. "Here's what I know." He gave CJ information on Sara Margolin, partner of an IT consulting firm based in River Bend.

"Did you say she lives in River Bend?" CJ felt the hairs on the back of his neck stand up.

"Yeah," came the hacker's distracted voice. "Shit! Someone's getting real interested in me." Click, click. "I'm going off line for a few days. I gotta make a new identity."

"What about our deal?" CJ tried to keep his voice down.

"You'll hear from me later. Things are just hot right now." The line went dead.

CJ threw his phone toward the sofa cushions and swore.

"What is it, darling?" asked Madeline. As the phone flew through the air she floated into the room in a very expensive lounging outfit.

"We're screwed. David had his people lock me out of the system. My guy can't find any way in."

"The offshore money?"

"They have our accounts blocked there, too." He didn't want to talk about the other accounts that he and Theo had been watching for years. But River Bend seemed to hold the answers to everything—Rothman, Mahaffey and, now, that Margolin woman.

"That's our money. We worked hard for it. I have plans." Madeline stood nose to nose with CJ. He pushed her away, walked toward her well-stocked built-in bar, and poured something from one of Madeline's handy decanters.

"If you want this money, you better come up with a plan. I'm all out of ideas." He paced the room. "My guy can't get into anything. Do you understand that? He's all I've got working for me since I can't get to my office."

"What do you mean, can't get to your office?"

"David has changed all access codes on the buildings and the guards have been advised that I am not to enter." He sneered at her. "Face it. That bastard has us boxed in."

Madeline paced the room herself as CJ flopped on the couch, sipping his second drink. After some time she said, "We just need to get at his hacker, you know that woman you say is fake."

CJ struggled into a sitting position. "My guy found her and says her name is Sara Margolin. She's a widow with three kids and lives in River Bend. She's a real computer consultant. My guy says she works on some real advanced crap and has some powerful clients." CJ studied his notes.

"Not much else. She did a closed-door training with Templeton Inc. tech managers last Monday and then Quinn whisked her and her family away. I think they're in River Bend now."

"River Bend?" Madeline was thoughtful. "Isn't that where you told me one of your partners lives?"

"And where one died," CJ whispered to himself. To Madeline, he said, "Yeah, Kip Mahaffey. He's in jail."

"Could he have partnered with this woman to take our money or to ruin us as part of some deal for his arrest?"

That thought stopped CJ. He rolled the idea around, adding the information about Rothman dying in River Bend. And the fact that Theo had traced another signal to River Bend, a signal that first appeared after Rothman's death. Was he looking at some sort of conspiracy? Ideas circled in his mind, scenarios formed and reformed.

"Let me run something by you," he said to Madeline. For all her fashion focus and negative intellectual capacity, CJ respected her killer instincts. He didn't like to admit that he was only skimming funds small time until she caught on and developed their complex system.

Once he had her attention, he laid out facts and concluded, "I don't know how, or if, any of this is related, but something is happening and River Bend is the place."

"I never heard of this town." Madeline was a big city girl and measured a city's worth by the availability of high-end shops.

CJ shrugged. "Nevertheless," he waved his arm in the general direction of Raleigh city limits, "that's the town where little Miss Computer Consultant resides. And she seems to have David and Quinn's attention." He stared at his partner and dared her to come up with an idea to recover their losses.

"I think we should visit River Bend and have Quinn's new girlfriend undo her damage." Madeline gave CJ a look he had come to dread. She was planning something nasty. He wondered again how he ever got into this alliance. Yeah, he reminded himself, there was all that sex. And she had used sex to learn everything—his marriage problems, his skimming of funds, his other affairs. "Well?" She tapped her foot waiting.

"River Bend it is." Capitulation. Later he'd have to reclaim his leadership role. And after that he'd make his final move and leave her behind while he and their money disappeared.

"Let's get packing." She left the study and ran up the stairs.

They were staying in Madeline's condo, as she liked to say, the best place Templeton money could buy. It had three bedrooms and as many baths as well as a state-of-the-art kitchen which CJ had never seen used. It had been easy to leave Margaret's place and move in with Madeline. There was so much space. Her condo came with two underground reserved parking spaces. He'd be comfortable here until this thing was resolved. With that thought he ran up the stairs to look for her. She was packing. "Why such a hurry?" he asked.

"It's just a matter of time before the Templetons have us arrested," she snarled, "If we can be found, that is."

"We can only disappear if we get our money," CJ reminded her.

"That woman blocked us, so she's going to have to unblock us." Madeline threw some blouses into a suitcase.

"She can't be doing all this alone," argued CJ. But Theo was certain that she had a role in creating some of their problems.

"Whether she is or is not, it's obvious Quinn's interested in her and I think he'll trade her safety for our money." Madeline was pleased with her solution. She pushed CJ out of her way and walked out of the room calling over her shoulder. "We're going to River Bend. Get ready."

But he paused. Could this Margolin woman be involved with his other accounts? Could she have been skimming from Rothman's old accounts for years? Maybe a trip to River Bend *was* necessary. If she wasn't the hacker Theo was tracking, maybe she could be forced to help use her resources to find the other thief. CJ frowned at the way things were developing, but Madeline said move and he did. He had one final thought. What if this Margolin woman was taking Quinn and David for a ride and all her IT consulting was an even bigger scam than his operation? That, he concluded, was a heartwarming idea—someone bringing down the Templetons!

* * *

Lynn ran into Sara Margolin having a quiet lunch in the Main Street diner. "Alone?"

Sara grinned. "Tilda is at drama camp and the boys are hiking with some friends." She threw her arm out. "This is as alone as it gets because

I still have some clients waiting for me this afternoon." She closed her menu. "Join me?"

Lynn slid into the bench opposite Sara. "You can bring me up to date on your new friend." She wiggled her eyebrows.

"You mean Quinn and you sound like my mother." Sara scowled. "Only Mother doesn't smile when she asks. She thinks Quinn has ulterior motives."

"Does he?"

"I hope so!" Then she laughed. "I've known him since college and suddenly this renewal of our friendship has my heart fluttering." She blushed. "Isn't that so high school? But I haven't felt like this since Josh."

The waitress took their order and Lynn studied her friend. "How are all the kids with this?"

Sara laughed again. "Like they belong together. Quinn left his son Colt behind for a visit." She used finger quotes. "I think Colt is plotting to stay here. He's already making friends and talks about starting high school here, playing on the soccer team. He has it all planned. My kids love him. And he is very sweet and down to earth even with all his family wealth."

"What's the shadow on your rosy horizon? Mr. Templeton?"

"Do you mean David?" Again Sara had to grin. "Once he understood the company computer problems and his son-in-law's involvement, I became his golden girl."

"Wow!" marveled Lynn. "No worries. No bad vibes. Now what?"

"I don't know where Quinn is." She wrinkled her brow deep in thought. "He, well, he, ah, ..." She blushed. "He has kissed me and implied interest." Sara hung her head. "I'm trying to figure this out. Any signal from him and I'm sold." She took a taste of her salad. "Am I too bold? Is this too fast? Am I crazy?"

"Yes, yes, yes," cheered Lynn, "Go for it!"

* * *

David and Quinn left another meeting of their staff and attorneys. It was a sad situation, but not bleak. Sara seemed to have discovered CJ's machinations just before extensive money losses. As they walked into David's office he slapped his son on the back, "You were great in there."

Quinn turned to his father, surprised. "Dad, I do have a brain." Then he said, "Thank you. I felt I owed you and the company for having allowed all this to happen."

"We both owe your friend, Ms. Margolin."

"Mouse *did* save us." Quinn had a pensive look on his face as he looked out the window, staring at the state legislative buildings in downtown Raleigh.

"Son, I think she saved more than the company." David patted Quinn's shoulder.

"What do you mean?" Quinn was warmed by his father's touch and the affectionate sound in his voice.

"You've been working here for a decade. Or I should say you've been treading water here for a decade. Today you showed up to work." Quinn opened his mouth to argue but David continued, "I've wondered if you were unhappy or over your head or something. And today you were everything I'd ever hoped to see. You cared, you understood the problems, and you listened to solutions and made some great suggestions. You became the next Mr. Templeton."

"What? You're leaving?" Quinn's mind raced to process this conversation.

David motioned Quinn to take a chair at the small work table. He pulled up another chair. "No, but I have been wondering if I had to wait for Colt to grow up to have a family member ready to replace me. I'm ready to power back. I've been ready but I've been waiting for you to step up. Today you did."

"I'm sorry I let you down," said Quinn. This was one of the most meaningful conversations he had ever had with his father.

"But you haven't!" David shook his head. "I can't explain it. It's like all of a sudden you're ready." He rested his hand on Quinn's wrist. "That woman did it."

"Mouse?" Quinn gave his father a soft smile. And David knew he was correct. "Colt likes her."

"And you?" asked his father.

"And me, too. More so than anyone I've met before." He gave his father a shy smile. "Am I too bold? Is this too fast? Am I crazy?"

"Yes, yes, yes," cheered David, "Go for it!"

* * *

"I need help." A soft voice floated into his thoughts.

Dusty looked up to see that Marianna, his mother-in-law, was standing at his office door. It was unusual to see her in the sheriff's department wing of the courthouse. In fact, Dusty didn't think she had ever been there. How had she found him? How had she gotten past the electronic door, the sign in register and . . .

"I see you found him." An older deputy smiled at her, clearly smitten with the charms and beauty of the retired actress. Marianna gave the man her starlet smile in thanks, and he reluctantly moved on. And that explained everything.

She looked around Dusty's office. "Are we alone?"

He looked around the empty office and looked back at her. "Did you come to confess to a crime?"

"No. I told you I need help." She took a seat at Tee's desk, smoothed her skirt and rested her clasped hands on the desktop.

He raised his eyebrows in question, "I thought you were running a drama school." She fidgeted, cleared her throat and sat straighter. "You sure you're not here to confess something?"

"Rory's drama camp," she nodded. "But it's over for the day." Her eyes danced as she blurted, "They bought my series!" She almost levitated above the chair. "My scripts and the concept have been optioned by a production company that already has several programs on various pay per view channels."

"I thought it was a sure thing last month when they sent in Casey Handel." Dusty referred to the law enforcement consultant who had come to town to look over, well, he wasn't certain what he looked over. But he had been present at the FBI raid and Kip Mahaffey's arrest.

"Casey was the first review," explained Marianna. Dusty looked confused. She continued, "The producers sent Casey to evaluate my story credibility."

"You mean to make sure your characters were realistic law enforcement officers?"

"Exactly. Now the producers want more detail and that's why I need you."

"To act?" Heaven forbid!

She laughed then blew out her breath and visibly calmed herself. "I should be more professional. This isn't my first option." She became flustered again. "I mean. I've worked on projects that got so far and nothing more happened. But a team is coming to town and wants to chat with me and my local consultant."

"Consultant for what?"

"Policing protocol." She shrugged, "You know, the person who helped put flesh and credibility into my characters." He stared back in confusion. She scowled. "They want to know who has made certain my scripts are accurate for police procedure. And you have to meet with them and be my consultant."

He threw back his head and laughed. "Last time we talked about this project you told me that I would be a woman and have an affair with Mars. Now I'm your consultant?" He referred to the producer's idea that the Dusty character in Marianna's script be a woman with the Mars character as a love interest.

"Well, yes." It was obvious to Marianna. "You are my inspiration. But the producers who hold the option think Dusty should be a woman. It's not my idea or my original proposal!"

"Shouldn't your consultant be a woman? What about Tee?" He was enjoying this discussion.

"I'm going to suggest her to the producer as the information source for women policing issues. I think they might agree, and then both of you can earn money and get your names on the credits."

"Earn money?"

"I know you both would be paid but I don't know how much." She shrugged. "After all with so many policing and crime shows around there are plenty of consultants available. But you and Tee would help keep the flavor of my small-town characters."

Dusty wasn't certain what she meant, but he thought it sounded interesting and he would like to help Tee earn extra money. She had those three kids to feed. And he wouldn't mind a little extra for his old age. He walked over and took her hands helping her to her feet. "Of course, I'll help you." He kissed her cheek and walked her out of the office as she began to tell him about the production team who would be coming to town in a week or two.

* * *

"Here's our first edition," Trina Healey bragged as she flipped a magazine onto Lynn's kitchen counter while she held the baby snug at her shoulder. "We have the distribution boxes at several grocery stores and are mailing magazines to those folks who have subscribed. We also have our online edition running, offering updates on issues to keep our readers current." The baby gave out a gurgle in support or congratulations.

Last Spring Lynn had helped Trina present her regional parent advice magazine to several potential investors. The investors were excited about the concept. Trina had recruited a world-famous photographer, Delsey Ledges, to come into town and help populate the first issue with her photos. Delsey had delivered more than anticipated. With the help of Mutt Mason, a nurse at the local health clinic, she delivered evidence that uncovered a drug operation run by a local lawyer, Kip Mahaffey, and the health clinic executive director, Margaret Eliason.

The story broke before the magazine was ready for print, but in the first edition of the new magazine Trina offered her readers an in-depth story with detailed information only available to her readers because law enforcement owed her and Delsey for finding the drug distribution outlet and the characters managing the operation. Success!

"I noticed your marketing all over town." Lynn placed a celebratory bottle of wine and glasses on the counter and took the baby to plant a kiss on his forehead.

"One of Michelle's clients has a PR firm. She got us organized and out there." Trina poured a glass of wine for herself and Lynn. "The community college has suggested that we run an online weekly or daily edition with current local news and announcements. They liked our first effort and the journalism students are eager to do more."

"That's good, isn't it?" Lynn saw Piper walk in through the front door. Handing the baby back to Trina she placed another glass by the bottle. She also found a stray bag of pretzels.

"It's more than I was prepared for," moaned Trina, finally getting to her reason for the visit. "Success can be breathtaking."

Before she could launch into her worries, Piper flopped into a chair after filling a wine glass. "School starts in three weeks." Her voice sounded as though it came from a tunnel. "I still need four teaching assistants, two bus drivers and a fifth-grade teacher." She emptied her glass. "And I don't even want to hear the word mask!"

"Content!" Trina almost danced around the kitchen. She kissed the baby. "I needed ideas for my e-edition." She hugged Lynn. "You always solve my problems!"

"She never solves mine," griped Piper.

"I could use this interview as the basis for an e-report on my website." Trina handed the baby to Piper as she sat at the table and jotted notes on a stray carryout menu.

"This is an interview?" Piper looked around for a camera and kissed the baby.

Lynn had been paging through the magazine. "This looks great and your cover story about the health clinic and Kip with Delsey's photos looks professional."

"It is professional! I already got a call from a national magazine asking if they can run the story with my magazine byline." She stuffed her notes in her pocket and grabbed the baby. "I gotta go and give my reporters-in-training assignments for our next e-edition." She was out the door.

"You wanna learn how to drive a school bus?" Piper asked her best friend as she drained her glass. Lynn poured her more wine.

CHAPTER ELEVEN

Rory called Lynn, excited about the opportunity to work with the Templetons. It seemed Quinn had made him comfortable and had given him all the support he needed to move forward on reorganizing the family foundation. "Here only two days and everything is perfect, sweetie," he sang over the air. "I feel a little guilty about drama camp. Please do me a favor and visit Marianna at the Little Theater today. She and Bryce are delighted with the class this year. And Quinn's returning to River Bend this afternoon." He lowered his voice. "They have a private plane that flies him everywhere." He chuckled as Lynn wondered if she would get an opportunity to speak. But he continued, "He can't stay away from our Sara. That man is in L-O-V-E!"

Lynn laughed. "I'll keep an eye out for him. Hurry back, even Nelda misses you."

"I do not!"

"I heard that!" He lowered his voice, again. "Sweetie, you won't believe what I've found in just two days. That brother-in-law was a piece of work. He has taken the foundation board on expensive junkets. They did an Alaskan cruise one year. For quarterly meetings he takes them to spas and resorts around the country."

"Yikes!"

"Our Sara caught them just in time." Rory was finally silent, just breathing into the phone.

"Are you all right?" Lynn asked, concerned about Rory's uncharacteristic silence.

"I'm just wondering what else I'll find." He went on to explain, "This brother-in-law didn't even try to hide anything the last year. I can see why the staff left."

"Are you tempted to take on this as a permanent job?" And leave me, Lynn worried silently.

"I honestly don't know," he admitted. "But Quinn hasn't offered anything. He needs to see me perform first."

"He'll love you," Lynn moaned.

"We'll see. Gotta go, sweetie."

* * *

"Lynn, didn't you just love those kids?" asked Marianna, after wrapping up another successful summer drama camp day. Lynn had taken Rory's advice and stopped to visit the Little People Little Theater program as the youngsters prepared for the performance that would be presented to their parents and anyone else who was interested in rough, unpolished entertainment. It would happen Friday evening.

Lynn had enjoyed every skit she had seen. She would return Friday evening with her husband and a few friends who needed to see this program and maybe think about making a donation to the Philanthropies to renew the funding for next year. She was laughing as she hugged her stepmother. "Thank you. This was the best medicine for a hectic summer. I know a few donors who might like to be a part of this in the future." They moved to the side of the lobby as parents and kids found one another at the end of the day. Lynn waved to a few that she knew and frowned at the thought that she knew fewer and fewer young parents every year.

She and Marianna chatted while the theater lobby emptied. "Thanks again. I'll see you Friday." Lynn pushed open the door and walked out under the marquee. A little girl was standing at the top of the steps scanning the parking lot. "Tilda?" Lynn called, "Did your mother forget you?"

The little girl shrugged. She was still in some ghoulish make-up and the remnants of a tattered zombie costume that would be part of Friday's finale.

"Come with me," offered Lynn, "I'll take you home. You can tell me about drama camp."

It was a short drive to Sara's place and Tilda talked the whole way, enacting her role and the roles of all the other nineteen youngsters in the program. Lynn was enjoying the trip but came to an abrupt stop as she was flagged by a local policeman.

"We have an incident, Ms. Powers. We're holding traffic for a bit." The officer looked over the neighborhood. Lynn pulled to the side of the road and tried to catch sight of her husband or a friend who would fill her in on the situation.

"You stay in the car, Tilda. I'll go look for Dusty." She was gone. It only took a few minutes to find Dusty at the command van. "Why can't I take Tilda home?" she asked as she poked her head in the van.

Dusty scowled. "That's Sara's daughter?" Lynn nodded. "Sara's having some trouble. Someone has taken her and some children hostage."

"Sara?" Lynn looked further down the street and realized that the road was empty for the next three blocks, with Sara's house in the middle of the zone. She opened her mouth, then closed it. What questions could she ask? Dusty was doing all that he could and there were too many people to protect—neighbors, police, Sara and the children. She nodded to Dusty and went back to check on Tilda.

The car was empty! She waved to the officer who was detouring traffic. "Where did the little girl go?"

"I don't know, ma'am, I've been busy with this traffic."

Lynn scanned the street. Dusty and his staff had it cleared. Where could Tilda be? Lynn walked away from her car and away from Sara's house. When she thought she was out of sight of the patrolman, she dashed into a yard to get to the back alley to work her way to Sara's block and back yard. She ran through neighborhood yards, tiptoed across streets and followed the alley that ran behind Sara's place. She was certain she knew where to find the little zombie.

Where Sara's back fence joined the garage that opened to the alley, Lynn saw a SWAT officer struggling with a dog, or something. She moved closer. Tilda! The man was holding the little girl as she struggled to get free. He had one arm around her little body holding it tight to his and one arm around her head with his hand over her mouth. She was flexing her little body trying to break free.

Lynn got his attention as she reached to take Tilda. The office looked relieved. "Ma'am, we've got a situation." Now that he had a better opportunity to study the youngster he gave Lynn a puzzled glance. Some of Tilda's zombie make-up had transferred to the patrolman's clothing and hands.

"Yes, I know." Lynn gave a weak smile and tried to arrange Tilda's hair in a less zombie-like style. Her usual unruly curls were dusted in a zombie gray powder. It looked as though she were wearing a cap made of flexible pipe cleaner pieces.

"Mommy needs my help," said Tilda letting both adults know that she was very displeased with them. "I have to go help." Her attitude transcended her costume.

"How do you know she needs help?" asked Lynn.

"That's the bad man's car." Tilda pointed to a Porsche hidden in the alley several trash cans away from Sara's yard.

"Do you know who has taken the hostages?" Lynn asked the officer. He whispered into his headset.

"Yes, ma'am," he replied, "Ms. Margolin was able to get a message to someone through her computer. But thank you for pointing out the car. I've shared that information with command." He straightened his gear. "Could you and the little girl -" Tilda had disappeared!

They looked around. There she was slowly moving through the back yard, around toys and trees and shrubs and shadows getting closer to the house with every step. The little zombie assault force of one.

Lynn was about to challenge the officer, wondering why there was only one person guarding the back, when she saw another SWAT officer close to the house swoop in and grab Tilda in the same confining hold as before.   But Tilda settled down as the officer seemed to be speaking with her. He pulled his hand away and she nodded. They inched closer to a back door that seemed to access a landing with a short flight of stairs going up to the kitchen and a short flight going down to the basement.

"Who's that officer?" asked Lynn.

"Danny." And Danny waved to the man in the alley signaling him toward the house. The man looked at Lynn with a firm, steady gaze that suggested she stay put.

"I'll stay here." Resigned that she would miss the action, Lynn watched as a third SWAT officer appeared from the neighboring yard by scaling the fence.

Two men ran toward Danny and Tilda as he worked a basement window open. He stuffed the little girl into the basement and stood by the back door. Soon it opened and he grabbed Tilda before she could escape up the stairs into the house. He handed her to the backup officer then nodded to a third officer to enter the house and the detective followed.

The remaining officer was left to wrestle Tilda again. Ignoring instructions, Lynn rushed to his side offering to take the youngster.

"Stay close to the house until we get these kids out," said the grateful officer as he handed off the zombie and moved inside the doorway. From her location Lynn could see the first man acting as point standing at the kitchen doorway. He did nothing but hold his weapon ready to fire at anyone entering the kitchen as Danny crawled across the floor.

The detective dragged someone to the door. The body was taken by the backup officer and thrust at Lynn. She and Tilda rushed to grasp one of the twins, pulling him outside against the protection of the basement wall in case there was shooting. The officer returned with another person that Lynn and Tilda dragged out of sight. It was Colt. He was bruised and bleeding from a cut above his eye. Danny came out of the house with the other twin. The point officer backed out the door, carefully closing it while keeping his weapon ready to protect the children. One of the officers breathed, "Fifteen seconds."

Danny and the backup officer each lifted a boy while Lynn and Tilda struggled with the remaining twin. They raced toward the alley while the point officer protected their retreat. Once Danny placed Colt in the alley protected by the garage, he ran back into the yard and took the twin from Lynn. She scooped up Tilda and ran behind him into the alley. The backup officer had already begun to cut the duct tape from one of the twins while Lynn and Tilda did all they could to remove the sliced pieces of tape and try to make the boys comfortable.

"Who else is in there?" Danny asked the boys as an EMT appeared with water and a medic kit.

"Mom," replied one of the twins.

"CJ and my mother," said Colt. "My mother has a gun and so does CJ." The officer relayed that information over his mouthpiece.

"Which room are they in?"

"They're all at Mom's computer," said Paul.

"They're shouting at her and threatening to hurt us," said Rob.

"Does my dad know what's happening?" asked Colt.

Danny shrugged. "Who's your dad?"

"Quinn Templeton."

Danny asked a question in his mouthpiece. "Yes, he's being restrained at the command van." Some instructions came for Danny over his headset. He nodded. "He just flew into town and was stopped at the barricade. They're sending him back here." Just then they heard Quinn shout as he ran down the alley to the children. He scooped all four of them into his arms, hugging them as he tried to check them for wounds and missing body parts.

Lynn and the EMT helped Quinn move the children down the alley away from the house as Danny gave them a nod. He and the two SWAT officers raced back to the house. They were going in. Lynn grabbed Tilda. The EMT gave his kit to Colt and picked up a twin. Quinn carried the other twin and pulled Colt by the arm. They raced out of the alley as they heard popping sounds and breaking glass.

At the end of the alley the EMT stopped, spoke into his own mouthpiece and put down Rob. "It's over. I've got to attend the hostage." The man took his kit from Colt and ran back toward the house.

"Mouse?" cried Quinn. He put down Paul and ran after the EMT, Lynn and the children followed.

The street in front of the house had come alive. All the neighbors had come out of their homes. There were emergency vehicles, a TV truck and a local newspaper photographer. CJ and Madeline were handcuffed to a gurney where they were being treated for inhaling tear gas. Sara was stretched out on another gurney with a mask over her face. She was unconscious.

The children were in a panic as they rushed to her side. Quinn got an update on her condition and pulled the kids into his arms. "She's fine. They hit her on the head and tried to run out the back door. She breathed too much of that smoke. She's going to the hospital and we'll follow the ambulance." Her children seemed to understand. Quinn and Colt took the three youngsters away from the scene as Sara was slipped into the ambulance.

* * *

Lynn raced to her car and followed Quinn and the children. Once she arrived at the hospital she made a few calls, alerting Charlotte and Janet about Sara's condition and what had happened at the house. By the time she got to the ER she found Sara sitting up on the bed with Tilda, still in her zombie makeup, tucked under one arm and one twin on either side of the bed holding her hand. Colt was holding onto Quinn because it looked to Lynn as though Quinn was having a rough time. Colt looked like he had enjoyed the whole adventure, even with his black-eye and a few facial cuts.

Sara spotted Lynn as she pulled back the curtain. "I've called your mother and Janet," said Lynn. "I'm certain they'll be here soon. How are you feeling?"

"Fine." Sara grinned. "This is the first time I've been involved in one of your crimes."

"What does that mean?" demanded Quinn, looking pale and concerned.

"Lynn always gets involved—you know, dead bodies and robbers and kidnappers."

"Wow!" Colt breathed a sigh of adoration.

Quinn just stared at her.

"My husband is a detective," she explained.

"I know that," said Quinn, "He lets you solve crimes?"

"No, I don't," growled Dusty as he stuck his head into the area. "She won't listen to me." He reached over and took Tilda's hand. "Nice work. You were really brave."

"Brave?" asked Quinn and Sara together.

"She helped the SWAT team get into the house and pull the boys out," said the detective.

"The boys didn't get tear gas?" asked Sara. "I'm sorry, Dusty. I was going to rant at you because I thought you took risks with my boys." Sara thought over what she had heard. "You risked Tilda?" She almost screeched that accusation, then coughed up tear gas inspired phlegm.

"Danny always had her protected." Dusty kind of shuffled his feet.

"You sent her into the house?" Sara didn't think Dusty understood her concern so she raised her voice a few decibels. "Alone?"

"She volunteered." The detective looked around the room for help.

A few more decibels. "She's seven!"

"Maybe she convinced Danny she could do the job? Besides she was the only one who could fit through the window."

Sara glared at him.

"But we got the boys out." He thought that was a point in his favor. "That fellow had duct taped them up and left them on the kitchen floor. My team carried the boys out." He looked at Sara. "Then we lobbed the gas."

"Here you are," said Charlotte with relief, pulling off the hospital's mandatory mask. "I've been all over this hospital." Her husband followed right behind. The space was getting crowded so Dusty pulled Lynn out into the corridor with him, happy to escape an irate mother. And a grandmother as soon as she heard about Tilda's adventure. The nurse's eyebrows scowled above her face covering and they replaced their masks.

"How did you get involved with this?" Dusty asked his wife, ready to hear a preposterous explanation.

"I was at the Little Theater where Tilda is taking a drama class. Sara didn't come to pick her up, I guess because she was being held hostage. So I took Tilda home and she refused to stay in the car and ran around trying to save her family. I had to help her."

"Since when do you think a six-year-old knows what has to be done?"

"She's seven." Lynn liked getting the last word, correcting Dusty in the process.

CHAPTER TWELVE

Dusty was off to work early the next morning. He said he had to deal with out-of-town lawyers. Lynn understood. The people who had assaulted Sara had lawyered up—they had resources to command some big-time lawyers from another part of the state. Anyway he hadn't made coffee this morning and she had been in a rush because she had an early morning meeting with the Philanthropies' policy review committee. So she left all her houseguests sleeping. They needed rest after crazy yesterday. Charlotte and Carter Macauley kept Quinn because Charlotte was certain Quinn had designs on Sara. And her tear gassed state, Charlotte was certain, made Sara vulnerable. There was no home for Sara and the kids to spend the night since Dusty's staff had blown out her living room windows. That's why they were at Lynn's—Sara and her kids. They could sleep late, thought Lynn, because she and Dusty had things to do.

As she ran out the door Lynn sent a quick text to Piper to solve the house guest problem. She would handle breakfast for the guests. She already had provided Jason and Colt with beds for the night. What were relatives for, Lynn wondered as she stacked papers at her desk, enjoying the quiet office as opposed to what Piper was facing in Lynn's kitchen. Her seven-thirty committee members arrived.

She yawned and wondered why she always seemed to have board members who liked early morning meetings. They had worked fast and she was now free at eight-thirty AM! She couldn't decide whether to visit the bakery, or the diner on Main as a place for breakfast. Then she checked her calendar. Another meeting at nine! So she decided to walk to the coffee shop in the business park—only three doors down from her office.

"Nathan!" she called as she walked into the shop. "I thought you had breakfast at home?"

"I'm meeting an old friend," said her favorite donor and good friend. He stood and smiled as a man walked through the door. "David, over here."

"I'll leave you alone," began Lynn.

"No, please stay and meet my friend." Nathan smiled at the man and said, "David, I want you to meet my good friend, Lynn Powers, the director of the River Bend Philanthropies." He turned to Lynn, "And this is my friend, David Templeton."

Lynn gasped, "Quinn's father?"

"You know my son?" David stopped and thought. "Of course you do. You sent us your friend Rory. Thank you for that. He's doing a fine job."

Lynn sort of thanked him but wasn't sure what else to say. How much did this man know about yesterday's adventure and which side of the family feud was he on? She tried to recall all the details of the hostage situation and the computer stealing. He did like Sara, didn't he? She finally decided to play it safe. "Are you here to visit Nathan?" She smiled sweetly.

"Really, Lynn," chastised her old friend, "He's here because of that thing that happened at Sara's. It was reported all over the national news. David just flew in from Atlanta."

"And I want details before I meet with my son!" David was every inch the executive in charge.

"Because you're angry at him?" Lynn was having a difficult time reading this man's response.

"Why would I be angry? Where is that coffee you promised me, Nathan?"

"Right away." Nathan scurried to the counter and ordered three large black coffees, calling over his shoulder, "No talking until I get back."

Nathan returned quickly followed by a young man carrying a tray with coffee and scones. "David, you're very lucky that Lynn could join us. She'll know everything. Her husband is the chief of detectives and she helps him solve crimes."

"I do not," she protested.

"Were you there at the hostage situation yesterday?" Nathan challenged Lynn.

"Yes, but -"

"I told you, David, you'll get all the information you need." Nathan sipped his coffee, sat back and waited.

"Mr. Templeton, -"

"David."

"David. I happened to be giving Tilda . . . do you know Tilda?" He nodded. "Well, I was giving her a lift home from drama camp where she had spent the day being a zombie. You know, make-up and costume." David snickered and that relaxed Lynn so she continued, "We got to the neighborhood and couldn't get to the house because of the hostage thing. Tilda ran away from me and tried to sneak into the house to rescue her mother. You had to see it—a little zombie sneaking through Sara's back yard."

Now David was laughing. He wiped his eyes with a napkin. "I rushed here with no information expecting a horrible outcome from what I had seen on the news. This is so much better."

Lynn patted his arm. "Let me give you all the details." But her cell beeped and she jumped. "I forgot, I have a nine o'clock appointment. Nathan, they're all staying at my house since they blew out Sara's front window. Piper said she would be cooking breakfast for them. Go join them." She gave Nathan a kiss on the cheek and rushed to her next meeting.

"Come on, David, I have to hear the rest of this story." Nathan hustled his friend out of the coffee shop.

* * *

The men arrived just as breakfast was getting into full swing. Charlotte and Carter had shown up, along with their house guest, Quinn, to help Piper cook. Two dogs had staked out large portions of the kitchen floor just in case some of that bacon tumbled their way. Piper was shoveling mounds of scrambled eggs as Charlotte distributed bacon and hash browns. Carter was taking drink orders as he stepped around dogs and Janet.

"Janet?" he demanded, "What are you doing here? Isn't there food at your place?"

"Uncle Carter," moaned Janet, supporting her very big belly, "I just had to see Sara and these kids."

"Tim let you drive over here?"

"No, I didn't," called Tim from the laundry room where he was changing a diaper on baby number two.

"Nathan, are you here for breakfast, too?" shouted Charlotte over the din as two men stumbled through the door and Nathan handed her a bakery box.

"Yes, my dear, I can't think of a better place to eat." Nathan dragged David Templeton to the center of the room.

"Grandpa," shouted Colt as he struggled to his feet, pushing back his chair, just missing a dog and Janet's baby number one, a very energetic toddler.

"Pop?" Quinn called from another room. He was carrying another chair into the kitchen. Stopped. Counted heads and disappeared to look for more chairs.

"Where's Sara?" called David.

"In the shower," offered Tilda between bites of bacon. "She said she could still smell the gas."

"What gas?" David paled.

"The tear gas," explained Colt. "She was knocked out. The police rescued me and the guys before they threw it in the house." David gasped as he studied the black eye and bruises on his grandson.

Colt grinned as he rubbed his eye. "Uncle CJ. I tried to tackle him." Colt rubbed his chin. "He's quicker than he looks."

"What about Madeline?" asked David. "Did she allow this?"

"Nah, she screamed and swore at him. So they taped us up." Colt grinned in delight as David looked on the verge of a panic attack. Charlotte and Piper put Nathan's pastry contribution on the table as everyone sat for breakfast. Hands reached for the pastry plate. Bacon was passed. More juice was poured.

Janet squealed. "My water! It's time!" All the adults in the kitchen gasped at once. Tim appeared at her side in a panic.

"The kids . . a car blocking the drive," Tim babbled.

"I have my security man out front. We'll get you to the hospital." David ran to the front of the house and waved to his security man. The man bolted from the SUV, unfazed when David explained that they had to beat the stork to the hospital. Tim, Janet and David rushed to the SUV as the security man started the engine. They were off in a flash as Tim pulled his cell phone out to warn the doctor.

Quinn and Charlotte got the kids settled back at the breakfast table while Piper and Carter rounded up Janet's two children.

"I thought I heard Janet," said Sara as she walked into the kitchen. Quinn caught his breath as he looked at the slender woman with wet hair and bare feet, dressed in a big t-shirt and someone's jogging shorts. "Where is she?"

The crowd exploded.

CHAPTER THIRTEEN

Four somber men sat in the DA's office early on a Friday morning. "Are you certain you want to drop all the charges?" asked the DA. Dusty sat beside him, shaking his head.

"Yes." David Templeton turned to the attorney beside him. "Mr. Grayson, I assume you have received all the paperwork from my legal staff?"

"Yes, sir." The four men turned to see Quinn enter the conference room.

Dusty stood. "Mars will be bringing the two of them here in a few minutes. I have to get back to my office." He shook hands with everyone and left the office. The DA excused himself also. "No charges. I'll get the paperwork completed for you to sign, Mr. Templeton."

"Tell me your plan, again," Quinn requested from his father as they sat and waited with Mr. Grayson. "And do you think she'll take it?"

"Money or jail? What do you think?"

The men stood as the door opened again and Mars ushered in Madeline and CJ. They had been in the James County jail for three days and were wearing the uniform they had been issued at their arrest. Neither one of them looked fresh, clean or happy.

"What is this?" snarled the woman, "another chance to humiliate us?"

"Please be seated," said David, "I have a proposal."

She started to speak but CJ said, "Shut up, you cow. I want to hear this offer. I don't appreciate being locked up with those psychos." CJ had spent two nights in a cell next to a homeless man.

"Do you think I met a better class of people in my cell?" snarled Madeline.

"Enough!" David was at the end of his patience. He gave a nod to H. Lawrence Grayson, his River Bend attorney.

The man began, "Templeton, Incorporated is willing to drop all charges and relinquish claim to the funds already held in the account in the Cayman Islands. In addition, the corporation will deposit five hundred thousand dollars a year into that account for the next ten years, provided neither of you contact the family again during that time."

"My son -"

"Yes, Madeline, your son," snarled Quinn. "He won't see you for ten years. You may send presents and cards. He will get them and I'll encourage him to respond to any letter or card or present he receives as long as I have an address." He doubted that there would be any contact over those years from her.

"As I was saying," said H. Lawrence, "after ten years you are free to contact any member of the family but must understand that you may be denied any meeting or additional funds."

"What does that mean?" snarled CJ.

"It means," said David, "that you can knock on the door, but we don't have to answer."

"And if we refuse?"

"You'll be held without bond and be charged with crimes that go beyond the jurisdiction of this state. In federal court, you're on your own," explained the attorney.

Madeline gave Quinn a hateful stare. "You can't take my son."

"You can write to him and you can see him and talk to him in ten years." Quinn glared back at her.

"What about Margaret?" asked CJ, "She can't agree to this?"

"Wanna bet?" snarled Quinn. "She wanted you to do real time. It took all we had to convince her that this was a better option."

"When you sign these papers," explained H. Lawrence, "you are also agreeing to a divorce without cause from Mrs. Kirtley. She agrees to an additional settlement of joint properties." He handed CJ a sheet of paper.

CJ studied the list. Margaret kept all the stock in Templeton, Inc. and subsidiaries as well as the main house and two of the cars, along with some smaller items. She gave him all their other stock, the house in Hilton Head, three cars and a list of property and other items that she obviously didn't want.

"As for you, Ms. Templeton," H. Lawrence continued, "We are offering to buy your condo in Raleigh." He placed a check in front of her for triple the value of the condo, "and you agree to leave the Raleigh area as soon as you can pack up."

"My friends -

"You'll find others," offered Quinn. "Maybe even some who will care about you."

"That's enough, Quinn," cautioned David. He turned to CJ and Madeline. "We'll leave you to discuss this. You may call your attorneys." He pushed a phone toward them and the four men left the room.

After talking with their attorneys, CJ and Madeline were ready to negotiate, somewhat.

"We have some questions," said CJ. "First, although we are not to contact the family, what happens if we see one another, you know, we all happen to attend the same event or we visit the same vacation spot?"

"We'll all be civil," replied David. "That excludes Colt, of course. He's still a minor and he is not to be approached at any time." He set his lips in a straight line for emphasis, then continued, "Or there will be no more money."

Madeline tensed in her chair. "After ten years, that's no longer an issue, correct?"

"Correct," replied David, "By then Colt will be able to make his own choices."

"When does this clock start ticking?"

"I've had your Porsche serviced. This detective will take you to it." He nodded to Mars who had been a silent witness to the discussions while providing security for the meeting. "You can leave as soon as the papers are signed and you are processed out of jail." He looked at Madeline. "You should be out of the Raleigh condo in ninety days." He nodded to her, "I can have some packers assist you when you return to Raleigh, if you like, readying your things for storage or transfer." He turned to CJ. "Margaret is out of town for a month or two. I have security staff at the house. She has already packed your belongings. But you're welcome to take items that you feel are personal. The security staff will help you move your things to storage or transfer them some place."

"What about access to the offshore accounts?" asked CJ.

"As soon as you sign, any holds will vanish," David explained.

"We had clothing in the car," barked Madeline as she pulled at her jumpsuit.

"We touched nothing," said Quinn. "It's all still there. The car has been in the police lot since your arrest." He and David stood, nodded to H. Lawrence and left the office.

The discussion ended and H. Lawrence spent an hour with the prisoners as he watched CJ and Madeline sign the stack of papers. After the signings and additional instruction from H. Lawrence, Mars led the prisoners back to the jail for release.

* * *

CJ and Madeline left the jail in the clothing they had worn at their arrest. They were so happy to be released from jail that they jumped in his car and raced back to Raleigh. For most of the dash down I-40 eastward Madeline cursed and complained. "I'll get even with that son of a bitch one day," she repeated over and over.

CJ kept his counsel throughout the drive, nodding his agreement and making sympathetic noises. Mentally he was making his own plan to get even, to get all the money and to get away from her. He had to stay at her place for a few days until he figured some things out. How could he get sole position of their joint accounts? Where could he hide to avoid Madeline's wrath? He pushed his car to the limit, miraculously without meeting the highway patrol, and arrived in Raleigh in record time.

Madeline rushed from the car as he slid into the parking slot for her condo. "I'm so glad I held out for possession for three months," she said as she slammed the car door. During the jail negotiations David had wanted her out of Raleigh and out of her condo immediately. She had argued that she needed time to plan for the next phase of her life while needing time to close out her Raleigh life.

CJ had been entertained by her dramatic display and also her skill in handling David. Following her into the elevator he said, "Let's shower and go find some dinner."

"I'm throwing these clothes away," she declared.

He agreed. He had enough of his things at her condo that he could do the same. "That's a fine idea. Margaret bought me this jacket anyway."

* * *

Friday evening the Little Theater was packed with Tilda's fans. Even the twins and Colt were in place, mostly because they had heard a story from Jason about him and his friends tackling a would-be murderer once, years ago, as they volunteered to take coats or something in the lobby.

Dusty was even there because Lynn had cajoled him by saying, "One of your own is on stage tonight."

"What do you mean one of my own?" He had a funny feeling about the question.

"Tilda, the SWAT member who got your team into the house."

"She's not on the team," he reasoned.

"Did she get them into the house? And because of her work, did the rescue go off like clockwork?" She raised her eyebrows, waiting for him to deny Tilda's role.

"Damn."

So Dusty and his staff and their children were all at the Little Theater. The performance was all everyone expected, but they applauded with enthusiasm anyway. And all the detectives' children begged to attend drama camp next year.

In the lobby, after the show, David Templeton pulled Lynn aside. "I think you should suggest that Rory send a grant application to our foundation next cycle." He winked at her and went to bring a bouquet of flowers to Tilda, the best zombie on stage.

The lobby was filled with noise and excitement. There were cookies and juice for everyone. David found his son and said, "The plane will be here Monday."

Quinn frowned. "I'm not ready to go home." It wasn't a challenge, just a statement.

"I know that." David smiled at his son. "I can see what you and Colt have found here. You get that woman to marry you. You and your son need her family."

"I know." Quinn clapped his father on the back. "Thanks, Dad."

Colt spotted his father across the lobby and rushed to his side. "I met some of those guys at soccer camp." He nodded toward a group of teens at the punch table. "They said if I lived here I could try out for the high school JV team when school starts." He turned to his grandfather, "I mean, I would like -

"I agree with you, son," replied David, "You should try out for the team." Colt grinned and ran back to his friends.

CHAPTER FOURTEEN

"What are we doing here?" Mouse asked as Quinn took her hand and dragged her into the backyard of a house in Dancing Creek, the exclusive older neighborhood in River Bend. She looked around. The kids had disappeared.

"Dad wanted me to check out some property," he explained as he pulled her further into the secluded backyard. "I've been thinking," said Quinn as he massaged her hand, "We've had a pretty good time these last few weeks."

"I've been held hostage," Mouse reminded him, "The kids have been threatened. Your father thought I was a gold digger. My parents didn't like you." She thought a moment. "I guess my family finally realizes what a great guy you are. And your dad isn't such a bad guy."

"I wasn't talking about our relatives." Quinn stopped and turned her to face him. "I want to talk about us." An embrace and a longing kiss focused her attention.

They parted. "You and me?" Her eyes warmed. She licked her lips.

"You and me and those crazy kids." He put his arms around her and pulled her to him for another long, lingering kiss, the kind he had been trying to initiate for the last weeks. She slipped her arms around his waist and kissed him back with enthusiasm. When they separated, he asked, "Does this mean we're on the same page?"

Mouse smiled at him and traced her finger along his lips. "I was beginning to think that I was a few pages ahead of you."

He kissed her again, enjoying her body pressed against his. "When did we ever have time? Mysteries, robbery, mayhem -"

"Mom?"

"Kids," sighed Quinn in frustration.

"What is it, Tilda?" asked Mouse, staying in Quinn's arms.

The little girl seemed to be unfazed by her mother in Quinn's embrace. "Colt said I have my own room, but it's not in the attic." She took a moment and studied the two adults. "He says the attic is for the boys and their games. He said I can't go there unless they ask me."

"What are you talking about?" Mouse let go of Quinn and knelt to be eye level with her daughter.

"Our new house." Tilda pointed to the house on the property they were visiting, showing her disgust at Mouse's lack of understanding. "Colt said when we move in, 'cause you and Quinn are getting married, I can't go to the attic and play. So I need a baby sister. Then we can keep the boys out of our room." She studied her mother's face and amended her request, "Or a kitten."

"Married?" Mouse asked Quinn as she stood to face him.

"That's where I was going with this conversation."

"I guess we were distracted." She smiled at him and walked back into his arms.

"I didn't expect all this help." He looked down at Tilda who was now very interested in the conversation.

"Colt said I get a TV in my room and we're putting a swimming pool there." She pointed to the back of the house.

"Swimming pool?"

Quinn frowned, then cleared his throat. "Okay, here's the plan. I bought this house and Colt is going to River Bend High School in the fall. And since we have so much extra room, I thought we could invite you and the kids to live with us, you know, like a family?"

"Can we, Mom?" The kids were jumping up and down. She didn't know when the boys had joined them.

"Yeah," came soft encouragement from Colt.

Mouse left Quinn's arms and turned to the young man. "We have your approval?"

"Yeah," he replied with a shy grin. She gave him a hug and a kiss on the cheek.

"As long as Colt approves," she said to Quinn, "I guess we have a deal."

* * *

As CJ walked out of the shower, his cell rang. It had been days since he had used it and had only last evening plugged it into the charger. Not eager to talk with anyone since his return to Raleigh, he had put it aside. This afternoon was the first time it had burped with a call. He checked caller ID. His hacker? "I thought you went underground?"

Theo whispered, "I have but I want to see you. We need to talk alone and in person."

"Yeah?" replied CJ, intrigued. "Meet me at the palace in one hour." That was code for the office that the old Starships endeavor had leased years ago. When all the partners seemed to die so conveniently, CJ had continued the lease because he often needed a legitimate business address for his embezzling efforts. Ending the call abruptly, he went to find Madeline. Knocking on her bedroom door, he stuck his head in to find her standing naked in front of her closet. "I have to go to the house to get more of my things," he announced when she turned to face him. He was only wearing briefs. At that moment he knew the partnership was over. Beautiful Madeline, naked, had no allure. "I'll bring back something to eat."

She studied him, seeming to have reached the same conclusion. "I'm not hungry. I'll see you when you get back." She returned to studying her closet.

CJ arrived at the office in the well-maintained business park early. He wasn't certain if the other offices were back to full staff or were maintaining remote working schedules. The business park with manicured landscaping and well-organized parking areas presented a solid business image. As he walked into the lobby the hacker came out of the shadows. They exchanged nods. CJ took the elevator and Theo took the stairs.

CJ let the man into the office then closed and locked the door. "What's wrong?" They hadn't met face to face in maybe two years. Theo was a man of indeterminate age and racial origins. Sometimes CJ thought he was Asian and other times he could see hints of a South American Indian heritage. Their association had been going on for almost ten years, but they had never gotten to the stage of exchanging life histories.

"We gotta talk." Theo sat on one of the visitor chairs as CJ moved behind the desk. "I found the guy." CJ raised an eyebrow. "The guy who took the money." The hacker was getting excited. "I know I told you I had to go underground. Well, I didn't have anything to do so I started back tracking the signal he left at the account when he stole the rest of the money." Theo grinned. "He's sharp, but I'm sharper."

"So you found him?"

"Not quite, but I'm close. He's somewhere in the western part of the state. I need a week or two and I'll have him. The signal seems to be somewhere close to that River Bend, but not quite."

"You sure it's not Margolin?"

"She's too clean. She doesn't have to sneak around, she can just get the Army to open doors. This guy is doing some slick shit."

By this time, after his River Bend arrest, CJ understood that Sara wasn't the person who had taken the Rothman money. And Theo was right, she had other ways to access accounts. "What do you propose?"

"I want us to stay off line. I got you this burner phone." He flipped a package onto the desk. "It only has the number to my phone." Now Theo looked him in the eye. And CJ understood that another partnership was changing. "I find this guy and get the money then it's fifty-fifty. Afterward I disappear and we got no more business."

CJ did some mental calculations. He had ten million with Madeline. He could end that partnership tomorrow and have all ten million. The thief took about five million in the first raid of Rothman's account. There was no telling how much he would find when he tracked down the man. He'd have to give Theo something. "We don't know how much is left of Rothman's money. What about everyone else's money?" CJ suspected that there had been millions stashed under various identities because he had known that Garson had recruited several more investors than CJ had ever met.

"Someone, I think the Army, put some watchdogs on those accounts." He shrugged. "Maybe it was the FBI. Someone got curious when your friend, Mahaffey cleaned out his account." Neither man knew that someone else had emptied those accounts years ago.

CJ was confused. "You think the Margolin woman and her friends tied up all Garson's accounts?"

"Yeah," nodded Theo. "They must have followed Mahaffey's trail and looked for related accounts. Who else knew about the money?"

CJ agreed. "You're right. We were the only ones who knew about the accounts. How did Margolin or the FBI miss Rothman's account?"

"I think he had some accounts in that Mahaffey cluster. This stuff we're going to recover, he was keeping separate." The hacker grinned. "Nobody seemed to trust anybody."

And that, thought CJ, summed up his financial partnerships. All those years of illegal financial dealings and all he could account for besides his own funds was about seven million. There was more someplace. Maybe it was time to claim what he could and cut his losses. "How about we just say you get three mil?"

"If all we find is seven mil, that's a nice round number."

"But how do I know you're gone and won't hack me?" CJ was a little nervous. He was learning that trust didn't exist in cyber space.

"You're right," said Theo, "I can always find you on the internet. But I've been around long enough that I know you have some ugly friends." He didn't look over fifty but he had been in the hacking game almost since it was invented as a career option. Theo was ready to retire with all his funds, especially the anticipated influx from this last job. He would quietly ride out compound interest in a sedate investment account already set up that was following all the financial laws of the land, ready to underwrite his retirement. The rewards of a successful criminal life.

"And I would find you, too," threatened CJ in a voice that told the hacker he wasn't the only computer guru around. CJ sat up and took out a note pad from a desk drawer, anxious to begin the last act of this partnership. "What do we do now?"

"Nothing until I pinpoint this guy." Theo stood. "I'll call you next Monday at 4 PM and we'll go from there." He walked out the door.

CJ sat at the desk and thought, unaware of passing time until he realized that it was dark in the office. It was summer so he must have been sitting and thinking for several hours. He smiled, pleased with himself because he finally had a plan. He called Madeline.

"Where are you?" she demanded.

"I got distracted packing up my stuff. I'll see you in about thirty minutes. Can I pick up some food?"

He returned to her apartment with the food offering. She was aloof. "I wondered where you were." She pouted.

He sighed, adopting the role of a plagued ex-husband. "I found that Margaret had taken somethings I wanted. And she threw my clothes in trash bags." He tried to look oppressed. "I packed up a few things and think I should run down to the place in Hilton Head to see what she's done there." He unpacked the food as he talked. "You work on your move here. I'll see what's with the property down there." He gave her his sincerest smile. "Maybe we can resettle there once I clear out her stuff."

"That sounds like it might work." Madeline was void of any ideas. She was too unsettled by the actions of the last week. Hilton Head was as good as any interim location as she planned her future.

"Give me a week to clean up that place while you get you shit together here."

"It's not shit!" she shouted. Shocked at her response, he reached over and rubbed her shoulders. "I learned how to talk tough in jail," she frowned in explanation.

"I guess we'll look back on this as an enlightening experience." Or as the end of our partnership, he thought.

* * *

David Templeton found himself spending a lot of time in River Bend. He had never been to the town until last week. Today he was recovering from the scare of the hostage situation that threatened his grandson and negotiations with the kidnappers, better known as his son-in-law and ex daughter-in-law. He was still in town wrapping up some of the technicalities with regard to Madeline and CJ's arrests.

"I don't know what we'll find in the foundation, what damage that fool did to us." David sat in a lovely home in Dancing Creek complaining to his old friend Nathan Taft.

"What is the problem?" asked Nathan. He was delighted to be on the inside of this investigation. Well, inside was relative, he was getting his gossip straight from David. He didn't have to fabricate trips to Lynn's office and pump her for information.

David sipped his coffee. "I made an offer. Madeline and CJ took the offer, and all the charges will be dropped."

"Did Sara agree? After all her children were at risk." Nathan liked to be the devil's advocate.

David nodded. "Quinn's been talking with her and she wants what will be best for her children and for Colt." David smiled at his old friend. "She's just what my son needs. I think he's figured it out." David winked because he had promised not to mention the engagement until they had talked to that friend of Lynn's about scheduling the ceremony.

David's phone pinged. "Excuse me," he told Nathan and scanned the message. He smiled at his old friend. "Well, I guess I can tell you to clear your calendar to attend a wedding on Friday."

Nathan grinned. In addition to being on the inside of crime solving, he loved a good romance. They talked for some time in Nathan's library in the house at Dancing Creek. Finally, Nathan said, "You're welcome to stay in the guest house as long as necessary. Do you have any ideas about filling your time here until Friday?"

"I've got to fly back to Raleigh to get some things done and make plans to fly a few family members here for the wedding. But before I leave I want to meet that woman, Audrey Decker, who runs the group home program here. She does some exceptional work."

Nathan laughed, "That's the name of her program, Exceptional Children. Just ask Lynn, she'll help you make introductions."

* * *

Jason, dirty and sweaty, walked into the kitchen. Lynn followed, just as sweaty. Dusty stared at his family, sniffed, smelled no dinner. He waited for an explanation. After Lynn finished gulping a tall glass of water she said, "We moved Connie and the kids."

"Ugh?"

"Doug's moving next door."

"I know." He looked at the two tired movers and was grateful Doug hadn't asked for his help. "Doug told me Emily needed more assistance with those kids."

Lynn finished the rest of her drink. "It seems that Emily is unable to keep up with just Lucia's assistance. She wants Connie's help raising the children and since she and Doug are in the will as guardians it made sense to Emily that they move in now."

"Doug was worried that I wouldn't want him in the neighborhood." Dusty searched through the carry out menus he had strewn across the kitchen counter.

"What?" Lynn scowled. "Why don't you want him here?"

"Calm down. I told him it was fine with me." He scanned Chinese, Thai, Uncle Chicken. "I just hadn't realized Emily needed more help."

Jason who enjoyed his new adulthood perk of grabbing a beer said, "Juan moved out. He is making enough money to afford his own place." He finished the beer and looked in the pantry for some snacks and placed a few opened bags of various chips on the table. "He has a girlfriend, too." Dusty handed him a menu.

"So does Lucia." Lynn wiggled her eyebrows.

"She has a girlfriend?" Both men were surprised.

"No, a boyfriend and you'll never guess who."

"Who?" Two men were now curious.

"Umberto!" Lynn looked smug as though expecting a drum roll. Both guys looked stunned or confused. "You know she bakes those pastries and cookies from Mexico?" They both nodded. "Emily suggested she talk to Umberto about using his ovens to make bigger batches. He liked her recipes. And now she bakes once a week and he sells her baked goods. And." The guys waited. When she was certain she had their attention she said, "Juan moved out because the apartment he shared with his mother was getting crowded." She used finger quotes with crowded.

"Ah," nodded Jason. He liked to demonstrate his worldly understanding of life.

"Umberto?" Dusty was startled by the news. He had known the baker for years and had never seen or heard a hint of any dating, or other stuff.

Lynn nodded. "Yolo says when the ovens heated the kitchen they seemed to heat him, too." Yolo was Umberto's cousin and Lynn's friend. "She thinks this is a serious relationship."

Piper and her two sons walked into the kitchen as dirty as Lynn and Jason. "Will said text Uncle Chicken. He's gassing his truck and will pick up the order." Jason's fingers danced on his phone screen.

The newlyweds tumbled into the kitchen as dirty as everyone else. "Mom?" Doyle gasped. "Does Umberto really have a girl friend?"

Piper nodded. She gave her new daughter-in-law a hug. "Love is in the air." All the guys groaned. Jason increased the carry out order. He

125

had to get used to Doyle and Lori in the family mix. He remembered how much Doyle could eat.

Lori looked around the kitchen with her dark dancing eyes. She had wondered what life would be like living near her in-laws. She remembered her father's caution, "Piper is crazy." In Lori's opinion Piper wasn't alone. She hadn't realized Lynn's role in Dusty's investigations. Just the other day there was that tear gassing thing and a little girl and zombies. Doyle hadn't made much sense because he kept laughing. Married life was going to be interesting.

CHAPTER FIFTEEN

Emergency meeting. Frank's six!

Lynn scanned her phone. Sara was calling a widow's meeting for tonight. She smiled to herself. She had an idea that the group would hear that another member had decided to end her widowhood. She quickly texted Piper who wasn't on the circulation list. She also sent Rory a quick text. Her phone rang as fast as her message had hopped through the ether.

"Sweetie," he laughed into the phone. "Is it true?"

"I don't know yet, but I'll let you know for sure this evening." With that Lynn got to work and hoped there were enough leftovers in the refrigerator to feed Jason and Dusty this evening. She was going to party!

Of course, she still had a full day's work to get done. Today it included an introduction. David Templeton wanted to meet Audrey Decker. She brought them together in her conference room. "Do you need me here?" she asked, distracted by plans for the evening party at Frank's.

David shook his head. "No, thank you for everything, Lynn. I just want to get to know this lady."

Audrey blushed. "Mr. Templeton, I'm flattered. You fund such innovative programs. I want to learn from you."

Lynn smiled at her guests. "It sounds as though you two have some admiration to share." She stepped out of the room and closed the door.

"Mrs. Decker, my foundation funds programs that I hope will be innovative. I've followed your programs and find they also offer exciting opportunities for success."

"Thank you."

"I have to ask why you have never applied for funds from our foundation?"

Audrey looked embarrassed. "We have. In the last three years we have submitted proposals I thought met your foundation's criteria." She swallowed. "But, the denial letter told us we had not met the foundation's threshold for innovation nor had we included measurements for success."

"I'm sorry. You may have heard we've had some leadership problems in the foundation offices." David quietly added to the list of CJ's sins.

She smiled. "I know you've hired my friend Rory Prentiss to help reorganize." She thought about her next remark. "Rory is a good man. He will get the foundation back to the image you want for a family foundation that is a leader in so many ways."

"Thank you for that." David gave her a teasing grin. "Of course, you may have an inside track with your friend at the helm."

Audrey took a shaky breath. "Rory stands by his friends. I miss him here."

"That's quite an accolade. My son hired Mr. Prentiss. I'll look forward to working with him." David checked his watch. "I have to return to Raleigh." He frowned thinking over the demands of collecting family for a quick wedding and keeping an eye on Quinn's responsibilities at the office while he and Mouse honeymooned. "Can we set a date two weeks from today? I would like to meet you again and have an opportunity to tour one of your group homes."

"That would be great. I like lead time to set up a tour. The clients need to be prepared for visitors. Otherwise they become very upset." Audrey impressed David with her professionalism and her advocacy for her clients.

"I understand. My son is in a group home in Raleigh." He mentioned the name of the program.

"Ah," Audrey nodded, understanding. "I knew they received funds from your foundation and I knew they had resources to try some exciting ideas." She smiled at David. "I hope your son prospers in that facility."

"He does. I want to take those ideas to more facilities."

"You have, Mr. Templeton," Audrey assured him. "My program has borrowed extensively from those innovations. Sometimes we've added our own spin and think that has made a good idea even better."

"So I've heard," said David. He checked his phone. "My ride is here. In two weeks we'll talk more." He stood and collected his notes.

"Certainly." She stood and held out her hand. "Thank you for initiating this introduction. I look forward to our next meeting."

David took her hand. "I do, too. But I must run." He opened the door and called to Lynn, "Thank you!" And hurried to the parking lot.

Lynn dashed in to get the scoop from Audrey. "Well?"

Audrey grinned. "He wanted to meet me! He asked why we don't ask for money from his foundation. He wants to see our group home next week."

Lynn hugged her. "Sounds like your programs are going to get some new funds."

"Yes. He sounded so eager to learn more and help us. Thank you." The young woman seemed to dance out of the office.

"It's you Audrey. You've grown a program that folks notice."

Audrey hugged her again. "Well, he'll visit again in two weeks. I wonder if we have time to re-carpet and repaint everything before then?"

Lynn laughed as she ushered her friend out the door.

* * *

That evening at Frank's Tavern the ladies gathered with anticipation. Sara had arrived early and ordered the usual, pitchers of beer, nachos, wings and, as a celebration, a box of cannoli from the bakery. Harriette came in with a bouquet of daisies. Piper and Lynn wrestled a string of helium balloons and decorations through the door. Piper shouted to Frank, "Double the order Frank. We're moving to the back room!"

"What?" shouted Sara over the chaos because the bar was filling with women. Her mother and two aunts came in followed by Amelia Rawlings and her daughter-in-law, Penny.

Ronnie Dowd walked in and announced, "Janet can't come so she sent me. I brought my sister." Michelle Grayson waved to the growing crowd.

Teniquia LaMont and Trina Healey walked in with Angie Valeri. Angie was an old neighbor of Sara's, and she explained, "I had to bring the rest of Dusty's staff. I knew Lynn would be here."

"Are we the last?" asked Allison Reid as she dragged Tovah Fleischer into the back room. While Tovah was heard to say, "I won't know anyone." Several women shouted, "Hey, Tovah!"

The ladies all greeted one another. Frank muscled his way through the door with beer and food. As he left he whispered to Lynn, "Thanks for the heads up!"

Someone started a chant and they all joined in. "Announcement! Announcement!"

Mouse stood on a chair, waved her hand with an engagement ring. "I'm getting married."

"Ooh, aah!" Piper and Lynn stood on chairs and unfurled a banner exclaiming congratulations.

"When?" came a call from Penny as she poured more beer for someone.

"Friday!"

"What?!" a chorus gasped.

Sara blushed. "He doesn't want to wait." The gang cheered.

CHAPTER SIXTEEN

Proposals and weddings were on Quinn's mind. But he couldn't ignore the family business. He scheduled a Teams meeting at Lynn's office to talk with Rory and David. "Thank you for letting us use your place," he said to Lynn as they settled in her office to each view their laptops, she at her desk and he at the small work table, as the meeting screens invited entry. "I'm glad you have time to join us. Neither Dad nor I understand all this nonprofit stuff." he grinned. "We're big capitalists."

"Hey, sweetie," Rory's image waved from the laptops. He was the host of the meeting.

"I'm on, too," David Templeton nodded across the ether.

Quinn said, "Hey, Dad. I asked Rory to give us a report of his initial impressions. I know you've only been on the job a week, Rory. Just tell us your first impressions and a broad assessment of where the foundation stands."

Before their eyes Rory seemed to become a different person, very serious and very concerned. "Thank you, Quinn, for telling your staff at the trust offices to be as helpful as possible. Gilda is a treasure. She has a marvelous network and has been able to recommend people on your staff to advise me." He looked down at some notes. "I found a mess here. Mr. Kirtley had driven off your best staff and had populated the offices with a few of his sycophants. He added additional staff, calling them interns. It appears they are offspring of board members or old fraternity brothers. The board of the foundation is a rubber stamp made up of a few of his cousins, one or two old girlfriends and again a couple of fraternity brothers." Rory rubbed his forehead. "Let me just tell you what I've done and it should explain my recommendations. My first morning I met the staff. This foundation this size should have a staff of twenty or so. There are maybe a dozen people here, all Mr. Kirtley's people. After meeting the staff I called Gilda and asked for an HR person, two people from the trust accounting offices, and two attorneys from somewhere in the Templeton Corporation." He grinned out of the laptops. "She gave me some great folks. Monday afternoon we set out an action plan and started working it. I fired the foundation staff. The HR representative put together a severance package that seemed to please everyone except Mr. Kirtley's executive assistant." His eyebrows wiggled. "I think she has a more meaningful relationship with the boss after hours." Both Quinn and David growled unprintable words.

Lynn laughed at them. "So Tuesday morning the office was empty?" She was intrigued by this close-up account of a foundation's almost meltdown.

Rory shook his head. "No, I had all those people from Gilda's network. They audited the books, read all the grant files, and we called in an IT guy to clean all the computers. Each evening we go over what we've found and plan for the next day." He looked into his screen. "These are fine people. We'll have this place ready for the new director. The attorneys wrote a letter to the board members thanking them for their service and terminating their board participation. It was a great letter, talking about foundation reorganization and redirection." He chuckled.

Lynn interrupted. "Did you remember to call Beth?"

"Who's Beth?" called out David.

"Beth Seymour. She's an attorney in the AG's office. She used to work with Mr. Grayson before she took that job."

Quinn jumped in. "I don't think we want to go high profile. Can't we keep this in-house?"

"Not to prosecute," explained Lynn. "Beth can quietly help identify the bogus nonprofits. But she will also be helpful if you want to pursue any charges against people around the state."

David scowled out of the screen. "Let's get our foundation back in order first."

With that directive they spent another hour listening to Rory's plan and offering suggestions. "Thank you, Rory," concluded David. "Let's do this again next week." They all signed off.

"Thank you," Quinn said to Lynn as he packed up his laptop. "Can I get you lunch or something?"

"No, I have other things to do today. But you're welcome to use our offices when you're in town." She smiled. "You can use Rory's office. He won't mind."

Quinn paused and thought about her offer. "Thank you. I do need some place as a base. Mouse is busy with her work and Charlotte makes me nervous."

"She's just watching out for her daughter."

"But we're getting married Friday!"

Lynn laughed. "Charlotte will believe it when she sees it."

Quinn moaned in frustration. Between kids and a vigilant mother-in-law-to-be, he couldn't find time alone with Mouse for more than a quick hug. . . . well, and maybe a kiss or four. He couldn't wait until Friday.

* * *

These weeks without a drug high preyed on Bart Decker. It had taken time but he had finally learned where and how to find some drugs locally. Or had someone found him? Sometimes he was blurry about things. The guy who handled the purchase liked to meet in open places, like the park, in daylight. Bart had remarked on the time and location.

"Out in the open," remarked the dealer. "How does that look guilty?" He took the cash and placed a pouch on the picnic table. "We're two dad's letting our kids play in the park." The man's daughter played with Bart's daughter in the toddler playground.

The man called to his daughter and she scrambled into his arms. "See you next week." He strapped the youngster in her car seat and was off.

Bart continued to let his daughter, Maya, play. Audrey was at work and he had left the boys at home alone. They might have caught on to the transaction. Maya seemed to just enjoy being alone with her father. His stomach churned. Yeah, she was alone with her father as cover for his drug buy. He hated himself and he hated the drugs. But most of all he hated that man who had stolen his wife.

Maya waved to him as she climbed a little castle and was soon distracted by another child. They climbed and shouted and giggled. Bart slumped against the picnic table. The other parent was watching everything. It gave him more time to brood and place blame. It also gave him time to plan. He had to get away this evening and enjoy these new drugs. It was something different the guy said but should give him the same feeling as the shot.

The dealer had known he had lost access to his regular supplier. Bart had to give that some thought. Someone was keeping track of his drugs. And as good businessmen they didn't want to lose his patronage. Someone in the supply chain had passed his name and contact information along to a replacement supplier. How much did they know about him? They must have known he needed something to keep him going. In some part of his mind Bart didn't like being manipulated, being exploited for a weakness. But he didn't have any weakness, he just had an unfaithful wife.

He got to his feet, smiled at the helicopter parent watching his daughter, scooped up Maya, made her giggle and got out of the park. Bart was struggling with his demons and with what remained of his conscience. Possessing new drugs gave his demons more power. This evening he would leave for the forest, his refuge, to try the new stuff. He could tell Audrey he had a job interview in the evening because he had babysitting duty during the day. Yeah, that worked. He'd tell her he'd be home late. Because, he had to babysit again tomorrow—and all the other days until he found himself a job.

CHAPTER SEVENTEEN

Quinn had pushed hard to convince Mouse to marry quickly. "Everyone will think I'm pregnant," she had argued.

"That'll never happen," he had frowned, "because we're never alone."

"Besides Margaret is coming to town with Jimmy. My whole family will be here." He kissed her again. "And your mother won't trust me until some minister blesses us."

"Mom?" Some kid had interrupted another private moment wanting something.

Quinn grinned as the youngster had just proved his point and Mouse laughed. "You win," she had said then turned to her child.

So today was the day. It was a small ceremony on the grounds of Taft Manor Museum and Conference Center. Afterward there was a luncheon with a quick toast and congratulations offered by David. Quinn hustled Mouse to a waiting SUV and they disappeared in a cloud of dust.

"But the kids?" gasped Mouse. Quinn had moved things along so quickly once she agreed to marry him that she realized there were many unanswered questions. Mouse paused. She wasn't a person who leaped. She thought things over. Who was this man that he could sweep her off her feet—sweep her with three kids—off her feet? Then she smiled to herself, she knew. She loved him. She valued his friendship years ago, but now she had seen him in action—a man devoted to his father and his son. A man who respected all those he met. A man who was not defined by his wealth, but by his heart. But she did have questions as they raced to . . . she didn't even know where they were racing!

"Gracia and Ray will tend the house and kids for a few days," explained Quinn.

"Which house?"

"Dusty's brother, Carl, is already working on the renovations for the new house. We should be in about mid-October."

"Does that mean we'll be living in my house? The window's repaired." She grabbed a hand grip as Quinn took a curve in the road.

Quinn grinned. "We'll stay at your place until our house is finished. Because we need a bigger place with more privacy."

"My house is in a quiet neighborhood."

"We need privacy from all those kids," Quinn explained as he reached across the console and ran his finger along her chin. "Just once I want to kiss you without someone saying, 'Mom?'"

"We've been alone."

"But not long enough to . . . ," he wiggled his eyebrows at her.

She laughed. "So where are you taking me?"

"We have a condo in Vail. It's not the season, so we should have plenty of privacy for the next week." He pulled into the airport and spotted the company jet near the general aviation hangar.

"Vail? In your plane?" They were racing toward the general aviation hangars. "I only brought something for overnight. You didn't tell me I needed more. I thought we would just go to an inn or something for overnight." Mouse was upset as she waved her big mom bag. "What will I wear?" She looked down at the lovely summer dress she had just been married in. "I can't wear this for a week."

"We'll shop when we get there." Quinn had all the answers. She frowned and he continued. "When are you going to accept that you will never have money concerns again? We'll buy whatever you need for our honeymoon, even if you think you need a new car." He helped her out of the SUV and they waved to the pilot. Quinn grabbed her arm and almost ran to the jet.

Once in the air Mouse turned to him and asked, "Shouldn't I have signed a pre-nup or something? You can't really mean that I can spend and spend."

"We don't need a pre-nup. I'm not going anywhere. Are you?"

"No." She clutched his arm as the plane seemed to jump into the sky.

"There you have it." He took her hand.

"How can you be so certain?" She held his hand and ran her fingers over his knuckles.

"You fill my heart," he answered. For several weeks he had watched Mouse interact with Colt and thought his heart would burst as he witnessed her tenderness toward his son. He and Colt had found the future they had been seeking.

They talked about the kids and the hectic life four children would bring when Quinn asked, "You never answered Tilda. A kitten or a baby sister?"

She smiled at him and said, "Both."

Quinn grinned. He didn't know if he could wait until they got to Vail before he . . . He sighed and knew that he could wait. Throwing Mouse down in the aisle of a small jet wasn't exactly honeymoon quality love.

* * *

Bart Decker had just been turned down for another job interview. He couldn't even get in the door for a face-to-face talk! It was finally dawning on him that his arrest, even though he was not serving time, meant many doors had closed to him. His wife was now the sole support of the family. She had to keep her job and he had to make certain she didn't leave him. They'd have a little talk tonight once the kids were in bed. He rubbed his head because something didn't feel right with those new drugs he tried yesterday. He was supposed to feel on his game, but he felt on edge, ready to brawl.

"I haven't seen that boyfriend in town lately." Nothing like tossing a match into gasoline. Bart wanted to shake things up. Audrey had ended her affair with a gentleman who was consulting with a local group of nonprofits. He and Audrey had begun a relationship after he moved his developmentally delayed brother to her group home. She had ended the affair shortly before Bart had been arrested in the drug raid. Tonight Bart was going to demonstrate his power as her husband. He rubbed his head again.

Audrey didn't know how her husband discovered her secret. But over the last weeks he had made several oblique references to an affair, but this evening he brought it out in the open. She stared at him, surprised and confused. "I won't give you a divorce," he announced.

She was standing at the kitchen counter cleaning up for the night and getting the coffee ready to brew in the morning. Turning to face him she asked, "A divorce?"

"I've known about that boyfriend of yours." He towered over her and pushed her back against the kitchen counter. He looked around to make certain the children were out of sight. "What would your board of directors say? Or the families of your clients? They think you're so perfect." He lowered his sneering voice and in a harsh whisper said, "You make sure you toe the line and maybe I'll let you keep your reputation, because I won't let you do anything else."

"I told you it was over weeks ago." They had skirted this discussion for weeks. But something was different tonight. "I don't understand what more you want."

"I mean," he growled in a low threatening voice, "if you want to keep things away from your friends and the kids, you'll do things my way from now on." His eyes drilled into her. "Everything."

"I'm not the one with a record of drug possession," she spat back as she stood up to his challenge. This confrontation had been brewing a long time. She was ready to battle as she faced him, fists clenched. He pushed her with unexpected force and she went flying across the floor, hitting her forehead against the cabinet edge.

"Dad?" Both parents looked up to find that the two older children had witnessed Bart's action. He swore under his breath, gave her a threatening look, and left the kitchen.

Audrey shivered. She heard him walk out of the house and heard his truck drive away. It was time. She had to make some decisions, decisions she had been putting off for months. Her financial situation jockeyed with the safety of her children as her primary focus. Could she manage? With her salary could she support and protect her children? A smaller house, maybe? Paying for a divorce lawyer might cost up front but in the long run, it was time to leave her marriage, such as it was.

"Mom?" Two youngsters huddled in the doorway, frightened.

Audrey got to her feet. After working with Salley Connelly and the domestic violence programs through the years, Audrey had resolved long ago to leave her marriage at the first sign of abuse and assault. Once it happened, as she knew, it would happen again. "Go pack a few things," she told her children. "We're going to Grandma's." As she spoke she found her phone and made a call.

* * *

Mouse stepped out of the plane into the early evening in Vail. She squinted as she thought about all the things she didn't pack—sunglasses were now at the top of her list. But the place looked beautiful, and so different from River Bend.

"Come on, slowpoke," urged Quinn. "We've got a lot to do before we get to the condo."

Mouse got down to the tarmac and thanked the pilot for his service. She moved toward Quinn wondering what more surprises this day would hold. "A condo? Why do you have a condo in Vail?"

He wrapped his arms around her and nuzzled her ear, whispering, "I had to find someplace to hid out from those kids." She swatted at him, embarrassed in front of the pilot. Quinn laughed and took her hand pulling her toward a parking lot. "Come on. We don't have to wait for luggage." She rolled her eyes at him and clutched her big mom bag with its change of underwear, a pair of shorts, a blouse and a few cosmetics. Quinn squeezed her hand. "A few winters ago Colt said he was interested in learning to ski. Several of his school friends had gone up to Boone to ski. Dad said he used to ski and the next thing we knew we had a place in Vail. We usually come here over the Christmas holidays and a few three-day weekends before spring."

"And when do you find time to get to Montana and Colt's horse?" Her voice had a real challenge, as in how many houses did he need?

Her tone of voice was lost on Quinn. "We find time in the summer for a few weeks, like other kids would go to camp. And sometimes we go to Montana for Easter, usually if it's one of those late April Easters." He stopped at a red SUV and found the keys in the door pocket. He helped her into the passenger seat and headed out of the airport.

They arrived at a lovely, gated condo community with several buildings scattered on a mountainside. Quinn signed in with the gate guard and picked up a decal that would identify them as residents. "We're up there." He pointed to a building at a higher elevation on the slope. We're near the top. I hope you like heights."

He parked the car in a shelter and led her into the building. With his key card he activated the elevator. "There are extra keys in a drawer in the kitchen." When they exited the elevator they stood in a well-decorated and maintained common area. "That's our door and the other belongs to our neighbor. I have no idea if anyone is in town. Some very nice folks." He unlocked the door with his elevator card and ushered Mouse into the condo.

She gasped. "It's beautiful!" And rushed to the windows to look out onto the mountain range. Quinn unlatched the sliding door and escorted her out onto the terrace for a better look. "I can't even see the other buildings."

"Yeah, Dad likes that feature best. Come on I'll give you a tour. He took her hand and walked her through the living area, the kitchen, some storage and laundry rooms, as he explained, "We keep our skis here and all our gear so we don't have to load the plane when we come. The kitchen is OK."

"You and David and Colt take care of yourselves without a cook when you come here?"

"Sort of," he blushed, "There are a lot of carryouts and several services that provide meals. Samuel joins us sometime and so does Ray. He helps us keep Colt contained. There are staff quarters beyond the kitchen." He led her upstairs.

"You have two floors?" Mouse felt like she was in a castle.

"I think we have one of the roomiest places here. Dad wanted it big enough so that Margaret and CJ could join us."

At the top of the stairs he pointed out David's, his, and Colt's rooms. The room Margaret used was on the first level. "CJ never came here and I think we were all happy about that." He stopped at his room and took her in his arms and kissed her. She held onto his arms and seemed to sway. As they broke apart he grinned. "Do I make you dizzy?"

She gave him a quick kiss and said, "It's you or hunger."

"I prefer to think it's me, but I'll find us some food then have you all to myself for the rest of the evening."

As Quinn moved around the condo, opening window shades and checking the status of the property, Mouse returned to the terrace to stare at the mountains. Even as the sun set she marveled at the colors splashed across the mountain ridges and crevasses.

Quinn found her and asked, "Do you want me to order in or take you out?"

"Let's just spend our first night alone, with some carryout." She walked into his arms.

* * *

It was midnight by the time Audrey had gotten the children organized and to her parent's place. Her mother was pacing the kitchen when she arrived. "Are you all right?" Her mother was as frightened as the children.

Audrey, a small gauze patch on her temple, carried Maya into a bedroom and returned to the kitchen. "Help me settle the boys and then we can talk."

Once the kids were in bed Althea Wilson asked, "Now what? Although I have to say I'm glad you left. I haven't liked this whole arrest business."

"Ah, Mom, I don't know what's next. I'm just tired. I appreciate your concern."

Althea patted her daughter's hand. "I know, dear. Your father and I have been so worried, especially after that arrest." The two woman sat at the kitchen table speaking in low voices.

Audrey nodded. "I think we're seeing the symptoms of withdrawal."

"Withdrawal?"

She nodded. "I think Bart needs more drugs and he hasn't found any. I think that has put him on edge and made him dangerous." She brushed away a tear. "And my affair didn't help the situation."

Her mother sighed. "I don't pretend to understand your behavior, but you are our daughter. We can't approve your behavior, but we will stand by you."

Audrey stood and hugged her mother. "Thank you. I know I had a part in ruining my marriage. That's why I can't be placing all the blame on Bart. But his action this evening changed our marriage dynamic."

Althea hugged her back. "Get to bed. You're starting to sound like some therapist on TV." Audrey released a tearful chuckle and kissed her mother good night.

* * *

Making love for the first time was a real conversation stopper. The silent room vibrated with unspoken words. They rested in bed, naked, clinging to one another, but saying nothing. Mouse sighed. Quinn held her tighter. She rested her head on his chest, her hand resting at his ribs. He caught her hand and held it. There seemed to be so much, and nothing, to say.

Finally he asked, "Are you okay?"

She burrowed deeper into his arms, not ready to see his face, his eyes. "He loved me."

Quinn knew she meant her dead husband. "I know. I saw the two of you together. He was a man who had found what he was looking for."

She finally pulled back to look at her new husband. "But?"

Quinn smiled. "But how can I love you and you love me and there's a love in your past?"

She nodded. "I feel like a child. I feel confused. But I do feel loved." She kissed his chin and rested her head on his shoulder.

He raised himself on one elbow and gazed at her with an expression more serious than one she had ever seen on him. "It's our time now, Mouse. We weren't ready for this relationship fifteen years ago. You were ready for Josh and I wasn't ready for anything. I was the fool. I could have paid attention to people around me and found a woman who wanted to be Mrs. Templeton forever. Instead I was conned by Madeline. I think she plotted our whole relationship like some military assault. And she succeeded."

He lowered himself and drew Mouse back into his arms. "Just remember that the time wasn't right for us back in school. But it is right, now. I can feel it. I've felt my world expand. I see a future for us and those kids that will be filled with everything a family should be. And I see you as the person I will be with from now until I die."

Mouse looked into his eyes again. "I see that, too. I'm just surprised. And so in love."

Quinn drew in his breath as he remembered a feeling from his college days with Mouse. She made him want to be better, to succeed, to be all the things he could be. What more was there to say, he kissed her and made love with her again.

CHAPTER EIGHTEEN

After assaulting his wife in front of his children, Bart Decker had run off to think about his family and their future. He wasn't happy with his actions. He wasn't happy with Audrey either. Most of this was her fault. Assigning fault to his wife made it easier for him to return to the house. Heading back home, he planned to accept her apology for upsetting him and life would go on as usual. When he returned to the house, the family was gone! She had probably run to that fairy guy, Rory.

Bart raced to the house in Dancing Creek. It was dark. No cars. She'd probably gone to her mother's place. Audrey's response was not what he had expected. She should have been waiting at home for him to return, not to ask forgiveness, but to allow him to explain. Of course, the only explanation he had was that it was her fault. She had provoked him. She had suggested he was not a success as a husband and father. He loved those kids. He needed something to help him think. Maybe alcohol. It was just sitting in the cupboard of the empty house. He'd wait for her at the house and think about things. Take the edge off with a little something to drink while he waited.

Alcohol and anger don't mix. Bart had not found the satisfaction in alcohol that he found in drugs, and soon the house was in shambles. Looking over the mess he had created, he decided to pack up some of his things along with some camping gear in case he had to rough it for a few days until she came to her senses. And until she cleaned the place up. After all, this was all her fault.

And he would need money. Taking one last drink, he nodded to himself. He had a plan.

* * *

143

David Templeton had encouraged members of his small family to attend Quinn's wedding. He had even chartered a bigger plane to accommodate them. With Quinn taking the corporate jet to Vail, he had had no other choice. But it proved a wise decision. The plane was bigger and was more comfortable for his aging aunt, his two sisters and a cousin or two. Margaret had taken responsibility for Jimmy who had been delighted with the trip. His attendant had suggested a mild relaxant to keep Jimmy's panic attacks in new situations under control. It had proved to be a great idea. The young man had arrived with the family on Thursday, enjoyed time with Sara's children, rested at Nathan's guest house and enjoyed a walk in the nearby cemetery.

As the plane raced back to Raleigh on Saturday morning, Margaret Templeton Kirtley found her way up the aisle to sit with David. "I like Mouse." She laughed. "And I love the nickname. And I'm jealous. Quinn found what we have both been looking for."

"Don't say that," chided David, "you make me feel as though I denied you a life."

"Oh, Dad, no." She took his hand. "You taught us so much about living and sharing. I think the lesson finally sunk in with Quinn." With a rueful grin, she continued, "I, on the other hand, still have some learning to do."

David pulled her into an awkward airline seat hug. "Not you, my girl. You always seemed to know what you wanted."

"But it wasn't what I needed." She sat quietly holding her father's hand. With a sigh, she finally said, "I went after CJ because some other girls thought he was cute and charming. I never looked at character. But at the time, I don't think I had character either. I was too rich and pampered."

"Did I give you too much?"

"I wish you had made me work for some of it. You gave Quinn a job. Why not me?"

David looked at her, puzzled. "I have no answer. Did you want a job? What can you do?"

She shrugged. "I don't know if I do. I don't know what I can do. But I know I'm as smart as CJ. He barely got through law school. He never sat for the bar. When we first married we would play chess. He told me he had played in college."

"You know how to play chess. I taught you."

"And I always won. After our first year of marriage we never played again." She chuckled. "That should have told me something." She sat up straight. "What if I wanted a job, what could I do?"

"We need a new cook at the ranch in Montana."

She giggled and rested her head on his shoulder. "Be serious!"

He studied his daughter for several minutes. Tilting his head in deep thought, he said, "Why don't you take a few months to build your new life and new friends without CJ? Take some chances, find some challenges, enjoy your life."

The pilot announced that they would be landing soon. David patted her knee. "We can't let Quinn have all the fun." She kissed his cheek and tightened her seatbelt.

* * *

The first morning of his new married life and Quinn was delighted. Mouse as his wife and lover made the world whole. He felt like a new man. He opened his eyes slowly fantasizing about the way he would greet her this morning and she—she was gone! She couldn't have gone far, he realized. She had only one change of clothes and no car. He had her trapped in the condo. It was just a matter of tracking her down.

Descending the stairs he saw her leaning on the balcony rail enjoying the early morning Colorado crisp air. She looked tiny against the mountain peaks and he could see her hair being kissed by a morning breeze. She was barefooted and wearing a t-shirt, probably his, and what appeared to be a tattered pair of jogging shorts, maybe Colt's. It was difficult to tell, the t-shirt was almost too big.

"Morning, Mouse." He had her in his arms and was kissing her before she could respond.

She greeted him with enthusiasm. "This place is beautiful." She turned her back to him and he wrapped his arms around her as they shared the scenic beauty.

Finally, when it was time to speak, he asked, "What are you doing up so early?"

"My biological clock says I'm on Eastern time. So I thought I would get up and make some breakfast, then shower."

Quinn was nibbling her neck and his hands were exploring under her clothing. "Mouse, you're not wearing any underwear," he teased as his hands caressed her rear.

"I only have one change of underwear," she grinned, "I thought I would put it on after my shower." Her hands tunneled under his sweat pants waist band. "Hmm. No underwear?"

"I was in a hurry, in case you were trying to escape." He kissed her again. "I have an idea. Why don't we shower, then have breakfast -"

"There's only coffee."

"- shower, then have coffee, then go find some food and clothes for you."

And that's how their first day of marriage began.

Once everyone had on underwear and had breakfast, Quinn took Mouse out to shop. He didn't know much about women's clothing stores, but he knew where his sister and ex-wife shopped. Arriving at the store, Mouse glanced at a few price tags and said, "I can't spend this much on a top and skirt."

And he said, "Yes, you can. I think it looks great. And you need something dressy for dinner. And shoes. And maybe some jewelry."

Recognizing Quinn and noting the dazzling wedding band set on the woman he was escorting, the sales clerk welcomed, "Mr. Templeton, I think I know what Mrs. Templeton will need for your stay here. She and I can work together. Why don't you do your other shopping and be back here at twelve-thirty."

Quinn understood the offer and the woman's interest in a sales commission. "Great, just in time for lunch." He nodded to his co-conspirator and rushed from the shop.

When he returned Mouse was surrounded by bags and boxes looking defeated. "I can't buy all these things," she protested as Quinn walked into the store.

He turned to the clerk. "Does she have at least three outfits to go to dinner?" He mentioned some exclusive restaurants. The woman nodded. "Does she have shoes and accessories?" The woman nodded. "Is there anything she needs that she didn't find here?" He handed over a credit card.

"If you plan to hike or other outdoor activity, you'll have to visit one of the outfitters."

With a wave and thank you, he picked up the bags and boxes and headed out of the shop. Mouse picked up the rest and followed.

Once in the car she said, "We spent too much."

"No, we didn't. We still need some hiking clothes and boots and maybe a jacket or something." He drove through the town.

"I only bought two pair of underwear and no bras. I couldn't spend that much money on those things."

"Not to worry," he smiled, "I found a store and stocked up on undies."

"What?" She grabbed a hand grip as he took a sharp corner.

"I found a few things I thought would look great on you." They pulled into the front entry of the condo complex. "And I picked up a few things for the kids." He hopped out and gave directions to the security man. He stuck his head back in the car and said to Mouse, "I ordered some lunch, too. It should be here in half an hour." At the parking area a young man appeared with a luggage cart to help ferry the purchases up to the condo. Mouse trotted behind while Quinn rushed ahead to unlock the elevator.

Once settled in the condo, Quinn said, "Show me what you bought. Show me what you like best."

She smiled at this generous man she had married. "I bought this extravagant lounging cover." She pulled a lovely robe from a box. "I thought I would enjoy wearing this even at home when I get breakfast for the kids. The tag says it's washable." She placed it over the back of a chair. Then she pulled outfit after outfit from the packages and displayed each with appropriate accessories. Quinn studied the display.

"Did you pick these out or did the saleslady?"

"Once she explained the type of places we would dine, I told her what I liked and we sort of worked it out. Do you like everything?"

"I think you'll look great in all the outfits. But maybe underdressed. So I got you this." He pulled a jeweler's box from a small bag and watched as she opened the surprise. It was a smooth and understated ensemble, earrings, necklace and bracelet—gold and diamonds. Mouse gasped.

"This is beautiful." Tears came to her eyes. "How could you know it would be so perfect?"

"I know you, Mouse. I've known you for fifteen years. I guess I just didn't know how well." She ran into his arms.

Lunch arrived before they could be distracted by other things. And Quinn got to display his purchases. He pulled t-shirts out of one bag as he indicated which shirt went to which child. "I forgot my camera so I got this." He swung a small digital camera from a strap. "I think Tilda will like it when we get home." He pulled up a final sack. "You need underwear," he proclaimed and opened a bag filled with lacy panties and matching bras. There were also two very sexy garments, to which Mouse rolled her eyes and Quinn grinned.

"After lunch," he announced, "We'll finish shopping. You need some hiking boots. But first lunch and then a fashion show." He held one of the filmy garments up in front of her. She blushed.

CHAPTER NINETEEN

When Bart left River Bend he was like a homing pigeon. By breakfast he was in Marshall, a quiet town in a neighboring county north of River Bend. "What do you want?" asked his mother as she buttoned a quilted robe over pajamas.

"I had a fight with my wife."

"She finally throw you out?"

"Nice talk!" he scowled. "She was the one having an affair. I left."

"Yes, but you got caught with those drugs," his mother reminded him. "Am I supposed to support you?"

Now Bart was angry. He had expected a warmer greeting. "I can take care of myself. I thought I'd look for a job here with some of my old friends."

"As long as you're here," she said as she began pulling breakfast food from the refrigerator, "you can help me."

Bart resigned himself to being asked to clean the gutters or mow the yard. "What do you need?"

"I sold this house."

"What?" Bart felt himself in an eddy, his entire life was spinning out of control.

She shrugged. "The market is hot. I plan to move to grandaddy's place. I had renters there. I couldn't sell that place for as much as I'm getting for this place."

He looked around the house of his childhood and noticed the boxes and piles of belongings. "How much did you get?"

"Enough that I plan to work two more years and retire, maybe move to Florida." His mother worked for the state at the county extension office and had for decades. By his calculations she would have a nice pension. And he might have a place in Florida to visit once his life settled down. No Audrey. No kids.

He thought about his grandfather's house. It was along one of the country roads surrounded by several acres that hadn't been farmed in years. It was a good place to hang out. He'd just have to find some kind of life here for a few years. He couldn't ask his mother for money because she had been sending him funds that he told her he needed to help with bills for the kids. After his arrest she learned that she had been supporting his drug habit.

As his mother prepared breakfast Bart finalized a vague future. He'd stay in Marshall. He'd find a job. He had visited several ATMs and withdrawn all the cash from the joint accounts he shared with Audrey. She had a job and he needed money. Besides this was all her fault.

Damn, he needed something now. Liquor just didn't do it.

* * *

Audrey stayed with her parents over the weekend. After speaking with Rory, she felt very organized. The kids were safe with her mother and she would stay at Rory's place, close to her office. Returning to River Bend she planned to go to the house to get a few more things. But first she stopped at the ATM. All funds had been withdrawn!

Angry, Audrey called her attorney. "Darlene, I need a lawyer. I want a divorce."

Darlene Porterfield, a young attorney who had set up a local practice within recent years and currently served on Audrey's board told her to come to the office. Darlene wasn't that busy. Folks in River Bend still had a hard time with female attorneys, especially those not from here and not affiliated with a local law firm. Fortunately for Darlene, attorneys like Jim Hoefler and H. Lawrence Grayson respected her independence and ability. They often sent cases her way. It was enough to slowly build her reputation and keep her lights on.

"Calm down," the attorney advised. "First things first. Is this sudden?"

"He hit me the other night. I moved me and the children to my mother's."

"Have you been back to the house? Withdrawn any money?"

Audrey screamed. "I went to the ATM. It's empty!" She had thought divorce would be straight forward until she learned she had no resources! "I haven't been to the house."

"Come to my office now!" Click.

Audrey stumbled into Darlene's office looking every bit as though she was at the end of her rope. Darlene poured her a cup of coffee, settled her at the work table and said, "No money? Savings?"

"I stopped at the bank. It's all gone." Audrey clutched a Styrofoam cup.

"Is your pay check direct deposit?" Audrey nodded. "Call your office and cancel that. When is your next payday?"

"Friday."

"Good. We'll have new accounts set up by then." The attorney very efficiently went through several routine steps laying the groundwork for divorce proceedings. At one point she was thoughtful. "You had an affair and he has an arrest for drug use. Sort of balances out. We'll just have to see how his attorney plays it. Do you know which came first?"

Audrey just stared at her. "I have no idea."

Finally Darlene ran through a list of chores that Audrey had to complete. "Let's go to your house and get your things."

When they arrived it was obvious from the street that the draperies on several windows were askew. Darlene immediately called the police, reporting that her client was at her residence after being away for several days and noticed signs of breaking and entering. The dispatchers advised her to wait for a patrol car for assistance. Within minutes a police officer appeared, took Audrey's key and did a routine inspection of the home. "Ma'am, it appears there has been some vandalism." He escorted Audrey through her home. The master bedroom was asunder. Audrey's clothing was thrown around, drawers from the dresser had been upended. The only rooms not harmed belonged to the children. After her inspection the officer waited for her response.

She took a deep breath. "My husband and I quarreled Friday evening. The children and I have been staying with my parents in Brevard."

"He assaulted her," added the attorney.

"Are you pressing charges?" asked the officer.

Audrey was mute but Darlene said, "Yes, we need a record of the assault and this destruction for the divorce filing." The officer looked at Audrey. She nodded. It was beginning.

* * *

After convincing Madeline that he would prepare his house on the coast for them, CJ was on his way to Hilton Head and to freedom. His first action after his arrival was to hop a quick charter to the Caymans and withdraw his money. Because he didn't trust Theo, he wanted his banking done face-to-face and without Theo's knowledge. Within the span of a day, he had flown to the islands, closed his account, opened an account at a friendly international wealth management firm, taken possession of a credit/debit card assigned to that account and ordered checks for an account that would allow him to withdraw funds at their partner bank in the states with minimal tax issues. The flight back to Hilton Head was quick and carefree.

That evening he called Madeline and asked encouraging questions. Which club would she like to join? Did she have an opinion on boats, you know, sail or motor? Madeline fell into the excitement of planning a move. He called again the next day with more questions and descriptions of the shops and restaurants close to their place. He quoted docking fees for the imaginary boat and asked her opinion about colors as he talked about repainting some rooms.

He didn't call the next day or the next. When she tried to call him she learned that his phone number was no longer in use. She called the Hilton Head police. They reported that the house was on the market and the owner had told the realtor he would be out of town for a few weeks. She called the realtor and demanded a phone number. He only had the disconnected number.

Madeline had a funny feeling. She accessed the Cayman account— EMPTY!

* * *

"Rory?" Lynn greeted her friend, "How's life at a real foundation?"
"Oh, sweetie, that's not why I'm calling."

"Is something wrong?" Lynn could sense his distress over the airwaves.

"Yes." He heard Lynn gasp into her phone. "Not here. Not the foundation!" He rushed to explain, "But there. Audrey needs your help. Bart attacked her the other night. She put the kids at her parents' place but she's staying at my place and I don't like her being alone."

They talked for some time as Rory tried to tell her specifics without breaking his promises to Audrey, "She hasn't seen him since that night, but I'm worried."

"I'll go visit her and see what I can do."

With that promise, Rory ended the call and Lynn started to plan for Audrey's safety.

* * *

Five days into marriage Quinn had gone out to run an errand, leaving Mouse to relax and enjoy the balcony view that so enchanted her. Quinn let himself into the condo and saw her out on the balcony. And at that moment she looked as though she were in deep thought about something very serious and important to her. He was sure he was right. He knew Mouse.

She stretched because she had been staring at the view for a long time. Her thoughts focused on her children and the changes that would happen in their lives. She didn't know if she wanted them to understand the enormity of Quinn's wealth. Yes, it would give them advantages. But life in River Bend had advantages, too. How would she balance it all? And how could she explain it so that Quinn would understand?

"Do you want to come in and talk to me?" he asked as he stepped out beside her.

"How did you know?" She slipped into his arms.

"I know you, Mouse. Something is making you uneasy." He pulled her back into the room and sat with her on the couch. She put her feet up on the coffee table reminding him of their old college days when they sat on his porch and talked all afternoon. He took a deep breath. "I bet you're starting to wonder how life will change for you? And your kids?"

"How did you know?" She snuggled against him.

"Dad and I talked about it," he explained, resting his chin at her temple. "We've seen many of our friends marry people from the outside." Here he made quotes with the hand not embracing her. "You know what I mean?" She nodded.

"I wonder what I've done to my children by marrying you and all your wealth." Mouse furrowed her brow as she tried to imagine the future.

"In what way?"

She took his hand as they both sat with their feet propped on the coffee table. "I want them to work for things they want. I want them to study hard and learn to take care of themselves, and each other. I want them to have summer jobs. I want them to earn things, not have things handed to them."

"I want the same things for Colt."

"But Colt already has everything. A ranch in Montana? A condo in Vail because he wanted to learn to ski?" She frowned and leaned away to look back at him. "I think Colt is terrific and I think you want the same things for him that I want for my kids but he starts several rungs above my kids." She blew out her breath. "Am I making sense?"

Quinn put an arm around her and pulled her back to his side, running his lips along her brow. "I don't understand everything, Mouse, because I've always had all this. But I appreciate that you have goals and standards for you and your children. I think I can respect what you want for them. I think it'll be good for Colt, too. But, I'm going to give your children everything, every opportunity, I give Colt. So we all go to the ranch and we all ski and we all go to the beach - - -"

"You have a place there, too?" An accusation!

He thought a moment and wondered if he should mention the place in Hawaii. David had purchased it when they invested in a ranch on the Big Island several years ago. He decided against it because he had never taken Colt there—at least not yet. "I think that's all. You know about all the houses we use."

"You use?" Mouse caught that little slip.

"We might have a place in Hawaii but it's more for business. Colt has never been there."

"And the beach?"

"Margaret uses the beach house more than we do. It's old family property on the Outer Banks." He kissed her hand. "Just know that your little tribe is now mine, too. I will always treat them as I treat Colt."

"And I'll always treat Colt as though he has been mine from the beginning."

* * *

They would be returning home tomorrow, but Quinn had a sumptuous evening planned. Mouse had gasped when he announced that dinner was black tie. He had sent her back to the clothing shop to find the supportive salesclerk. The woman had done another outstanding job. Mouse looked beautiful. She looked sophisticated and poised, wearing an off the shoulder soft silk barely blue to almost white dress, cinched at the waist with a thin rhinestone belt with long chords and tassels tracing down the slim floor-length skirt. She also looked delectable, but he could wait until after dinner. They would be attending a popular summer fundraiser for the Arts Guild. The Templetons had been supporters of their Kids Draw program since purchasing the condo.

It wasn't often that a member of the family was in town to attend this function so Quinn had been delighted to find this opportunity on his arrival. He knew several of his acquaintances would attend, even some famous names. He hoped Mouse would enjoy herself. He had viewed this honeymoon as an opportunity to let her see what life as Mrs. Templeton might offer.

Then he frowned at himself, at his smug attitude. Of course, Mouse knew what to expect. She had walked into the Templeton mansion and held her own against David's challenges. Quinn still chuckled at the way David's bravado vanished when Mouse turned out to be a high-level US Army computer consultant. She had succeeded with his father at their initial meeting. In her lovely, calm, confident way, she didn't take any prisoners.

She was quiet on the drive to dinner, reading through the evening's agenda and silent auction opportunities. "It's very beautiful here. I do want us to bring the kids." She smiled at him as she placed the brochure on the console. "Do you plan to buy something?" She glanced down at the information.

"I might. You can, too. If you see something that we could put in our new house. Or just something that you like. It's all for a great cause."

"How much can I spend?"

"As much as you like."

She frowned at him. "You know what I mean. There have to be limits."

He grinned at her. "Now you're making me nervous. Madeline could spend money. She needed limits. Have I misread you?"

She smiled back. "I mean five hundred, a thousand. Those kind of limits."

"Sure," he nodded, "Five or a thousand per piece."

"Per piece?" She kind of squeaked.

"You may see more than one thing that you like." He clasped her hand as he pulled to a stop to let the valet take the car.

They walked into a buzzing room. Quinn whispered, "People turn out to see the celebrities." He nodded toward a famous musician and his actress wife.

Before he could move them further into the room, a woman called, "Quinn?" in a voice that made his skin crawl. "Madeline told me to be on the lookout for you and," she turned and looked down her nose at Mouse, "your new wife."

Mouse smiled. Quinn cringed because he saw the mischief in her eyes. "I'm Sara Templeton." She took the woman's hand. "I haven't seen Madeline since the day she held me hostage at gunpoint and threatened my children. We didn't get to finish our conversation because of the tear gas. And you are?"

Quinn wanted to laugh out loud. But he said, "Sara, this is Portia Marsden Daniels."

Portia was saved from further conversation because a man called out, "Sara!" in a booming voice, making heads turn. Before Quinn could focus on the man behind the voice, the stranger had Mouse in his arms and was swinging her around in a great bear hug. She giggled as she told him to put her down.

"What are you doing here?" demanded her friend.

"I'm on my honeymoon." Mouse pulled her dress back into position and didn't even want to think about her hair.

"Who's the lucky devil?" The man scanned the crowd, overlooking Quinn.

"I am." Quinn stuck himself between Mouse and her admirer.

"Tag Olvero, this is my husband Quinn Templeton," said Mouse as she introduced the men.

Tag returned Quinn's handshake. "You one of those Templetons from North Carolina? I know David."

"He's my father."

Tag grinned then enveloped Quinn in a bear hug, almost lifting him off his feet. "Damn. Glad to meet you. David was one of my first investors."

"Olvero," said Quinn deep in thought, "Not SeedTag?"

"Best idea I ever had and David believed in me. I'm making you fellows richer." Tag slapped Quinn on the back.

Quinn stumbled a little as he said to Mouse, "SeedTag is -

"I know," she nodded, "Janet and I designed Tag's backoffice software and data management functions."

"How's my girl Janet?" asked Tag. He had one arm draped around Mouse.

Quinn said, "Just had a baby girl. Dad helped with the delivery." He liked this outrageous fellow.

Tag howled. "You're kidding!"

Quinn took his arm. "Let's get a drink and we'll tell you the whole story."

The night was a huge success for the Arts Guild. Mouse found several works she thought would go in their new home, including a set of kitten prints for Tilda's room and an oil landscape of the mountains that just spoke to her. She was embarrassed as Quinn gave her a questioning look when he noted that she had spent three thousand dollars for it. She blushed. He wrote his check with a flourish. Five thousand dollars for silent auction items was nothing compared to what his ex-wife would have spent. "Oh, no," he said as he gave her a teasing elbow, "another wife who spends money."

As they were leaving Tag barreled over to thrust a small, delicate, porcelain angel into Mouse's hands. "That's for Janet's baby." When she took it he reached into his pocket and retrieved a lovely piece of Native American jewelry. "That's your wedding present." He kissed her cheek and bid them good night.

Portia sidled up to Mouse. "Sara, I'm sorry we didn't have more opportunities to speak. I hope we see one another again." She gave Mouse a half smile and scurried after a quartet of women mincing toward the door in spiky heels and designer dresses.

Quinn bent and whispered, "Those are ex-wives. They don't know what to make of you. You hung out all evening with all the eligible men."

Mouse didn't want to gloat. "I didn't know I'd run into two other clients."

"You knew two of the new wave of billionaires. I've got to learn more about your business," he said, "but I've got other things on my mind tonight." She blushed.

CHAPTER TWENTY

For several days Bart Decker was the perfect son. When his mother went to work he packed and moved cartons to the old family farm house. He cleaned out the renters' debris from his grandfather's house and cleaned his mother's house for the buyers because the closing was in three weeks.

As a reward, he found several of his grandfather's old medications. Evidently the renters had never looked at the back of the closet. His mother had probably stored them along with granddaddy's clothing and other belongings, planning to sort everything another day. The meds were old but did take the edge off. He also tried to connect with old friends. No one had a job for him. A few of them had heard about his arrest and were wary of associating with him.

By the end of the week he thought he had to find something. He wouldn't go back to River Bend and that dealer. Audrey probably had police waiting for him. But his body had this undefined craving. Where? How? He was restless and edgy. He had an idea! Maybe there was something back at that cabin. Maybe the distributor had set up new supply lines. He should check it out!

"I've worked hard," he told his mother. "I was thinking I'd go talk to Audrey and see my kids this weekend. Take them camping." His real plans included looking for drugs and spying on his wife. Nothing his mother needed to know.

She patted his shoulder. "You did." She had been surprised at his cooperation. "I'm real pleased. You take a break. Bring those babies for a visit. I sure miss them. I'll finish packing things here and next week you can finish cleaning up for the closing."

He smiled. If he could find some of those pills, he'd do anything she wanted. "I will. I've put all my things at granddaddy's. If Audrey agrees, once we get settled we can have them up to visit the new place."

His mother was delighted. She had missed seeing her grandchildren. She had known Bart and Audrey were having problems. Maybe they were coming around, reconciling. She looked forward to their visit in a few weeks.

* * *

Dusty paced the living room. Marianna had called informing him that the Hollywood consultants had arrived. She was bringing them by the house for introductions. Lynn laughed at him as she did her usual Saturday morning half-hearted pass through the house with a dust cloth. "This isn't an audition."

"I don't know what they expect me to do." He was really nervous. He thought this is what it would be like for a spaceman to meet aliens from another planet.

They turned as they heard the kitchen door open. "Knock, knock," called Marianna. As Lynn and Dusty rushed into the kitchen she said, "I told them we are informal and this is the way to enter your house." She turned to the three people behind her as she explained, "My concept is based on a lot of interaction in this kitchen. Dusty usually hosts a breakfast crime-wrap-up for friends and family when he solves a case."

"I don't host anything," he growled, ignoring the strangers, "you all just barge in."

Three people grinned. Cameron O'Leary, a tall, older man with receding gray hair that curled around his ears, had been in TV since college, becoming a valued location scout. Giselle Trudeau, only a few years younger than Cameron liked to brag that she could trace her Canadian heritage back to that well-known political family. And as she liked to say, in spite of the family connection she had succeeded in the world of entertainment. Stacy Runyon, the youngster in the group, had arrived in Hollywood expecting to become a star overnight. Reality struck after three years but by then she had learned a lot about the production aspects of the entertainment industry and had become in demand for her organizational skills and her eye for detail. She also had a fresh, clear-eyed charm that usually attracted healthy young men.

"That's the character we want!" assessed Cameron giving Dusty a serious head-to-toe scan. "I know the director wants a romance but this guy can't be a woman." They all moved into the kitchen and began to talk about Dusty as though he were some lab specimen. One man and two women had a lot to say. They paced around the kitchen, took some photos with their phones, and helped themselves to the coffee on the counter.

"Who the hell are you people?" snarled Dusty. Lynn and Marianna snickered behind him.

As though he hadn't said a word, the older woman said, "He's a natural. Maybe we should audition his type instead of the director's idea."

"Remember," the younger woman said after sipping her coffee, "we're only here to look for set ideas and possible location sites." Another sip. "But I see what you mean." She nodded toward Dusty.

"Stop it, all of you," laughed Marianna. "I told Dusty you wanted to have his help with small town law enforcement procedures."

"That, too," said Stacy. She smiled at Dusty, "But you are a great character."

He wasn't charmed. "I'm a law enforcement professional. And I don't want my time wasted." He poured a cup of coffee and sat at the table. "I love Marianna and I will work with you because she asked me." He glowered around the table. "But I won't put up with your attitudes."

They all heard a thundering sound and Jason raced into the kitchen in only a pair of jogging shorts. "Mom," he shouted, "I need some clean underwear." He stopped as he noticed the kitchen of visitors. "Or maybe I need to shut my mouth?"

The older woman looked at Dusty. "Is he a law enforcement professional?" Even Dusty laughed.

Marianna jumped in. "This is my grandson, Jason. He's going to be a lawyer."

The Hollywood visitors bit their lips declining to reply. Lynn stepped in. "Now you see how this works. Dusty tries to be serious and professional and we all work very hard to save him from himself."

Piper walked in. "Is that Marianna's car? I want to talk to her about doing some drama classes at my school in the fall." She walked past the visitors, poured coffee and rummaged through the pantry for something to eat.

The dog walked in, sniffed everyone, and went to the pantry to help Piper.

Danny walked in. "Here are the rolls you wanted," he told Lynn, handing her a bakery box. He turned to Jason, "Come on, pal, we got six weddings today. We need your help!"

Jason dashed into the laundry room, came out with an arm full of clothing. "Five minutes."

Lynn turned to the visitors. "Help yourselves to a pastry." Piper already was. They watched the tiny principal slap a large jelly donut on a plate. Lynn continued, "This is Danny Valeri, one of Dusty's detectives. His family owns the bakery and Jason is going to help him build wedding cakes this morning." Jason raced back into the kitchen dressed in what everyone assumed was clean underwear beneath his bakery shirt and trousers. Danny stood waving from the door encouraging the cake assembler to hurry. Soon the door slammed pushing the cake crew onto their morning business.

"Do you want to see my office?" Dusty asked. But he didn't look serious because he had powdered sugar on his upper lip.

* * *

"Where have you been?" Rory screeched into his phone, finally connecting with the consultant who had had an affair with Audrey Decker.

James Thurman sighed. "I was doing a retreat in Yellowstone for an environmental group. We all gave up our phones and computers for the duration. What's wrong?"

"That son of a bitch hit Audrey!"

"Bart?"

"Yes." Rory sounded at his wit's end. "I can't help her. I'm in Raleigh on loan to the Templeton Foundation. She's staying at my place."

"The children?"

"She has them stashed with her parents. And she's gotten an attorney and filed charges."

"It's about time," said James, not knowing how he should feel since he was a party to ending the marriage. "What do you want me to do? Has she asked for me?"

"She's real clear that she'll handle this," explained Rory. "She thinks the assault was a one-time thing. But she admits the marriage is over." He heard James huff into the phone. Rory continued, "I wish you could get there and just make sure she's okay. I can't leave here."

"What are you doing?" James hadn't heard about Rory's work with the Templetons.

Rory said, "You won't believe this." And he went on to explain the drama at the Templeton Foundation. "Quinn hired me to sort things out."

"Quinn?" James chuckled, "Sounds mighty friendly."

"He just married a woman in River Bend. She's the one who found the trouble. Lynn and I helped him work out a plan. But I told him I don't want a full-time job."

"If you're going to be looking for a new CEO of the foundation," offered James, "I have a list of really good candidates."

"You do?"

"Folks always ask me for recommendations when I finish a reorganization job. Or organizations I've worked with ask for names if a long-time executive staffer is leaving."

"Forward me your list. The Templetons are eager to get back to being a topnotch foundation."

"I'll do that," James promised, "And I'll get to River Bend as fast as I can."

"Thank you," whispered Rory. "She needs us."

* * *

Mouse and Quinn returned from their honeymoon to what would soon become the norm for Quinn's life. Ray and Gracia, the two Raleigh staffers and honeymoon babysitters, hurriedly packed their car and took off for Raleigh. Ray said he had to register for his senior year classes. Quinn suspected he had a date. Gracia also seemed ready to return to Raleigh. Maybe she had a date, too.

That left Quinn in a house with four eager, energetic kids who wanted to report all the news of the last week. On top of that, Mouse's parents came to visit. Quinn thought that his new in-laws wanted to make certain Mouse was safe and sound. He wasn't quite sure what his in-laws thought of him. Even though he had married Mouse, they seemed to still be suspicious.

But they had brought dinner as Charlotte Macauley said, "We didn't think you would have time to cook." She glared at Quinn, "And taking this bunch to dinner could be expensive."

Mouse glanced at Quinn trying not to laugh.

After dinner they waved goodbye to the in-laws as Janet and Tim stopped by with their children. Mouse was able to give the new baby the gift from Tag Olvero. While the two IT partners caught up on business, Quinn helped Tim chase the toddlers around the house because Colt and the twins had vanished and Tilda said she had things to do in her room. Two cold beers and two diapers later, Quinn was exhausted.

The boys returned with a few friends, introduced them to Quinn, and he watched them eat chips and ice cream and drink a gallon of soft drinks while Janet's two toddlers begged at the table like little puppies. Quinn goggled at the activity and Tim sympathized and handed him another beer.

That evening in bed Quinn asked, "Was that normal this evening?"

Mouse laughed and kissed him.

* * *

Jason and Doyle sat on the front porch of the house. It was the house Doyle had lived in until he went off to college.   Now   he   was living there with his wife. River Bend High School was across the street. "Things have really changed since we graduated from there," Doyle said nodding toward the school as they watched the football team leave practice, the soccer team do laps around the block, and the band practice-march across the parking lot. All those activities started up even before fall classes were in place.

"Yeah." Jason felt he could almost see the changes happening.

"You're leaving for law school," Doyle reminded him. "I work for Will."

"And have a wife."

"Yeah." He always smiled at that reality. "She likes working for Kevin. She works from home a lot and goes to work at their clients' offices." Doyle slapped his knee. "She says this is a great place to raise a family."

"She's pregnant?"

"Not yet." The young man ran his fingers through his curly blond hair. "But she says working from home would make it easy." He grinned at his best friend.

"Aren't you scared?"

"What's scary about a little baby? All my family is here to help." He nodded. "You know my mom would be helpful."

"Or controlling."

"Or that."

"But a dad?" Jason had a hard time imagining his friend in a role other than sidekick. He thought of all the fun they had enjoyed through their high school years. What did adulthood have in store? Staring across the street at the energetic and horseplaying teens, he felt a stab of regret. Those had been great days.

"Those were great days!" Doyle echoed his thoughts. "We had some great times."

"Yeah." Forlorn.

"Man, what's wrong with you? We aren't dead yet!" Doyle poked his old friend. "We'll have some more great times. You'll eventually get out of school and come back here to be a scumbag lawyer. Patti Ann will come back and be a doctor."

"Patti Ann, a doctor," Jason mused. "She sure is smart." Patti Ann had been part of the college crowd but was beginning her second year of medical school not finding any time to return for lazy summer evenings with the old gang.

Lori came to the door. "Dinner, guys." She and Doyle had invited a few of their friends, better known as the college crowd, to sample Lori's cooking. The group of friends also planned to assess Doyle's man-of-the-house performance.

It was a perfect friends gathering. They reminisced about the old days while the future waited.

CHAPTER TWENTY-ONE

Mouse smiled at her husband. Her lips were a little swollen from all the kissing, her eyes somewhat glassy and vague from the remains of passion and her hair seemed to be everywhere, but Quinn thought she looked perfect. Finding time to make love to her was a challenge now that they were back home with a house full of kids. But he had gotten an early start on the day by waking her just before six. It proved to be a very satisfactory plan and as he looked at her in the dawn light he thought they might just have time for —THUD.

The kids were up and about. He and Mouse looked at one another and smiled. Another day was beginning in their new family. "I'll meet you here same time tomorrow," he whispered.

Another thud, a thump, and sounds of running water. It was time to get up. "I'll be here," Mouse whispered back, kissed him quickly and threw back the covers.

"Can't they get their own breakfast?" moaned Quinn.

Mouse stood at the side of the bed fastening her bathrobe, the beautiful cover she had bought on their honeymoon. "I have to get Tilda ready. Mother is picking her up at eight. They're going to visit our cousins in Hickory. They'll be home late tonight. Colt is running with the college boys every morning to get in shape for soccer. The twins have signed up for a robotics camp that starts today at the high school."

"So we'll be alone all day?"

"No, Colt will be here until soccer tryouts. I think that's at two. I told Janet she could leave her children here to play with Colt when she and Tim take Thel to a doctor in Asheville."

"We'll have the baby?" There was real panic in Quinn's voice.

"No, she's nursing. She'll take the baby with her. We'll just have two kids. And Colt." She gave him a very lustful grin and added, "But having the little ones here will get you in practice for -

"You're pregnant already?" He sat up and counted on his fingers. "We haven't been married two weeks."

"I'm not pregnant . . . yet." She smiled at him and knelt on the bed to kiss him again, then whispered in his ear. "But if you keep waking me up every morning, it won't be long."

He grinned and pulled her to him for a long kiss—SLAM.

"That was Colt going out to jog. I better get the rest of our family organized," she whispered and pushed away from him.

Quinn stayed in bed a bit longer listening to the sounds of his new family, amazed at how much living he had missed before Mouse and her kids and relatives thundered into his life. He cherished every minute of each new day. He thought about the day ahead. Babysitting? He and Colt were certainly in for a new experience. He had seen Janet's kids in action.

Quinn stretched out on the bed. Nothing urgent this morning. He could just listen to his new family and—the doorbell? Who would be calling this early? Then he heard his father's voice. Quinn jumped out of bed and grabbed some clothing. David might not understand the mayhem that was breakfast.

Thumping downstairs he heard David say, "I can get my own coffee, Mouse. But you can make me some of those pancakes that you're making for Tilda."

"Good morning, Dad," said Quinn as he walked into the kitchen.

David was seated comfortably in a chair beside Tilda, helping her pour syrup. He recapped the bottle and helped the youngster take some bacon off a plate. Once that was done he poured her a glass of milk. Then grinned at his son. "Good morning."

Quinn decided David looked very comfortable with breakfast duty. He poured himself some coffee and carried it to the table. Mouse handed David a dish of pancakes and looked at Quinn.

"The twins will be down in a few minutes. And Colt will be back in about a half hour. So you better eat with this shift." Mouse flipped a pancake.

"I'll have the same," Quinn nodded. "What brings you here so early, Dad?" David had stopped in last evening telling everyone he had driven in from north Georgia. As David explained, it was easier to drive than fly when the plane was in Colorado. Mouse had blushed.

"I'm returning to Raleigh today. Clay," the security man, "is servicing the car and will pick me up in about an hour. I should have called. I apologize for just dropping in. I've scheduled a tour of a group home and then we'll take off." He looked around the kitchen. "I was going to the diner and saw Colt run through town with some other fellows. I thought you must be awake and I've never seen a household like yours operate and I was curious."

"What do you mean?" asked Mouse. This was the norm for her household.

"Children, no maid or cook. It's very hands on."

"David," teased Mouse, "you've been very sheltered. This is what we do every morning. Once school is back in session, it will be very predictable and routine."

Her new father-in-law smiled. "I guess I'll have to come back to experience the morning school routine."

"It will be worth the trip," promised Mouse, "because by then Quinn is going to know how to make pancakes and bacon and even eggs."

"I will?" Quinn's fork stopped half way to his mouth.

"You'll have to be prepared for those days when I'm out of town working with a client," explained Mouse.

"Out of town?" asked Quinn. "You're still going to work?"

She gave him a challenging stare. "Yes." It was a short answer, but he got the message.

"But I'll have to be out of town sometimes," countered Quinn.

David cleared his throat. "Maybe a housekeeper or cook might be something that would be useful once you move to the bigger house."

"I can help cook," volunteered Tilda as she licked syrup off her fork.

"I'm sure you can," remarked Quinn as he tried to keep his plate away from her sticky place at the table.

"Hi, Mr. David," greeted Paul as the twins stomped into the kitchen.

And Rob added, "Mom, we need lunches, too." They each grabbed a plate and found room at the table.

"I really stopped by to ask about your furniture and clothes and things," said David. "You can work the travel arrangements out later." He was smug, thinking he had inserted his issue around the demands of the twins.

"What furniture?" asked Mouse as she placed more bacon on the table.

Quinn looked at his father because that sounded like a trick question. David cleared his throat. "We have some lovely pieces that belonged to Quinn's mother. I thought you might enjoy them in your new home. And there are all of Colt's things, bikes, sporting equipment."

Mouse handed out glasses of milk and started pulling lunch meats and bread from the refrigerator.

"Colt said he has three different bikes and tennis rackets and skis," said Paul helpfully between bites of pancake.

"And his own TV and computer and printer and scanner," added Rob as he drowned his pancakes in syrup.

"Are you going to insist I throw out my things because they're shabby?" asked Mouse as she slapped lunch meat on a helpless slice of bread.

Quinn looked at his father for assistance, again. "Why don't you all come down some weekend after the house is finished and, Mouse, you can select things that might fill in the spaces after you arrange your furniture." David sat back pleased with his solution. "I can just send one of Colt's bikes for now."

"Colt has a bike here," said Paul.

"Yeah," added Rob, "he bought it at the thrift store where he gets his clothes."

"He gets his clothing at a thrift store?" roared David.

"Mommy told him not to get shirts with bad words on them," Tilda offered as she finished her milk.

David glared at Mouse. Quinn cleared his throat then jumped in with an explanation. "Colt thinks his clothes look too neat. So we let him buy things at a thrift store, and help that charity," he added quickly. "Evidently he found a bike."

"He was using Mom's," explained Tilda, "but then she couldn't take me for rides. 'cause I can't go alone to Grandma's and Aunt Janet's. I have to get older."

Colt came charging into the kitchen acting as punctuation to the discussion. "I'm starved." Mouse handed him a plate of pancakes. "Hi, Gramps."

"Good morning. I saw you running with your friends. They looked like a fine group of youngsters."

"They are. They all go to college and they said when they're gone I can run with the detectives. They run all year. And," he put down his empty orange juice glass, "Jason said I can have his old job."

"Job?" By the sound of his voice everyone knew that David was hearing too many new ideas this morning.

Quinn cleared his throat. "What sort of job?"

"Jason says Mr. Nathan needs someone to help him work on his stamp collection. Entering data in his computer and keeping up his records." Colt took a gulp of milk.

"That doesn't sound like he'll be digging ditches," Quinn said to his father.

"I guess not." Sulk.

"Then Jason said, when I can drive I can work at the bakery."

"The bakery?" David was trying with some effort to stay in control.

"On Saturday, Gramps," explained the youngster. "They need someone to deliver wedding cakes and put them together." More pancakes and a strip of bacon. "Jason says it'll give me a skill and some spending money for dates."

"Dates?" All three adults in the kitchen cried out in unison.

Colt looked at each one of them. "I'm going to be in high school." As far as he was concerned that explained everything.

"Can I date, too?" asked Tilda.

"No," cried the adult choir."

* * *

James Thurman came rushing into town after a panicked call from Rory. Hearing that Bart Decker had assaulted Audrey had frightened both of her protectors. Rory felt helpless watching the drama from Raleigh. He had called James as a reliable option to assist Audrey at this time. And James had finally cleared his schedule to arrive in River Bend last evening. He knew he would find Audrey at Rory's house this morning.

He walked into the small cottage and wrapped her in his arms. Before she could ask he said, "Rory called me. Are you all right? The kids?"

Audrey took strength from his embrace then separated, moving behind the sofa to keep her distance from this good man. "The kids are with my parents." She gave him a shy smile. "Bart has trashed the house. I'm staying here while Rory is out of town. Then I'll think of something." She gave him a forlorn shrug.

He sighed with relief. "I've been so worried. I got here as quickly as I could. What can I do?"

"Nothing." She gripped the back of the sofa. "I have a lawyer."

"Does that mean . . .? Let me rephrase that. What does that mean for us?"

"Nothing. I can't stay in my marriage. It sucks the life out of me. I can't be two people, the successful community person and the cowed wife at home. You don't need to be involved. When it's all over we can talk. But I can tell you the divorce will be ugly, the kids will become pawns in his game and I will have to concentrate on surviving and keeping the kids protected."

"Can I help with anything?" James wanted to hold her but he understood. "I know I'm part of your problem."

She smiled at him. "You were part of my sanity and helped me see what life could be." She swiped a tear. "I have a meeting in an hour with a potential donor."

"I can stay in town and take you to dinner this evening."

"I can't deal with you and everything else that will be happening." She walked toward the door. "We'll talk when this is all over."

He nodded. "Let me know if I can help. I am somewhat responsible. I knew you were married." They stood facing one another. There was nothing left for them now. James cleared his throat, "I think I'll stop to see my brother before I leave town. Do you want me to move him to another location?" James' developmentally delayed brother had settled in nicely in a group home owned by Audrey's agency.

"No. He's doing so well here. We'll just have to make certain your visits don't include . . . ." She swept her arms out to encompass the cottage. She opened the door hinting that he leave.

He gave her a kiss on the cheek and left.

* * *

Bart sat in the old growth foliage of the quiet cemetery backing up to Dancing Creek watching because he knew Audrey was living at her friend Rory's place. He had been on his vigil since late Saturday night. This morning he saw James Thurman enter the cottage and shortly return to his car. The angry husband swore under his breath. "She told me the affair was over."

Bart followed James as he stopped for a coffee then drove to the group home where his brother lived. The brother was out in the yard and ran to greet James. They moved off to the back of the house, the place that Bart knew was kept for families to have private meetings. It was a small, converted sunroom that contained a TV and some easy games for entertainment. The staff waved as the men disappeared into the private space but were soon distracted by a bus that had come to pick up several residents for some activity.

Bart sat and watched and grew angrier. That son of a bitch would pay. He needed to hit the man to let him know who was in charge, who won this game, who was in control of the prize. Audrey couldn't divorce him now that he needed her paycheck until he found a new job. He got out of his car on a side street and walked around to the back of the group home seeking out his rival. Stumbling across some discarded building materials he picked up a piece of rusted pipe. Just gripping it and feeling its heft made Bart feel powerful and in-charge.

Looking through the trees he saw the two brothers gather some toys from a closet and carry them to a table. He eased closer to watch and listen. James carried on a simple conversation with his brother talking about the toys and his friends. In Bart's opinion, the guy was disgusting. Who cared what that kid had to say? He was dumb, dumber than dumb.

* * *

David Templeton had heard a lot about Audrey's programs for developmentally delayed adults. He had been impressed with their first meeting. She had a reputation around the state for her innovation and use of the best practices with regard to her special clients. On his first visit to River Bend he had met her, but Audrey's personal life and Quinn's wedding had interrupted further meetings. Today Lynn had arranged this get together, and he had arrived early at the group home, interested in getting a sense for himself of the home and its operation before the official tour.

David watched from the street for a few minutes. He saw a bus pulling away. Walking to the front door, he rang the bell. It was answered by a staff member who said, "If you're Mr. Templeton, I'm supposed to tell you to look around. I'm in charge of lunch today and I've got some cookies in the oven." The man looked David over with amusement. "Audrey thought you would be a little early. She'll be here soon."

"Thank you," smiled David, "What's for lunch?"

"Come in and I'll show you the place, then we'll talk lunch." As they walked toward the kitchen and the cookies, the man took a slight detour to point out the gathering area and the wing that had the bedrooms and staff office, pointing out how they had a goal of teaching residents to keep their rooms neat and clean.

The doorbell rang. It was Lynn. "I'm a little early, but there are usually some great cookies for a snack." She greeted the staffer and wiggled her nose.

The staffer laughed. "Lynn, you are like an army, you travel on your stomach. I'm making some oatmeal bar cookies this morning." He led them back to the kitchen and offered the snack. The two guests sat and waited for the oven fresh cookies to be sliced.

David asked between bites of a delicious cookie, "What else should I see before I meet Ms. Decker?"

"Have a look at the gardens. Our residents tend a flower garden and a small vegetable garden. We'll have their lettuce and tomatoes for lunch. They get such a kick out of eating their produce." He gestured toward the kitchen door to the backyard. "And there's a small room attached beyond the laundry that we use for private family gatherings. You get in from the outside. We find the families like to visit in private sometimes." He winked at Lynn. "The Philanthropies helped us furnish the room with toys and a TV."

Lynn smiled at the compliment as she and David took their bar cookies and walked out the kitchen door. The staffer took a moment and pointed to the gardens and to the path going around the house toward the family room. They heard the stove ding and he waved them on their tour as he answered the oven.

* * *

Bart Decker had had enough of watching that asshole James play with his dumb brother. He walked into the private family room, the pipe gripped at his side, and began threatening James. "She tell you it's all over? 'cause if she didn't, I am. You can get your ass out of this town and never come back. If I see you here again, I'll make sure you regret it." He tossed the metal pipe from one hand to the other.

"Threatening me is a step up for you, isn't it? I thought you only terrorize people weaker than you." James moved to push his brother behind him, away from the intruder.

"What do you mean? I don't threaten -

"That's not what I heard." James helped his brother move further away from the stranger. His brother was getting upset by the angry talk. "Everything's okay, Tommy," James reassured the frightened young man.

"You hear it from my whore of a wife?" Decker was enraged. He slapped the pipe across his hand.

"She's a good woman who works hard. She's loving and kind and you don't deserve her or those kids." James faced Bart almost daring him to act.

"I take care of what's mine," yelled the angry husband and he walked out of the room, slamming the door.

James and his brother talked and visited for a few more minutes because James was concerned that Tommy had been upset by the exchange. When the young man seemed calmed down James said, "It's time for me to go. Let's find your friends." It was the phrase he always used and his brother knew to put away the toys and return to the main house.

James opened the door and Bart hit him in the face and head with the piece of pipe. The man fell back into the room and hit the back of his head against the table. Tommy stood frozen not understanding what was happening. Bart stood over the prone man then smashed his head again in a fit of rage. As he swung the pipe for the third time he shouted with an explosive fury.

Finally out of energy, he stood heaving, and froze. He heard voices. Thrusting the pipe into the hands of the young brother, Bart dashed for the door and moved quickly away from the small room, running toward the back of the property to the side street where he had parked his truck.

* * *

David and Lynn walked slowly toward the flower beds as they munched their cookies and talked quietly. "The Philanthropies got the Botanical Gardens to send over a staffer to help set up the raised beds."

"I like how this community seems to always work together."

Lynn nodded. "That's the story of the family room." She pointed to the path that led to the private room. "The family room wasn't our money but a donation from one of our donor advised funds. We have a donor who had grown up with a DD sibling. She told us that this type of space would have been appreciated in those days by her family. The sibling, a sister, has been dead for years, but we named it in memory of her. It's called Daisy's Family Room."

They walked around the corner of the building and noticed the door was open and a startled young man stood at the entry with a pipe in his hands.

"Hello, young fellow," greeted David as Tommy Thurman stepped aside and allowed him to enter. David gasped, "Lynn, look!"

They both rushed to the prone figure. Lynn felt for a pulse. She pulled out her cell and called Dusty.

"He didn't do this," David began.

"Please stay calm, David, my husband will be here shortly." She spoke to Tommy, "Would you like some of my cookie?" She handed him the rest of her oatmeal bar in exchange for the bloody pipe he was holding, leaning it against the wall for Dusty's team to examine.

As they stood there waiting for the police, Audrey came around the corner. "Chet told me you were already here." She stopped, recognized her ex-lover's body and began to take heaving breaths. Lynn was at her side.

"Do you know him?" Lynn asked.

"The man I . . . told you about." She was hyperventilating.

Lynn led Audrey out to the yard to sit on a bench near the flower beds. By that time everyone could hear sirens. David befriended Tommy, asking him questions about the plants following the young man to the vegetable garden.

Chet came running into the yard. "The police. . ."

Lynn called him over to sit with Audrey as Dusty and Tee came out the kitchen door. Two more officers came from the side street into the back yard.

"He didn't do this," David kept saying.

Lynn went to Dusty and showed him the pipe she had placed against the wall.

Chet came forward. "We have security tapes." They looked at him. "Our grounds are always monitored because sometimes our residents walk off."

"Who monitors?"

"We do. The monitors are in the staff office. If someone is missing we just scan the tape to see when they left and what direction they were going. We count heads every hour, no one ever gets too far."

He led Dusty to the office. Chet pulled up the digital history and showed Dusty all he needed to see. Heaving a sigh, the detective went back to Audrey. "Your husband is on the tape."

Audrey sobbed. Lynn sat beside her and hugged her. "They've been having problems," she informed Dusty.

"Where can I find him?" asked Dusty.

"I haven't seen him for over a week." She clutched Lynn's hand and continued, "You'll probably find in your records that I was pressing charges for assault. He hit me and my attorney wanted it as evidence because I was beginning divorce proceedings."

"Do you know the victim?"

Audrey nodded, wiped her eyes. "James Thurman. His brother, Tommy, is a resident here. James and I had an affair."

Lynn saw Dusty's shoulders rise and fall. She knew he hated crimes of passion. He always complained and she always said, "Life moves on passion."

Dusty stepped away and spoke into his phone.

Audrey pulled herself together and took control of the group home staff and residents. Blotting her eyes, she turned to David, "Mr. Templeton, I'm sorry that you are here today. Thank you for being so concerned for Tommy." She nodded toward the body. "That's his older brother and guardian." She turned to her staff member. "Chet, please take Tommy inside for a snack." Chet nodded. She continued giving instructions to her other staff members who had gathered. "I think we should organize a picnic at the park for lunch." A woman nodded as she made a phone call to the bus driver.

Once her plan was in place and the residents protected from the investigation, Audrey swayed. David grabbed her and helped her back to the bench. He and Lynn sat with her as the drama of the police investigation unfolded.

* * *

Bart's mother was at work Monday morning worried that Bart hadn't returned Sunday evening. *Where are you?* she texted.

Her text pinged just as he was racing out of River Bend. He called her. "I got a job interview. You'll probably see me at dinner." He thought about what he had just done and wondered if the police would suspect him. He thought he should get to his mother's, pack his things and leave the state. He was driving toward Asheville and decided to stop at one of the local breweries to calm down and to make some plans. He needed something to help him focus and a cold IPA should do the trick.

As he downed his second draft, he received another text from her. *Why are police in my office asking about you?*

No idea. Just finished interview. He added a positive emoji to his text. Then he turned off his phone. He sat staring at his empty glass. Damn. Did someone see him? Did that dumb kid talk? What could he say? Bart was forced to think more about his fight or flight response. The bartender signaled about another drink. Bart declined and realized that he better pay cash for the beers. He had to go off the grid—no phone, no credit cards.

Camping! Good thing he had packed his gear. His mother had thought he planned to camp with the boys. He had set up a watch in the old cemetery instead to keep an eye on Audrey. Slapping the bar, he remembered that he had wanted to check out the old drug cabin for some left-over drugs. Camping for a few days would give him time to plan and do recon.

He stopped at a big grocery store and bought food and other supplies, mindful that he was now living with the cash he had on hand. He knew he could stay in the forest for several days while he came up with a plan. Leaving the state was becoming a priority.

CHAPTER TWENTY-TWO

"What have we got?" Dusty demanded as he walked into the office on a sunny, murder investigation day.

"Decker's in the wind," replied Danny. "We've had someone contact his mother. We have patrols in Brevard keeping an eye on his kids."

"And we have Sherri spending nights with Mrs. Decker," concluded Tee.

"His mother told the guys her son had planned to go camping and was having a job interview. She had no idea of where either event would be." Mars closed his notebook. "His probation officer hasn't heard from him since their first meeting."

Dusty scanned the white board notes. "Do we have someone looking in the forest? Campsites? Empty cabins?" His staff nodded.

Danny added, "We've even sent someone to check that cabin where he was arrested."

"Just keep doing what we're doing," replied Dusty.

* * *

With James dead and Bart missing, Audrey found that keeping up with the demands of her job held her problems at bay. One of the issues she had to deal with involved Tommy. She sighed. She couldn't ignore some of her problems because they were a part of her job. She walked into Darlene's office, "I have to deal with Tommy Thurman."

The attorney pushed a box of tissues toward Audrey. "In what way?"

Audrey placed a file on the desk. "James gave me power of attorney to handle health issues for Tommy and to make other decisions when he was unavailable." She riffled through some papers then passed the file to the attorney. "It's pretty common for me to have some responsibilities when my client's family might be unavailable." She took a tissue. "Anyway, please review the documents and see what we have to do about Tommy."

"How are you managing?" Darlene was becoming a good friend.

"The kids know Bart is in trouble. I haven't gone into detail. As long as they stay with my parents, they're insulated." Another tissue. "Tommy, on the other hand, is very confused and needs to see me often. My staff and I are trying to deal with that."

"Have the police given you any clue about Bart?"

"They don't want me living at Rory's alone, so Sherri Steiner, a policewoman, has moved in. She spends the night." Audrey chuckled. "She says guarding me got her off of night patrols. And she is grateful, because with Rory's security system in place, she gets to sleep nights." Audrey gazed out the window for a moment. "She parks her patrol car out front. I don't think Bart will bother me."

* * *

Closing in on almost three weeks of marriage Quinn got initiated quickly—errands, carpooling, food. Mouse told him she had some work to do in her home office as he accepted her shopping list and piled three kids into the car to be dropped off at various places. Colt declined to help him explaining that he was meeting some new friends later.

The youngster waved as the family Suburban darted from the neighborhood. He smiled to himself as he enjoyed the summer breeze in his hair while wondering if there was anything to eat, something to snack on before Quinn got back with more food.

"Colt," a woman called from a car pulling up in front of Mouse's house.

"Mom!" gasped Colt frozen in panic. "You can't be here. You promised to stay away. You'll go to jail."

"He stole all the money, honey," pouted Madeline as she climbed out of her car. "CJ cleaned out the account and disappeared with my money. You have to help me, baby."

Colt stood at the curb unable to move. His mother seemed to need help. But each meeting with her was confusing, sometimes frightening, and always painful. What would his dad say? She had to leave. As he wrestled with these thoughts, Mouse ran from the house and a dark SUV came to a screeching halt behind Madeline's car. The security man, Clay, was driving and his passenger, David, was on his phone.

Colt looked at the cavalry. Mouse was ready to protect him. She already had one arm around his waist. David jumper from the passenger seat of the SUV. Clay was on his cell as he positioned himself between the boy and his mother. "Mom says CJ stole her money," Colt tried to explain.

Mouse studied the woman, then asked, "Do you mean CJ took the money in that offshore account?" Her voice seemed to have a calming effect on David and the security guard.

Madeline cringed from David as Quinn arrived in the Suburban. "Get the hell out of here and away from Colt," demanded Quinn.

"Easy," cautioned David. "Are you all right, son?"

Colt nodded. "She says CJ took all her money." They all looked at Madeline.

David said, "Clay, please stay with Ms. Templeton. The rest of us are going into the house to talk." Madeline opened her mouth to speak but thought better of it. Clay opened the back door of his car and invited her to sit and wait.

In the house Quinn said, "We can have her arrested."

"No!" Colt looked terrified.

Mouse led him to a chair. "You sit down while we discuss this, Colt. We won't send her to jail." By her look she made certain David and Quinn understood that Colt's mother would be treated with respect. "Why don't I check into the truth of her statement? I can still get into that account. If I can't, Kyle will help." She sat at her computer and began her mysterious assault on the keyboard. Within minutes she had the beginning of an answer. "The account has been cleaned out."

"But did CJ do it alone or is this a plan they have to get more money?" asked Quinn.

"I'll contact Kyle and Janet. We'll trace the money from this account." She turned to Colt. "Honey, ask your mother to come in and offer her a Coke or something." The youngster dashed from the room. When he was gone, Mouse said, "No yelling at that woman. You will do nothing to upset Colt." She stared at Quinn and David.

"She can't keep holding us up." Quinn spoke as he stood at the window watching Colt talk with Madeline out at the curb.

"She gave you a great gift in your son." Mouse dared Quinn to argue with that statement.

"Aren't you going to call Janet and Kyle?" He was trying to contain his temper.

"I emailed them. Kyle's already got someone following the money." Her computer dinged just as Madeline and Colt came into the room. Mouse studied her screen as everyone waited. "Colt, get your mother something to drink and ask her to have a seat." She spoke while staring at her computer screen.

When Colt returned with a drink for Madeline, Mouse said, "She's telling the truth. CJ took the whole account and moved it someplace else. It's in an investment account and Kyle says CJ's passport shows he was in and out of the Caymans last week."

"That bastard," said Madeline through gritted teeth.

Quinn nodded to David and the older man said, "Let me make some calls and we'll try to straighten this out." He walked into the kitchen.

Madeline stood and started pacing the room. "I don't know why I ever got mixed up with you and your family," she sneered at Quinn. "All that money and you couldn't give me a decent settlement. I gave you plenty of sex and took care of the kid" she took Colt's hand, "for all the time you were in law school. I deserve something for my trouble."

Quinn opened his mouth but closed it with one look from Mouse as she cut her glance over to Colt standing beside his mother. Quinn took a deep breath and said, "I'm sorry Colt and I were such a drag. Maybe -

David returned to the room. "Here's our offer, Madeline. Five million which would have been your share of that account will be deposited at your direction."

"What about the money you promised for the next ten years if I stayed away? CJ got twice as much as me," she whined. "I shouldn't be punished for coming back."

"We'll honor our commitment as long as we have an account to transfer to," said David. "Be at my attorney's office in Raleigh tomorrow afternoon and he'll handle everything. Make certain we know where to make those deposits."

"What about the original divorce settlement?"

David and Quinn did some silent eyebrow twitching. Quinn said, "It will stay as it was originally laid out." Madeline would remain a pampered divorcee.

She took a last sip from her glass and gathered her purse. "I'll see you in ten years, honey." She tweaked Colt's nose. He stiffened and stood tall.

"Good bye, Madeline." He said it in a tone of voice that echoed David's.

Madeline shivered at the sound. Dropping her hand she clutched her purse, gave Colt a sad smile and walked out the door. Mouse went to Colt and hugged him. David walked onto the porch and signaled to Clay to let Madeline leave. The tone of Colt's dismissal told them all that Madeline was history. The youngster had found himself a real mother. And the Templeton family had a young heir to groom.

* * *

It was evening and the new family was enjoying a quiet home-cooked meal. Quinn couldn't figure out how Mouse worked all day, managed the kids and their activities and got food on the table. This evening she had prepared fajitas. He was mesmerized as he watched Tilda fill and wrap her warm tortilla and try to take a bite. He noticed his father also hypnotized by the youngster. "Dad, how did you get here at just the right time this morning? I thought Dusty said you could leave. Your part of the investigation is over."

David chuckled. "Clay and I had planned to leave but Nathan convinced us to stay for some party this weekend." He shrugged. "It was in the stars, I guess." He returned his gaze to Tilda and her wrap.

"Aren't these great, Gramps?" Colt was already building his second fajita. He paused. "Will Mom be all right?" He looked at the two important men in his life.

"She will, son," said David. "Your father and I will make certain she has what she needs and is safe from CJ."

Quinn's eye popped. David was certainly expressing a different attitude about Madeline than he had in the past. "What do you mean?"

"It's all Mouse," said David. He reached across the table and took her hand. "We needed someone with a different perspective to show us how to deal with Madeline."

Mouse gave David a grateful smile. "Thank you. You men just needed a little nudge toward chivalry." Then she grinned, "Besides I was just looking after myself. I didn't want to lose all of you. I would have paid her twice as much for the three of you."

Quinn winked at his father. "See how she spends money."

David's response was interrupted as Tilda's tortilla squirted out on to the table. The ensuing food crisis brought the family dinner back to what was important—cleaning guacamole off Tilda's favorite shirt.

After dinner, Quinn drove David to Nathan's. "Did Clay have dinner?" asked Quinn.

David replied, "I think he's made some friends here since we seem to be here so often."

They drove into Dancing Creek and took a quick look at the house being remodeled for Quinn's new family. "How soon will you be moving in?" David wanted to know.

"Don't worry, Dad," smiled Quinn. "We have a room for you."

"After dinner tonight, I might decide that it's safer to stay with Nathan. I'd never seen food fly like that."

Both men laughed at the memory as Quinn said, "I think we're going to see a lot of things we've never seen before."

CHAPTER TWENTY-THREE

"I think you should come to my office," was Darlene Porterfield's directive to her client.

Since Darlene Porterfield was Audrey's attorney for the divorce, Audrey had turned to her for advice on the Power of Attorney she held to act for James when Tommy needed something. She knew James had initiated the document so that any of Tommy's medical needs could be addressed quickly. Death was certainly not something that had been on James' mind. Audrey had wanted to know if the document was still in place or was there a family member who would be stepping up to care for Tommy.

Darlene had scanned the papers. "Why don't I contact the attorney who drew this up and advise him of James' death?"

That had been the conclusion of the discussion several days ago. And Audrey wondered what Darlene had learned that required a face-to-face meeting today. She walked into the office wan and demoralized. Bart Decker's drug arrest, then murder investigation had taken its toll. Audrey shoulders carried a burden almost too big. What else could happen?

Darlene smiled as her client took a seat.

"Is that a smile of sympathy?" Audrey was ready for more bad news.

"It all depends on you." Darlene spread papers across her desk. "I have been speaking with that attorney. It seems James Thurman also drew up a new will when he drew up the power of attorney. At his death he made you guardian of his brother and the manager of a trust for his care. When the brother passes, you inherit the balance of the trust free and clear. He also set it up so that you receive an annual stipend for shouldering the guardianship responsibilities." Darlene waited for Audrey to digest this information.

"But my divorce?"

"This inheritance and guardianship only involves you. Any inheritance only goes to you and any income from the stipend only goes to you. It will not be a part of divorce discussions or settlement."

"The police were still looking for Bart. He'll need more money with all the trouble he's in." Audrey tried to process this new information and Bart's potential interest in claiming his share of Tommy's funds. "Does Tommy have relatives who will challenge this?"

"It seems that there are a few cousins, but once they learn that James' estate is attached to Tommy no one will want to claim anything." Darlene thought a moment. "We might worry if the fellow dies within a year or two of probate. The cousins may make some claims. But I think we can prepare for that. If he lives longer, they won't think there is money left."

"How big is this trust?"

"That's an interesting question," mused the attorney. "The trust is the beneficiary of his retirement accounts and his life insurance. Because of the manner of his death, the life insurance will payout almost a million dollars."

Audrey swayed in her chair. "He was expecting to be murdered?"

"No." Darlene was quick to answer. "He shopped for a policy that would insure care for his brother should something happen to him and he bought the most comprehensive policy that would meet that goal." The attorney smiled at her client. "And his retirement account transfers to Tommy should he reach an age to activate it. Or it passes to you to be available when you retire. You might want to talk with someone in Michelle Grayson's office about financial planning. The retirement account will be a million plus by the time you or Tommy need it."

"If Bart is arrested and goes to prison, could he claim any of the funds when he is released?"

"That's a good question. By that time your divorce will be decades old, but you are receiving the inheritance while the divorce is pending." Darlene thought for a moment. "Let me talk with the other attorney. In the meantime, I'll make certain guardianship funds go into a trust account I'll set up in this office. It will be a checking account that I control. That's the only level of protection I can figure out right now. You submit bills and I'll reimburse you."

Audrey nodded. "Whatever you say. I'm just bewildered by all this. It's all I can do to attend to my job and my children."

Darlene nodded. "Talk to Michelle. She and I will take care of you."

That sounded soothing to Audrey who had been struggling to take care of everyone since this all began.

* * *

"I can't say I'm sorry to see you go," Dusty admitted to the three Hollywood types who had dogged him for a week.

"I'm just happy that you finally learned our names," said Cameron, the guy in the trio, as the others smirked.

"I was tired of being called Cameron," mocked Giselle, the older woman.

Stacy, the younger woman, grinned. She had met Jason's friends and had spent the summer evenings enjoying life with the college crowd. "I had fun."

Cameron growled. "That's what we get for creating opportunities for a young person." He glanced at Stacy. "She had all the fun and we worked."

Giselle gave Dusty a peck on the cheek. "You'll let us know what happens to that guy. Do you really think he's still around?"

"Yeah," said the detective. "He hasn't much money. He wants his drugs and he took all his camping gear from his house."

"But he could be on I-40 going west and be in Amarillo by now."

"That's if he had friends in Amarillo and if he was smart," said Cameron who had some law enforcement experience in his resume.

Dusty walked them to their rental car. "Drive carefully. When you get close to Charlotte you'll get into a lot of traffic."

Giselle smirked. "We're from LA. We invented traffic."

"Why are you going to Charlotte anyway?" The detective was curious.

"One of our clients wants us to scout a few locations."

They got into the car and waved to Dusty.

"Did you sign a big Hollywood contract?" The interim sheriff walked up and watched the Hollywood types drive out of the department parking lot.

"Don't you have something better to do than spy on me?" Dusty shook his head. "I feel like I've been under a microscope for a week. They didn't miss anything."

"Are you going to be in the show?"

"Damn, I hope not." He studied the ground and wrestled with his information. "I guess you should know they are hiring me as a consultant for this series. Marianna convinced them that me and Tee would be helpful when dealing with local color, procedure and interesting locations." He shrugged. "I won't let it interfere with my job."

Doug laughed. "I probably won't be sheriff by the time they come back for filming."

"Is the sheriff improving?"

"He's not getting worse," said Doug. "I just feel like I'm suspended. I can't make changes and everyone is just waiting for things to return to the old ways. I know that the old timers will go back to their old ways as soon as the old sheriff returns."

"I know what you mean," said Dusty. "You're doing a great job. I wish you were here for real."

"Thank you, that means a lot coming from you." Doug and Dusty nodded and silently returned to their offices.

* * *

Tomorrow was Piper's big party. Jason and the guys were sprawled in the grass as the dew settled. They were resting in anticipation of the morning frenzy when they would do all the rest of the prep work. They had done enough this evening unloading and setting up tents and rented tables and chairs. Tomorrow they would wrestle grills and bar supplies around the property.

"I don't even want to think about what else we have to do," moaned Jason. "Will and Dusty just sat and drank beer while they ordered us around."

"I think they're getting old," offered Jeff, the youngest fellow in the group.

"Don't let them hear you say that." Way, Dusty's nephew, was one of the older kids. He was working as a deputy in a neighboring county.

But, Stacy, one of the Hollywood consultants had drawn his interest. He was coming off of a memorable Hollywood inspired week.

"I didn't think we would see you," said Bryce. "That Hollywood girl seemed to be attracted to your skinny body."

Way grinned. "She had to go back to LA. But she said I should visit her."

All the guys snorted. Jason finally asked, "Will you?"

"I don't know."

Doyle's wife came over to get her husband. "Let's go, honey." The guys whistled and teased. Lori gave them the evil eye. They were silent. She reminded everyone. "My parents are getting in late tonight. We have to clean our house." Doyle groaned.

Bryce laughed and explained, "Lori's parents are coming for the party and staying at Doyle's. He's worried they'll think she's unhappy and take her home with them."

Everyone laughed. It was going to be another great party tomorrow.

* * *

"Yeah, Boss, " Fish responded to the ringing throw-away. He could hear music and glasses clinking in the background. The Boss was out partying. Fish looked around his dingy motel room.

"Fish?" whispered the Boss. "I hear that there's some big party tomorrow in River Bend that even includes police. No one will be watching that cabin. Let's meet up and look over the new merchandise."

"Got it." Fish yawned and finished his beer and cold pizza. He looked over the weapons on the other bed. No serial numbers and all in good shape. He'd have to get to that shack on the river and pick up the pills before sunrise. The Boss would want to make this a quick meet up and delivery. Yawn.

CHAPTER TWENTY-FOUR

Bart Decker had been living in the forest quietly for four days. He preened at the inherent intelligence that had inspired him to take the family's camping gear when he trashed the house. His wife was probably still trying to clean things up and hide everything from her important friends and board members. Bart shivered knowing the police had contacted his mother after he attacked Audrey's boyfriend. Was he dead? Who gives a shit, he thought. He delighted in recalling that stupid brother watching the entire event.

Whether the man was dead or not, Bart felt better that he had finally taken a stand, stood up for his family and his claim to Audrey. But four days in the forest was enough. She was probably ready to admit that she was wrong and she'd work while he got himself back on track. But he could sure use a boost right now. Maybe there's something that got left behind at that cabin, he thought. He cleaned his camp site, locked the food and gear in his truck—bears were a risk—and took off on foot for the old cabin.

Crouching in the rhododendron he watched the cabin for a short time from the ridge above. No action. He could see torn strips of yellow police tape flapping. To him that meant the police had no more interest in the location. Smiling to himself at his cleverness he started down the trail to the site of his many drug buys.

He stopped a moment as he got closer. Did he hear talking? He looked around and decided it must have come from some campers on the other side of the trees. He reached for the door and the knob turned silently. Pushing the door open, he froze. Two men were looking over a number of weapons and bags of pills spread across a table.

"Sorry, fellows," he stumbled and mumbled, "I didn't know someone was renting this place." The two men were as surprised as he was. In the few seconds it took for everyone to evaluate the situation and determine any level of danger, Bart grinned at the well-dressed older gentleman. "How're you doin'? Remember me? I'm Bart Decker. My foursome came in third and yours came in first at the hospital golf outing." He moved forward stretching out his hand.

The golfer returned the offered handshake. He chortled in that golfer-to-golfer way. "I do remember. You boys almost won on the thirteenth."

Bart nodded sadly. "It was me. I never miss that water hazard." He looked at the other man, a big, rough looking bruiser. "I'm sorry to interrupt." His eyes wandered to the pills.

"Don't give it a thought," said the golfer. "Mr. Fish and I have some business to conclude. Then we'll leave this place to you." The Boss never used names! At that point Fish knew that the Boss had no intention of letting this guy out of the cabin alive.

Bart looked around the cabin as he did some thinking. After arguing with himself, he decided that he would approach the older gentleman for a job. Golfers looked out for one another, right? "Do you own this cabin?" Both men looked at him. He continued. "If you do, you know I was busted for drugs here, and lost my job." Now Bart was in job interview mode. "I could use another job." He hesitated a minute before taking the plunge. "If this is your operation, I could step in. Mahaffey's gone and so is that nurse. You'll need someone to keep your clients satisfied."

The Boss looked him over, then nodded. "I see your point." He walked toward a window and looked out. After some thought he turned around. "You have experience with the product and are familiar with our procedures." Bart nodded eagerly. The Boss continued, as he walked back to the table, "We've been giving some thought to a new product, something that doesn't require a shot or a nurse." He gestured to the bags sitting next to the weapons. "Here's our new product." Opening a plastic bag he shook out four pills handing them to Bart. "Why don 't you try them so you can talk them up with our clients. Sometimes folks are a little wary about something new. You could make them feel at ease."

Bart took the pills and looked around for some water. "All four?" The Boss nodded. Mr. Fish handed him a flask that materialized from his coat pocket. "Thank you," said Bart as he popped the pills and gulped

191

the alcohol chaser. He walked around the cabin giving the impression that he was communing with his inner drug evaluating self.

When he swayed the Boss said, "Why don't you have a seat. The effects of these new drugs might be stronger than what you're used to. We'll wrap up our meeting and leave this place to you." He looked around. "We'll talk tomorrow."

Bart tried to focus on the man. "Do you mind if I just stretch out on this couch?" He was already feeling a buzz. "These feel mighty fine," he slurred.

Once Mr. Fish helped him to the couch, the Boss nodded and they began to clean up evidence of their meeting. Fish took the weapons back to the car while the Boss made certain that Bart was no longer aware of their actions. Fish huffed as he returned to the cabin. "Why do we have to park so far away?"

The Boss scowled. "Because of idiots like this. Let's get out of here."

"What did you give him?"

"Who knows? Some of that new shit those guys from South America are making." He looked around. "Make this look like a simple cabin fire, not arson."

Fish nodded and got to work.

* * *

Quinn and Mouse had returned from their honeymoon in plenty of time to prepare their gang for Piper and Will's annual end of summer party. It seemed the twins had grown out of everything in the days that Mouse was away. Tilda had lost every shoe she owned. Colt was the only one happy with his clothes. Mouse had sent him to the thrift store that supported the domestic violence shelter and he had come home with a dozen disgusting t-shirts and torn jeans. She had to laugh at him as he tried to reinvent himself as a normal high school freshman—and looking like a bum was a big part of his goal. At least he hadn't suggested tattoos or piercings.

But Tilda had cried because she wanted new clothes to wear, too, the spanglier the better. She wanted wedge sandals. To which Mouse said "No." Tilda cried and begged. Then she wanted a top that Mouse thought only a pole dancer would wear—when she was on her break.

She said "No." Tilda cried. Quinn solved the problem by telling Tilda she looked great in the t-shirt she had bought at Disneyworld.

By Saturday evening Mouse noticed she didn't feel that honeymoon glow any more as she found some cropped pants and a clean top, slipped into some sandals and climbed into the family car. Quinn grinned, gave her a kiss, the kids groaned and they dashed to the fun.

They arrived at Piper's in the big Suburban Quinn had purchased as the new family car. Colt was out of the car first to swagger in his faded t-shirt that memorialized a rock concert from a past decade and his jean shorts that he had frayed himself. Not to be outdone the twins had cutoff their own jeans. As Paul argued, "They're too short anyway for long pants." Mouse had to admit he had a point.

"Are you sure the kids are welcome?" Quinn asked as they searched for a parking spot.

"Yes. We've all attended in the past." Mouse stepped from the Suburban and grabbed Quinn's arm to walk across the bumpy field to Piper's yard.

"Who will be here?" he asked. They were all alone because the kids had scattered.

"Everyone you know in River Bend."

"Your parents?"

"And my aunts and uncles and a few cousins."

Walking into Piper's yard Quinn understood. People were everywhere. Children and pets running around. Music and food and long tables and folding chairs and hanging lights. Colt materialized at his side as Mouse disappeared. "Thanks, Dad. This is the greatest. These people like their kids."

"What do you mean?"

"We never went to parties together in Raleigh. Everyone was in their own box." Colt frowned. "Do you know what I mean?"

"I think I do." Quinn threw an arm around Colt and kissed his forehead.

"Ah, Da-ad." Colt pulled away from his father.

To save himself from becoming too sappy Quinn asked, "Do you need a haircut?"

"I was thinking I could let it grow. The guys at soccer camp all had longer hair. I don't think they get it cut every three weeks."

Quinn smiled. "Just don't let it get as long as Mouse's. I wouldn't be able to tell you two apart."

"Oh, I think you would." The youngster grinned at his dad and ran off to meet some of his new friends.

Surveying the crowd, Quinn realized that he had met several of the attendees in his few weeks in River Bend. He greeted his contractor, Carl Reid. His dentist who was Mouse's brother, his insurance man who was Mouse's other brother, and two of her uncles. His new cousin, Janet, and her husband, Tim, were there with no children. Tim explained that Janet couldn't hold her liquor and she embarrassed the kids. There was Quinn's new mother-in-law who liked him more this week then she had a few weeks ago when she suspected he had ulterior motives in his pursuit of her daughter. He did a slow study of the activity in the backyard. Families everywhere. A bar with plenty of hard and soft drinks, food and more food.

There was live music from a bunch of guys he didn't know, but he thought he recognized one of the musicians as one of Dusty's detectives. Then he blinked. His father was in the crowd.

"Dad?" he called, "I didn't think this was your kind of party!"

David strolled over to his son as he munched a hot dog. "Nathan told me I shouldn't miss this. It's the biggest social event of the late summer." He finished the dog and wiped his mouth and fingers on a mustard stained napkin.

"Dad?" called a breathless Colt. "Hey, Gramps. I didn't know you were here."

"Wouldn't miss it," replied his grandfather.

"Do you need something?" Quinn asked his son.

Colt grinned. "We have so much new family. Janet is Mouse's cousin so Tim, her husband, is my cousin, but he said I could call him 'Uncle Tim' like Jason does and he said that makes me his other nephew because a guy needs more than one to be a real uncle. I told him my Uncle CJ was out of the family and might go to jail. And he said every family needs at least one jailbird."

"Who is this man?" demanded David. "We don't need to talk about the crooks in our family."

"Calm down, Dad," said Quinn.

"But we're related to everyone, now," Colt continued, showing no concern that he might have an ex-uncle doing time. "Mouse had two brothers. Two more uncles! And cousins, we have tons. Some are real like the Macauley cousins but some are just for convenience."

"Convenience?" David was losing the glow from his hot dog.

"Jason says," explained Colt, "that sometimes you need family and so you should collect cousins and uncles."

"Need them for what?" David really needed another hot dog.

"He and Ricky said you need people around if one of your parents dies. Both their dads died." Colt looked serious for a moment then threw his arms around David. "I don't want you to die, Gramps." Hanging on to David, he turned to his father, "Or you, Dad."

David kissed his grandson on the forehead. "I feel the same, but it's good to have folks you can turn to in a crisis."

"Now we have enough relatives for loads of crisises." Colt stumbled over the word. "Come on, Gramps, and watch us play soccer."

"I need another hot dog first."

The two of them left Quinn standing in the yard. He looked for Mouse. She and the other new bride, Lori, were the center of attention with all the other women, showing rings, answering questions, getting hugs. As he took in the ambiance of the party Quinn understood what Colt meant. A few folks ambled by and introduced themselves then congratulated him on his new wife and family. No one among their Raleigh friends cared as much about family as their new friends in River Bend did.

As he moved in the direction of the bar he stumbled. Tilda was trying to fit between his legs as she ran from another youngster. He picked her up as she babbled. "He's a zombie. He's going to kiss me."

The little boy chasing her threw his head back and stared up as Quinn snarled, "She's mine, go find another girl." The little fellow spun around and charged in another direction.

As he held Tilda, Quinn asked, "When do you want to get that kitten?"

She threw her arms around his neck and squealed. "Can I tell Mom?"

"It was her idea," said Quinn. "Where do we get a kitty?"

"Miss Lynn will know," said Tilda. "she knows all the gossip. That's what Aunt Janet says."

"Then we'll ask Miss Lynn."

Tilda and Quinn got information from Lynn as she explained, "The James County Humane shelter is near Portage. Go out Highway 37—you can't miss it."

Quinn nodded, thanked her and released Tilda so she could spread the word about her new pet. He grabbed a beer and went in search of food. He managed to eat and walk while shaking hands doing the circuit of Piper's yard. One burger, two hot dogs and uncounted sides later he found an old Adirondack chair and sprawled in it to watch the fun. That only lasted a minute. Tilda crawled into his lap. She stretched her legs out so that he could see her toes.

"I painted my toenails," she announced. It was getting dark and Quinn had a hard time seeing the tiny toes as she smashed herself against his chest and pushed her feet out over his knees. He turned her so that he could hold her foot and get a better look. Each toe nail was a different color. To Quinn it looked like Tilda was balancing a little M&M on each toe—yellow, orange, green, red. All the while she was talking, so he tried to pay attention.

". . . and then I tried to do my own toes and they had to clean everything." Quinn squinted at Tilda's toes and could see traces of polish along her arch and between her toes. He was grateful someone with nail polish remover had helped his little girl.

All of a sudden he realized Tilda wasn't talking. Was she waiting for him to reply to some question or comment? He was screwed because he hadn't been listening. But she was sitting so quietly. Of course! In mid-sentence she had fallen asleep on his lap. He made them both more comfortable in the chair and he settled back to watch the party as the new dad to a little girl with M&M toes.

* * *

The evening was the usual for Piper's annual summer party. Dusty had enjoyed a chat with that new fellow, David Templeton. He knew everyone was delighted with Sara's marriage to the other Templeton. He sipped his beer and watched Doug move through the crowd with a surprising skill, almost what a politician would do. Hmmm. His phone buzzed. A few folks close by had heard the sound and looked at him. He gave everyone a scowled, sort of a nothing's-wrong-I'm-in-control smile. Moving off to the trees for some privacy he scanned the phone screen as he saw Doug out of the corner of his eye, also look at his screen. They're eyes met across the crowd. Dusty nodded toward the front of the house.

Out of sight of Piper's guests Doug asked, "What's this about a cabin?"

Dusty shrugged as he waited for someone to answer his phone call. He listened and replied, "He's with me. We'll be right there." He turned to Doug. "We need to use your car. Mine is blocked." They trotted to Doug's place and climbed into the car.

"Where are we going?"

"To that cabin where we caught Mahaffey. It's on fire."

Doug demonstrated his highway patrol driving skills as he got them through River Bend and into the forest in record time. They had to park along the old gravel road some distance from the fire. Emergency vehicles of all sorts had arrived earlier taking all the space.

A fireman spotted the car and ambled over. "Some campers saw the fire when it got dark. They called the forestry guys who called us. There was a body inside."

"Can we ID it?" asked Doug.

"Yeah, he probably died from the smoke. He was on the far side of the cabin from the fire." They walked toward the cabin, around hoses and other gear. "We got here in time. Another half hour and the whole place would have been engaged."

"He set the fire?" asked Dusty. "Or is it arson?"

The fire chief replied, "I got a funny feeling about this. It looks too easy, like he was heating some food and fell asleep."

Both Dusty and Doug looked at him in surprise. "Get the body in for an autopsy."

"That's our plan. We're waiting for the medical examiner. My guys got the fire out. You can see the body." The three men walked through the soggy remains of the cabin wall over to the sofa that had been draped with a tarp to keep out water and debris.

The chief pulled the tarp back and Dusty said, "Shit."

CHAPTER TWENTY-FIVE

Dusty dragged into the kitchen just as Lynn was making breakfast coffee. He was all covered in dirt and smelled like smoke. "I got your text," she said. "You're sure it's Audrey's husband?"

"Yeah, he had an ID in his wallet. I've been at the morgue." She handed him a cup of coffee. "Will you go with me to see her?"

"Certainly. When?"

"Let me get cleaned up and eat some breakfast." He trudged up the stairs.

He was back within fifteen minutes, warming up his coffee and smelling better. "I want to get this over with and get some sleep." He took the plate she handed him and sat at the table.

"Do you know what happened?

Dusty savored the coffee. "It looked like he was cooking something at that drug cabin and fell asleep. They have to call in an investigator because of the death."

Lynn shivered as she digested his words. "Are you suggesting arson?"

Dusty didn't want to tell her that the fire chief did, in fact, suspect arson, and possibly murder. "It's just routine procedure." He finished his pancakes and drained his coffee. "Let's go."

* * *

Quinn and Tilda followed Lynn's directions and arrived at the animal shelter just minutes after it opened. It was Sunday lunch time as they pushed through the door, Quinn saying, "I can't believe you're open on a Sunday afternoon."

The woman behind the counter smiled. "Sunday seems to be a great pet adoption day. Families riding around, coming from a picnic, see our

198

sign and stop in." She glanced over the counter looking down at Tilda. "Just like you and your daughter."

"We want a kitten, a girl kitten," Tilda explained. "We have too many boys."

"Kittens?" asked the lady.

"Brothers," scowled Tilda.

The lady smiled. "I have some great little girls for you to choose from. Do you want anything special? Any color? Who told you about us?"

"Miss Lynn," replied Tilda, "She said you would have a pet just my size." Her eyes roamed the room as if expecting small pets to fall from the ceiling.

"So this is to be your own pet? You won't share with your brothers?" The lady smiled at the little girl. "I had brothers. Sometimes they teased me." Tilda nodded her head vigorously. "And sometimes they took care of me." Tilda nodded her head reluctantly.

Quinn enjoyed listening to the conversation, but had to add, "Tilda promises that she'll take care of her kitten. Can you tell her about the responsibilities?"

The lady nodded. "Tilda, you have to make certain there is enough food and water. I'll give you some food samples and you and your dad can go shopping. I'll also give you a list of supplies and pet health records for you to take to the vet, you know, the pet doctor. You'll have to learn to clean the litter box and always find time to hug your kitten and to play with her." Tilda looked as though she were recording every word in her active brain. Quinn always enjoyed watching her process information. It was as though her thoughts made her thick curls dance.

"Here we are," said the lady as they stepped into a room that seemed filled with kittens. While they watched two little kittens tumbled with one another across the room, playfully nipping and swiping. "These are two sisters from the same litter. We've had them for two weeks. They're about seven weeks old."

Quinn watched Tilda think. He could tell she was wrestling with a big thought. He waited.

"They're twins?"

"Yes, two little sisters," replied the woman.

Tilda turned up her head to face Quinn. "We have to take both." He opened his mouth to object, but she continued, "Mom kept both twins.

She didn't leave one behind for someone else to get." She stared up at her new father. He folded.

"You have twins?" the lady asked.

"My brothers," said Tilda, nodding with all her curls bouncing.

The lady smiled. "Will you share the kittens with your brothers?"

"They're too old. And too big and Colt, he's even bigger. They would squish a kitten."

"Maybe they need a dog." Animal shelter workers can spot an easy mark.

"What kind?" asked the curious little girl.

"Tell me something about your brothers."

"They play sports and Colt runs with the big kids."

"I have just the dog," said the helpful lady.

"I bet you do," mumbled Quinn. She ignored his comment and led them into another part of the shelter.

Walking to a large cage she opened it and led out a Siberian Husky. "This dog loves to run. He is quiet and likes other animals. He'll get along with your kittens." The dog sat on the floor and tilted his head to look over the visitors. His eyes were an ice blue and he had the black and white coloring in the traditional markings of his breed. "He has papers so you know that he is well-bred. He does shed a lot." Tilda was already petting the dog and talking to him about the new kittens and explaining her brothers. The lady grinned at Quinn who helplessly nodded.

Two kittens and a husky to go.

* * *

Standing at the window of Rory's place Audrey saw Dusty and Lynn get out of a dark SUV. Her stomach turned. What other crisis had Bart created that she would have to solve? Lana the probation officer had spent the night but had left early to attend church services. Audrey remembered the old days when attending church services had been a part of her life. That had fallen away as her marriage crumbled. Sigh.

She opened the door for her guests. "Good morning." Lynn gave her a hug as they walked in.

Dusty stood in the entry. "We're here officially," he said. "Can we sit some place?" Lynn took Audrey's hand and led her into the living room.

Once they were seated, Dusty cleared his throat, "Ms. Decker, we found your husband dead last night at a cabin in the forest."

She gasped, clutched Lynn's hand and took a deep breath. "Go on."

"Some campers noticed flames and the responders were able to contain the fire before his body was burnt. We think he died of smoke inhalation. We'll be doing an autopsy and we would like you to identify the body. He had his wallet, but a family member is needed."

"I feel as though I'm on a roll-a-coaster," sighed Audrey. "These last few months have been terrible for me and my children."

"Where are they?" asked Lynn.

"They've been with my parents since the night Bart hit me." She was surprised by a tear that traced down her cheek. "I can be ready in a few minutes."

Dusty nodded. "Thank you."

* * *

Lynn and Dusty accompanied Audrey to the morgue. Lynn was certain there was no sadder experience. She had done the same identification when her first husband had been killed by a drunk driver.

Returning Audrey to Rory's place, Lynn asked, "Can we do anything for you?"

Audrey shook her head. "I've phoned my mother and Bart's mother. I'm going over to see my children now. Thank you for everything."

Dusty dropped Lynn at home and he ran back to the office to complete some paperwork. She was brewing a cup of tea when Piper walked in. "How is Audrey?"

"She's had a rough few months." Lynn made another cup of tea for her friend. "I told her we were here to help." Piper nodded. Lynn placed the tea on the table. "Sorry we didn't help with the clean up this morning."

Piper shrugged. "The boys and Will got it done. Come over for leftovers tonight."

As they sat quietly thinking about Audrey's challenges in the coming months, Nathan and David came into the kitchen. "Is it true?" asked Nathan. Lynn nodded.

Piper got out more cups and prepared more tea. "We were just talking about Audrey."

David sat at the table. "She is a fine woman. What happened?" He glanced at his friend. "Nathan tells me you always know the score."

"Sadly, today I do. I went with Dusty to inform Audrey then went with her to the morgue."

"Does she need anything?"

"She's with her family. Her children have been staying with her parents." Lynn sipped her tea as Piper found some cookies to place on the table. "She also has to deal with Bart's mother."

Nathan stirred his tea and asked, "He burned a cabin?"

Lynn shrugged. "They are investigating. I don't know anything more. They have to do an autopsy."

Nathan nodded as an expert. "An unattended death." David just sat bugged-eyed.

"When Dusty knows something, we'll all know something," Lynn reminded her friends.

David said, "I have to return to Raleigh tomorrow. Will you keep me informed about Audrey?"

Lynn nodded.

* * *

Quinn and Tilda arrived home after the pet adoptions and their shopping spree for supplies. Mouse screamed as the husky rushed into the house, happy to be out of the car and off a leash. The boys came running from all corners of the house anxious to see what had startled their mother.

"A dog!" shouted Paul, just in case the other boys hadn't noticed the leaping, licking animal. "Is he ours or just Tilda's?"

Mouse looked at Quinn waiting, along with the boys, for an answer.

"I have two kittens," announced Tilda as she put down a small cage and let the sisters out into the living room.

"Two?" Mouse drilled Quinn with her eyes.

"They're twins," he replied, "and Tilda said you didn't take one twin home from the hospital and leave the other for someone else to take. So we got both." He smiled weakly.

"And the dog?" Mouse was beside herself.

"That lady saw us coming," moaned Quinn. "She convinced Tilda that her brothers needed a pet, too."

"Weren't you there? Couldn't you stop this?" Mouse threw her arms out to the small zoo in her living room—kittens climbing the drapes, a dog sniffing everyone and everything while the boys argued over his name and Tilda unbagged all the pet paraphernalia.

David walked in to the mayhem. The dog rushed to him and soon had paws on David's chest. Quinn finally got the dog under control but David was covered in dog hair. "The lady told us he sheds a lot," was his helpless explanation.

David brushed his clothing. "I came to take you all to dinner. I'm leaving town in the morning," he said as he worked some dog hair out of his mouth.

"We can get carryout," suggested Colt. "We can't leave the house." He was sitting on the floor with the dog now sprawled across his legs.

"Great idea," said Quinn. "Mouse and I will go get something. You're in charge Dad." The parents disappeared.

"Where did you get these animals?" asked David.

The boys looked at Tilda. "We couldn't just take one sister 'cause they're twins. And the lady thought the boys needed a pet 'cause her brothers were nice to her."

"Isn't he cool, Gramps?" Colt asked. "Why didn't we ever have a dog in Raleigh?"

"They shed."

CHAPTER TWENTY-SIX

"What have we got?" Dusty asked his usual questions as he walked into the office.

"Maybe murder," reported Danny as he waved a clutch of papers. "The ME says the guy had a belly full of some drug. He says it was some fentanyl derivative, more powerful than he usually sees. Should he send it to the task force?"

"Tell him to send a sample to Claire, too," said Dusty as he paged through the report. "He could have taken the pills himself. Anything about arson?"

"The fire chief says his guy will be in this afternoon," replied Tee.

"How is Mrs. Decker?" The interim sheriff walked into the office.

"She's hanging on." Dusty looked at Doug. There was more to this case than the obvious. Where did Doug fit in? Dusty paced the office. He was in deep thought, causing the others to hold their comments. He finally looked at Doug, seeming to come to a conclusion. He looked at his staff. "Let's bring Doug into this discussion." They nodded. He asked, "What if Decker was set up by this drug crowd? What if he accidentally ran into someone at the cabin?"

"That's right!" gasped Tee. "You had me send out a notice that the cabin was no longer under surveillance by our department."

Doug took a seat to quietly listen to the discussion. His highway patrol experience did not routinely deal with murder. He would give it his attention because Dusty and the other detectives were giving him the respect for his position and responsibility as acting sheriff. "Please explain what we're dealing with. Murder?"

Dusty nodded. "This may be a murder set up to look like an accident."

"We suspect a leak in the task force, right?" asked Doug. "And you suspect this may be related to your ongoing drug investigation?"

The detectives nodded. They proceeded to present the information to Doug. After evaluating the evidence and debating all aspects of the case, Dusty said, "We are going to say this was an accidental fire. We're going to sit on our suspicions." He looked at Doug. "What do you think, boss?"

Doug was startled by the question. He had been worried about how he would be perceived, with Dusty as such a natural leader in the department. But Dusty, bless him, just signaled that he would respect input from Doug. The interim sheriff asked, "Do you all still think you have a bad cop in the task force?" All the detectives nodded. "Do you think the drug dealers orchestrated this fire?" Again they nodded. "Then if you want to keep them in the dark about your suspicions, I guess I agree with you." He looked at his friends. "How do you want to handle this?" He hoped they didn't want him to make a statement that made him look dumb and unprofessional.

Tee said, "Jasmine is waiting for the story. If I talk to her, it makes the fire look like an accident, not some murder that needs a high profile." And that's what happened. The story talked about a known drug user who overdosed. The implications for his family were heartbreaking. But what can you do about those druggies? Of course, Jasmine did her usual job, creating sympathy for the family and dislike for the dead man.

* * *

Colt was starting school as a high school freshman this morning. Quinn watched him thunder into Mouse's kitchen, ready for breakfast. He had started running with those detectives to get himself ready for soccer tryouts. Quinn had to smile. His son had found the life he wanted. "Morning, Mouse," called the youngster as he helped himself to a glass of orange juice.

"How was your run?" she asked as she handed him some pancakes.

"That married guy ran with us this morning."

"I thought they were all married." Quinn tried to show his knowledge of River Bend relationships.

"No, the guy that just got married, you know, like you, Dad." He grinned.

"You mean Doyle." Mouse grabbed the syrup from Tilda and handed it to Quinn to pour.

"Yeah. He told the guys he and his wife had dinner at some brewery." Colt grabbed the syrup, dealt with his pancakes, then said, "The guys said River Dog is a family bar." He looked at Mouse waiting for an explanation.

She smiled. "A few years ago three disabled vets came to town and started a brewery in Portage. That's a town up toward the river headwaters in the northern part of the county. They became a real success. They have food trucks and encourage families to have dinner."

"Can we go, Dad?" Colt had gotten the sing-song cadence of the plea from Mouse's kids.

"Can we, Mom?" The twins had just come into the kitchen.

"Have you ever been there?" Quinn asked Mouse.

"Yes." She looked sad. "I helped one of the guys and his fiancée set up some Zoom meetings with the parents when they planned their wedding." She sniffed. "He died from covid. I haven't been there since then."

"He had a wheelchair," offered Tilda. "He liked me."

Quinn looked at Mouse for an explanation, she just said, "I think we should plan on a brewery dinner tonight to celebrate the first day of school."

The motion carried.

* * *

For Quinn, driving into Portage and walking into the brewery was like going to another planet. All the men wore jeans or overalls and baseball caps. The women all had colorful manicures. But Mouse and her children seemed to know everyone. Colt even recognized a youngster from soccer camp. Soon the kids had vanished.

Mouse said, "They're checking out the food trucks and the Asian Market." She led Quinn to a high-top table with enough chairs for their family.

A petite woman in a bit of bling strutted over to greet them in her trademark Southern lilt. "Sara, honey, we haven't seen you in a while." They hugged. "Did you bring your new fella for us to meet?" She eyed Quinn.

"Shonda, this is my husband, Quinn." She turned to her husband. "Quinn, this is Shonda, she is Darwin Masterson's special friend."

"And Cooper's mama. Don't you forget that." Shonda gave Quinn a hug. "Quinn, honey, I know you're going to love this town. Why, since Granny shot my ex, life has just gotten better each day." His mouth opened but no sound came out. Shonda continued, "It was a nightmare in the making, Quinn, honey." She draped an arm around his shoulders. "Cooper crawled out through the hole in the trailer floor and ran to get help. My ex set the trailer on fire and tried to throw me in the flames. But that Granny is nobody's fool. She just aimed that six-shooter and he was done. Quinn, honey, she was upset. She got him in the heart but said she was aiming for between his eyes just like she shot her husband." Shonda hugged Mouse again. "Here I am talking and y'all must be thirsty. I'll get you one of our summer brews, Quinn, honey. You'll love it." She sashayed away.

Quinn stared at Mouse, flabbergasted. "What's wrong, Quinn, honey? Cat got your tongue?" She giggled. Before she could say more, she jumped from her chair and ran to hug an elderly woman. Returning to the table she said, "Granny, I'd like you to meet my husband, Quinn." The old woman dressed in work boots and an old housedress, looked him over.

"He looks to be a fine man. I met that boy o' his. Real polite."

Quinn nodded. "Thank you. I'm pleased to meet you."

"You stay here," Granny seemed to order. "The fellas will be by. I know Darwin seed you on his cameras."

"Thank you, Granny." Mouse hugged her again and the woman walked away, not greeting customers, but sort of giving them the evil-eye, making everyone behave.

"That was Granny with the six-shooter?" whispered Quinn. Mouse nodded.

The kids returned to the table. Colt was working his phone. "Dad, you just order on your phone and pay and the kids deliver and you tip them."

"I want dumplings," ordered Tilda.

"I know. I already ordered." Colt frowned at her. "It's Dad and Mom's turn." Everyone stared at him.

"You said Mom," Tilda reported.

Mouse quickly thought about responses and decided to say, "I hope you meant it." She walked over and hugged him. He nodded and rested his head on her shoulder.

"Do we have to call you Dad?" asked one of the twins.

Quinn thought about his answer. "No, I'm not ready to have three more kids. It's too scary. You'll have to wait until I get braver." Mouse's children looked relieved.

Shonda came back with the adult beverages and soft drinks for the kids. "Quinn, honey, this boy of yours is sure handsome." She toyed with Colt's hair. "You come up to Bernice's Beauty Boutique, Colt, honey, and we'll get you all styled for school."

"Do you cut hair?" asked Colt.

"Oh, honey, I'm the mani-pedi gal at Bernice's." She flashed her fingers and showed her toes through her high-heeled sandals. "You just come by, we'll get you ready to break hearts."

"Yes, ma'am." Colt liked the idea of becoming a high school heartbreaker.

Three young boys appeared at their table with food. Colt introduced them. "Guys, this is my dad. Dad, this is Cooper, Lucas and Caleb. They own this place." Quinn shook hands with each boy. "Dad, you have to tip them for bringing the food." Quinn took out his wallet and handed it to Colt who generously gave each youngster a ten-dollar bill.

Quinn looked at Mouse as the boys dashed off. "This is a pretty expensive place."

The rest of the evening passed with the other brewers and spouses stopping at the table to be introduced. Mouse knew Quinn had a lot of questions and hoped he would wait until they were in bed.

* * *

As Lynn and Dusty settled into bed for the night, he asked, "How was your day? I'm sorry I missed dinner." He settled comfortably under the sheets.

"Well, I got a call from the humane shelter. Quinn showed up and took two kittens and a dog and left them with a check for three thousand dollars. They were thrilled. All I did was tell him where to look for pets and the humane group thinks I'm a big hero." Lynn kissed his cheek and snuggled into his arms.

"Take the credit. Next month someone will blame you for something."

"That's philosophical."

"No, it's reality." He ended their bedroom conversation the way he usually did.

CHAPTER TWENTY-SEVEN

"Darwin, honey?" Darwin Masterson's eyes popped open. He hadn't heard that sort of panic in Shonda's voice since that night of the trailer fire.

"What?" He reached out to turn on a light.

She was standing beside the bed. "I thought I heard Cooper and went to check." She pointed to his phone. "When I came back that was flashing."

He scramble to sit up and grabbed the phone. Pressing some code and scanning the screen, he swore, "Who's that?" Shonda climbed onto the bed and kneeling leaned on his back to watch the tiny scene. "We got a prowler in my office." Darwin, IT director for River Dog Brewery and most of the businesses and the volunteer fire department in Portage, had the town wired with an emphasis on enhanced security in his domain, the tightly guarded room, above the brewery offices. As he watched the intruder, he sent a link from the video to Dusty.

In a snug bedroom in River Bend, Dusty's phone squealed. He grabbed it before the sound could awaken Lynn. "Too late," she mumbled, "I'm up."

They both sat up as Dusty scanned his phone. "There's a break-in at River Dog. Someone's trying to do something with Darwin's computers." He studied the screen and then made some calls. The first was to the dispatcher to get a patrol car to the site. The second was to Doug. "I'll pick you up in five."

"Dusty, he was asleep."

"But he lives next door and he's the sheriff."

"The interim," she reminded him as he pulled on clothes and ran from the room in his stocking feet.

Doug was coming out the back door when Dusty drove up. "You wanna fill me in?" he asked as he buckled up.

"There's a break-in at River Dog. Darwin sent me a video link. I got a patrol car dispatched."

* * *

Sherri Steiner was on patrol outside of Portage wondering what she could do to stay awake when she caught the call from the dispatcher. "I'm on my way."

When she arrived in Portage she parked on the backside of the volunteer fire department, knowing that she could go on foot and cover the front of the building and one end of the alleyway from that location. Collecting her gear, she quietly left the car, slipping into her vest. At the corner she heard gravel crunch and then felt a gun at her back. Shit!

* * *

"Who's patrolling out that way tonight?" the interim sheriff asked.

Dusty said, "You're the sheriff. Call dispatch and get in the loop. I'm driving." And he was, at a breakneck speed on the highway and hellbent for Portage.

"It's that little Sherri," groaned the sheriff.

"She can handle it. But the dispatcher can let you talk to her."

Doug spoke with the dispatcher and soon heard Sherri acknowledge. He shouted into his phone, "We're on the way. You be careful."

Sherri said, "I'm not alone."

Hearing that, Dusty almost stood on the gas pedal as Doug shouted, "Not alone?"

Another voice came on the radio. "Is that you, Dusty? This is Special Agent Wilson."

"This is Sheriff Doug Fiore. Special Agent? Are you FBI? And why are you here without telling us?"

Dusty chuckled. "Wilson's out of the Charlotte office. You met him on that Kip Mahaffey investigation."

Doug turned his attention back to the radio. "Special Agent Wilson, we'll be there shortly."

"No lights or sirens, please," requested the agent. "We've got the building surrounded and want to take this guy alive." Silence. "He's moving." The connection ended.

The men swore in unison as the car flew toward Portage.

* * *

Dusty and Doug arrived finding Portage Main Street in chaos. Sherri Steiner was enraged and looked as though she were ready to behead a very large fellow in FBI SWAT gear. CJ Kirtley, hands cuffed behind him, was as enraged as Sherri and was shouting in his best rich-boy-entitled attitude with all the Mastersons who had arrived in Darwin's truck acting as an interested audience. And close to the doorway of Bernice's Beauty Boutique, Claire Conti, agent in charge of the FBI Charlotte office, was gesturing with one hand as she clutched her phone to her ear with the other and shouted.

"Wanna get back in the car and go home?" Dusty asked the interim sheriff.

Doug studied the scene. "You handle Claire. I think she's sweet on you." Dusty rolled his eyes. Doug continued, "I'll deal with the guy in handcuffs. We know him, don't we?"

"That's CJ Kirtley. He's the guy who held Sara at gunpoint a few weeks ago."

Doug groaned. "I'll take him. I think I'll let Sherri bring that special agent down to size. What about all the Mastersons?" Doug squinted. "I think they even brought Granny."

Dusty snorted. "Watch out for her six-shooter." The two officers moved out to follow Plan B.

Doug approached Darwin Masterson who was standing in front of his truck. Zeke was leaning against the bumper. He was using his crutches because he had left the house so quickly with no time for his prosthesis. Kane Solomon was quietly surveying the activity made very dramatic by headlights from several vehicles. "Good evening," said the sheriff. "I think we have this under control. Is there somewhere you could all wait while we get organized?"

Zeke yawned. "We'll open the office." He nodded toward the entry next to Bernice's. "I'll get the coffee going."

"I'd appreciate that," acknowledged a grateful Doug. The Mastersons moved on and he proceeded to confront the perp. Doug listened to CJ's ranting and complaining as he watched Zeke through the storefront windows of the brewery office get the coffee going.

Dusty walked over to Claire and waved a hand attracting her attention. She said something into her phone as she indicated Dusty should come closer. He was cautious, moving slowly, but Claire grabbed him pulling him in to listen to the phone conversation. Out of the corner of his eye, he saw Zeke start the coffee.

* * *

Married life was all that Quinn had hoped, especially every night snuggled in bed with Mouse. Until tonight when they were both startled from a deep sleep by buzzing phones.

"Wha?"

"My phone, sorry," mumbled Mouse. "Hello." While someone replied to her greeting another phone kept buzzing. "Quinn, I think that's your phone."

"Wha?" He untangled from the sheets and grabbed his phone. "Hello."

Both of them listened, made responses, cursed and hung up.

Turning to one another with identical angry and confused expressions, Quinn said, "You go first."

Mouse was out of bed pulling on her honeymoon robe It was a calming garment. She took a breath. "Dusty is bringing the FBI over here. Some agent is angry at the General and I have to set up a late night online meeting with the agent and Kyle." She shook her head. "I have no clue what's going on."

"Maybe I can help," Quinn was pulling on some sweatpants. "That was the sheriff." He looked at the phone he had tossed on the bed. "CJ was arrested at that brewery in Portage by the FBI. He wants me to go to the jail and bail him out. The sheriff is coming over to speak to me, hinting that us rich folks better stay out of this FBI drama." He pulled on a t-shirt. "I have no clue what's going on."

* * *

By the time Sara and Quinn were dressed appropriately for late night visitors, a crowd was at their door. Quinn opened the door to the soft knock. He was glad they were trying not to wake the kids. He welcomed everyone by saying, "Coffee is in the kitchen."

Dusty walked in with a woman in remnants of SWAT gear. She was angry. The detective said to Quinn, "Danny's coming over with something from the bakery."

"They're open at," he checked his very sophisticated wrist thingy that Colt had encouraged him to purchase, "three-thirty?"

"Nah, he's got a key."

The woman barked, "Why are we here? I want to talk to Kyle."

Dusty said, "Special Agent Claire Conti, this is our host, Quinn Templeton, and his wife, Sara, knows Kyle."

Sara came to the door to help Quinn who seemed ready to send everyone packing. "Dusty, coffee's in the kitchen." She greeted her guests.

"That's his wife?" Claire muttered. She turned to Sara, "I want to talk to Kyle."

Sara, with her hair in a ponytail, dressed in an old t-shirt and jogging shorts, and barefooted, asked, "Who are you?" in a take no prisoners voice.

Claire smiled. "Tough girl, eh? You must be one of Kyle's secret weapons." She held out her hand to Sara. "Claire Conti, FBI."

Sara shook hands then pulled her phone out of her back pocket and scanned her text messages. "Kyle is sending a secure link in fifteen minutes." She smiled at Claire. "You have time for coffee." Danny walked in with three bakery boxes. She nodded toward him and the treats. "And time for a snack."

All this time several other people had drifted in. Quinn had remained at the door directing traffic to the coffee. He finally figured out that the SWAT geared people were FBI and the young woman in police uniform was a local deputy and the guy with her but not in uniform must be the sheriff. He knew that because, the other detective he knew, the one without the bakery boxes, a guy named Mars, greeted the man by saying, "Hey, Sheriff. Dusty bring you along?"

Sara had gotten Claire a cup of coffee and returned to the living room. Quinn was distracted by other matters as the new dog came racing down the stairs to greet the visitors with Colt running behind him, stopping to take in the activity and grinning. Collaring the dog he turned to his father. "This is so cool."

"You and the dog go back to bed," said Quinn.

"Are you kidding?" Colt gulped because he usually didn't speak to his father that way. "I mean he's too excited. Maybe I should take him outside to pee first." Quinn thought that sounded reasonable and nodded, then stopped in surprise as Tilda came out of the kitchen munching a pastry.

"The twins are making more coffee. Uncle Mars said we could have a snack and then go back to bed." She climbed the stairs, a little kitten at her heels.

* * *

Soon Kyle and Claire were yelling at one another across the ether with Sara as referee. The General shouted, "My office isn't at you beck and call. This isn't a police state. You have no warrant and you can't request unsubstantiated searches of offshore accounts."

"I know you can tell me what I want to know," Claire shouted in return. "We've been following this money and this is the first perp we've collared who has a connection. We're working under an order signed by our director to dismantle a drug and weapons operation."

"I don't care who signed what. The DOJ doesn't have any jurisdiction over this project."

While they argued back and forth, essentially repeating themselves, over and over, Sara moved to another one of the screens arrayed on her desk. Tapping, scrolling, tapping studying the data, she ignored the video argument and began to put two and two together. Before Claire could see anything, Sara punched a key and her screen dissolved to a screensaver photo of her children.

Claire and Kyle continued to shout at one another.

In another corner of the house Dusty and Doug were speaking with Quinn. "It seems the FBI has been watching some bank accounts and tracked some sort of signal back to your brother-in-law. They followed him to the brewery and arrested him." Dusty was explaining.

Quinn sounded confused as he asked, "Why?"

Doug shrugged. "We're hoping Claire will tell us more. We don't understand why he broke into the brewery. But he made it clear that you would have our heads and bail him out." The sheriff studied Sara's husband. "You don't look like you want to bail him out."

"It's that obvious?" Quinn ran his fingers through his hair.

Colt, who had allowed the dog a quick pee, was at his side. "Uncle CJ was stealing our money." Quinn looked ready to throttle his son while the sheriff just looked interested.

Back in Sara's office, Kyle asked her, "Can you set up a private talk?"

She looked around her space and found a solution. "Just one minute." She turned to Claire, "If you'll excuse us?"

Claire scowled but walked out of the sunroom/office. Sara followed her and called, "Sherri?"

The petite deputy replied, "Yes, ma'am?"

"I'm closing these doors to have a private talk. Please see that I'm not disturbed." Sara closed the doors. Sherri took her place as guard in front and by her stance dared any of those FBI agents to try to get through the doors.

In her office with Kyle on screen, Sara said, "We're alone."

* * *

Kyle who looked as though he were in pajama tops, squinted into his screen. "What's all this about?" He accepted a cup of coffee from an unseen assistant.

"I think it's a big mess of two cases converging," she said. She brought up the other monitors and did some tapping. Returning her attention to the General she began, "It's a confusing story, Kyle." She blew out her breath as she studied her other monitors. "I can see some jurisdictional conflicts." Kyle squinted out of her screen. He didn't like conflict. "Stay with me," she murmured in a placating voice. "Our part begins when we helped David Templeton learn about his son-in-law's embezzling." Kyle nodded. She continued, "Other characters who committed crimes in River Bend, names I only know because I've read some of their names in the local newspaper. Well, these other characters have offshore accounts linked to Templeton's son-in-law. One of the felons is a local attorney caught in one of Claire's drug raids."

"FBI? Drugs are usually local." He heard Sara clicking her keyboard. Then he heard her gasp. "What?" he demanded.

"Stay with me, Kyle. This is getting tangled. There is another guy who died trying to escape the police." Clickety click. Sara looked into the screen. "Kyle, I think I should speak with our local detectives. They might straighten this out before you and Claire go to war."

"I'm listening." Kyle sipped his coffee.

"Can I talk with Dusty, a local detective, and give you all the information tomorrow?"

He yawned. "Yeah, tell Claire I'm working up the chain of command." Kyle snorted. "Just make sure you're not alone with her."

* * *

Sara walked out of her office. Sherri smirked at the agents all gathered close by hoping to catch hints of the private conversation. Sara said, "Thank you, Sherri." Claire was standing in the middle of the living room ready to explode. Sara smiled.

"Claire, Kyle's going to check with his boss about just what information he can share to assist your investigation. He says your boss will hear from his boss and they will handle the paperwork to settle things."

Claire wasn't happy. "I'm in the middle of a drug investigation that involves half this state and maybe others."

"Kyle understands, but he has to operate under the mandate he was given."

Claire searched the room and nodded to her staff. "Let's get out of here." She turned to Dusty and Doug. "Hold my prisoner until you hear from me." She left in a huff, trailed by a half dozen agents clutching gear, coffee to-go cups and pastry.

Quinn and Sara looked around their house. Only local law enforcement remained. Doug turned to all the staff, "Let's wrap this up later." He turned to Dusty. "How about we all meet in your office about eleven?" Nods and yawns all around. They thanked the Templetons and shuffled out the door.

Sara touched Dusty's arm. "Can I join you at eleven?"

Dusty raised an eyebrow at the unusual question. "Sure." He followed his staff out the door.

Doing a sweep of the downstairs, Sara found the twins asleep on the long seating banquette in the kitchen. Quinn found Colt sleeping at the foot of the stairs, protected by the dog. Colt opened his eyes. "This was so cool." Quinn helped him up to his room followed by the dog, then returned to help Sara carry the twins to their beds.

As Sara and Quinn tumbled into bed, he asked, "What happened?"

She yawned in his face. "I'll tell you in the morning." She was asleep before he could ask another question.

CHAPTER TWENTY-EIGHT

"Mouse?" called Quinn, "Is anyone going to school? It's almost eleven."

She was dressed in her professional clothes and directing traffic in the kitchen. "They're going in late. Colt doesn't want to miss soccer practice and the twins want to tell their friends about the FBI raid."

"We weren't raided!"

She patted his arm. "I think Tilda may stay home." They glanced at the little girl resting her head on the kitchen table, Cheerios tangled in her hair. "I have a meeting. You're in charge." She dashed out the door.

Quinn's phone buzzed and Colt answered it. "Hey, Gramps! . . . . Yeah, it was so cool . . FBI and police!" Quinn snatch the phone out of his hands.

"Hello, Dad."

David was yelling so loud, everyone heard, "What the hell is going on there?"

"Let me go into another room, Dad. The kids are eating breakfast."

He pulled the phone from his ear as everyone heard David yell, "Breakfast!?"

Closing the door to Mouse's office, Quinn said, "Dad, please calm down. It was a very late night around here. We're all still tired."

"I just want to know why Kyle called me about CJ's arrest."

"It seems CJ tried to break into a local brewery last night. The FBI had been watching him." When David didn't respond to that statement, Quinn asked, "Do you already know about all this?"

"Sort of. Kyle wasn't real clear. He mumbled national security a few times. All I gleaned from the conversation early this morning is that CJ is in jail and the FBI doesn't care about him anymore."

Quinn was confused by that statement. The FBI sure wanted CJ's ass last night. "Do you want me to handle it here?"

"See what you can find out. I think they can hold him for forty-eight hours." David was silent a moment, then he asked, "FBI? Raid?"

Quinn laughed. "They caught him trying to break into a brewery and CJ demanded the sheriff notify me for bail. And the FBI wanted to talk with your friend, Kyle about something. So they woke up me and Mouse." He laughed again. "Colt was impressed to find FBI in SWAT gear all over the house at four in the morning."

"He is certainly experiencing a different kind of life," mused David.

"And he's enjoying every minute."

"Where has CJ been?" asked David. "Madeline told us he disappeared."

"It didn't come up in the discussion last night or early this morning," chuckled Quinn. "Ask your friend Kyle."

"So you still think you made the right decision moving there?" David's voice showed his displeasure with FBI midnight raids and brewery robberies touching Quinn and Colt.

"It's the best decision I ever made." Quinn wandered back into the kitchen to wave off the boys as they left for school. Tilda was still asleep at the table.

David chortled into the phone and then asked, "What should we do with CJ? You're close to the situation."

Quinn was touched. David usually took the lead, giving Quinn his marching orders. But things had been changing recently. "I think we can scare him because of the FBI investigation. I want him to move to the Caymans and stay with his money for a year or two, so I might suggest the long stay would allow the investigation to blow over. He has about 10 or so million there, plus the stock and property Margaret signed over."

"That's a start," replied David, "And more ideas than I have. Maybe you can chat with that attorney, Grayson, to put some formal context to the discussion."

"Good idea, I'll call him."

* * *

Tee walked into the office at the regular time reading a late night or early morning text from Dusty. *You're in charge. Meeting in office at 11. Later.*

She had scanned the message and snickered. Dusty had hauled Mars and Danny out of bed last night but let her sleep. She got the usual morning work done, returned phone calls, answered email, stonewalled the press because she had no information anyway. But promised to call the reporter, her friend Jasmine Fuller, as soon as she was in the loop.

By ten-thirty Dusty and Danny slouched into the office. Mars came a few minutes later. She smiled at the tired guys. "Coffee is ready and I ordered lunch for eleven-thirty. And Dusty, Claire wants you to call as soon as you're in. She said she felt guilty calling your cell."

As Danny and Mars brought Tee up to date, Dusty contacted Claire. "What's up?"

She huffed into the phone, "That General won't give me the information I need for this investigation. I have to wait for authorization through channels." Huff. Huff. "What he did say is that the perp isn't a part of my investigation. I have to trust that, so the perp is yours."

"He's not part of this drug thing?"

"No. All this computer tracing and I don't think we're any closer to the main man." She sounded tired and unhappy.

"I thought you had an undercover op going."

Claire scoffed, "They don't happen overnight, big guy. Don't worry. If we start to move I'll be in touch. I just got my operation funding organized last week." She sighed into the phone. "I hope this fiasco didn't ruin the set up. Talk to you later." She ended the call.

Dusty assembled his staff. "Doug will be here at eleven. And Sara Margolin, I mean, Templeton is joining us." The staff was as puzzled as Dusty. "She'll tell us when she gets here.

* * *

Sara arrived out of breath, followed by Doug. "Sorry," he apologized as he bumped into her. "That Templeton fellow had Herbie call me about that fellow Kirtley's status." They all looked at him. "I don't know what to tell him. So I said we would discuss this at our meeting."

"Is he Kirtley's attorney or Templeton's attorney?"

"Good question." He took the coffee Tee handed him. "Herbie is working for Templeton because he seemed to want us to cut this guy loose and scare him into moving to some island. But I don't understand all the relationships here."

They looked at Sara. She blinked. "Quinn and David were on the phone when I left the house. But I would guess they want to be rid of CJ, maybe exile him to the Caymans."

Doug shrugged. "I'll talk to Grayson again and see if he makes sense."

Dusty cleared his throat and asked Sara, "Why did you want to join us this morning?"

All eyes turned to her. She blushed then cleared her throat as she placed her laptop on Dusty's desk. "When I was talking with the General last night about Claire's case, I noticed some interesting relationships." She looked very apologetic. "Don't ask how I got some of this information. But some of it I just read in the newspaper about your cases. Let's just say real crime is better than fiction." Everyone was on alert.

"Should we be taking notes?" asked Mars.

"You might need a road map," she replied. Danny nodded and pulled the white board away from the wall. He had just cleaned off all the information about the Bart Decker investigation. A good thing because Sara didn't need to see their notes about a suspicion of murder. He stood ready to write.

Sara began, "I'm going to start with my involvement. With the General's approval Janet and I tracked CJ Kirtley's money schemes to offshore accounts. Last evening as I tried to help the General determine how much information we could share with the FBI, I found that CJ's offshore accounts were somehow related to Kip Mahaffey's money." That surprised everyone.

"But Mahaffey is an FBI case. We don't have anything to do with him."

"We-l-l-l." With that sound she had everyone's attention again. "Those accounts are also related in some way to that fellow Rothman and the Mastersons are in this somewhere."

Mars snapped his fingers. "That's why CJ was at the brewery!"

"Does that mean the Mastersons are in some offshore scam?" asked Tee.

Sara shook her head. "I think they were just helping themselves to Rothman's money." And that began her complex explanation of how CJ Kirtley, Rupert Rothman and Kip Mahaffey all intertwined. Dusty and his staff were able to help fill in the blanks and connect more dots. When she was finished she said, "Let me take this back to the General." She looked very serious. "I think there is another signal we haven't sorted out yet."

"That might be the drug connection we're working on with Claire." Dusty was pensive. "Be careful," he warned Sara. "You're getting close to some evil people."

She nodded. "I'll pass that on to the General. I shouldn't be involved much longer."

"What about the Mastersons?"

She smiled. "You need evidence of a crime and I won't give it to you. You wouldn't even know they were involved if I hadn't told you. The General will deal with them." Closing her laptop she declined an invitation to share lunch and checked her wrist thingy that did everything but cook. "The General is waiting."

* * *

When Sara left the room, they all stared at one another. It was an opportunity for Tee to hand out lunches. Everyone moved to the break area table. Mars got drinks while Danny moved the white board so everyone could read it.

"Now what?" asked Doug. They all looked at Dusty.

He was chewing on his jalapeño-chicken wrap and seemed to choke as he became the focus of the discussion. A gulp of iced tea. "Claire said that during her investigation into Mahaffey and while looking for some related drug activity in our part of the state she caught Kirtley nosing around some offshore accounts she thought were related to her case. They traced Kirtley's signal, found him, and followed him to River Dog. But when she asked Sara's client, the General, he wouldn't let her know anything about those accounts. But he did say CJ isn't involved in her investigation."

Doug asked, "Should we even be involved with all this?"

Dusty shrugged. "I think it's all above our pay grade. Today we learned that Kip Mahaffey and this Kirtley were in some kind of partnership with Rothman." He looked at Doug. "He's a guy who jumped from the parking deck and died when we were in pursuit."

"I think I remember that."

"Does that mean Mahaffey is in for more charges?"

"No." Dusty finished his sandwich and looked for cookies. "According to Claire, they got there too late to catch Kip pulling out offshore money. But they found these accounts and started watching. That's when they got Kirtley as he investigated the accounts that Claire says had already been emptied." Empty accounts? Drugs? They were all confused. "And she's pissed because the General won't give her more information. So Kirtley is ours because the FBI can't connect him to anything besides looking into an empty offshore account."

Doug snatched a cookie from the passing box. "You guys are great, lunch and entertainment. I'll give our Sherri credit for the arrest. I'll call Herbie to get Kirtley out of the jail. I don't want some rich guy suing us for giving him covid. It's still a risk in confined spaces." He tossed his trash in the container and waved as he left the office.

They looked at one another. "What does that mean?" asked Danny.

Dusty yawned. "We agree with Herbie and Quinn's proposal. Get this guy out of town. Mars, you go with them and look mean. Danny stay here and keep things under control. Tee and I are going to figure out what to tell the media about last night." He ate the last cookie. "And we still have a suspicious murder that might be related to drug distribution."

* * *

When Sara connected with Kyle he was eating lunch. Her stomach growled. She should have accepted half of Tee's avocado-bacon wrap. "I hope you've worked this out," the General growled around a large burger.

"I think I have an explanation." He nodded for her to continue. "We got involved. Or I should say I got us involved when we helped David Templeton track CJ Kirtley's embezzling." Kyle nodded. She continued,

"A few months earlier, Claire arrested a local attorney for some serious drug offenses and Medicaid fraud."

"FBI? River Bend?"

Sara scowled. "Don't interrupt. We'll never get through this if you do." She gave him her best mom's-in-charge look. "The local attorney and the director of a local health clinic were running a drug operation on the side. Claire was able to come in because they suspected fraud issues around Medicaid and Medicare funds. The man they arrested, Kip Mahaffey, was able to keep his offshore funds secret during the initial investigation. He managed somehow to deposit those funds into an investment management firm created by Kirtley to help move offshore money to legitimate stateside institutions. Mahaffey needed the money to pay for his defense. He'll go to prison for, I think, mismanaging some of his estate accounts, fraud and drugs." She rubbed her forehead. This was a complex explanation and she was hungry.

Kyle sipped his coffee, apparently entertained. "I know you're going to connect more dots."

"I am. Please bear with me. Based on what I can see in our tracking data, Kip Mahaffey had been in some partnership with CJ Kirtley. That's where you and Claire cross investigations. But we're not finished." She tapped more on her other screen. "Even before all this with the Templetons and Mahaffey, there was an investigation and murder, and several other deaths."

"How big is your town?"

Sara laughed. "This is very complex. In any case, I'll stick with the basics and try to explain why we got involved in a robbery at a brewery last night." She cleared her throat. "Back to that murder. The folks who own the brewery lost a cousin a year or two ago." Sara stopped and collected her thoughts. "She was murdered by some fellow and her family found a computer in her belongings. Our local police gave me some of this information. I can trace the family's actions backward now that I know they're involved. This family realized that their cousin was receiving a monthly sum for some reason from a man who died as he ran from the police."

"Let me get this straight. The cousin died and this fellow died. Did he kill the cousin?"

"No, she was killed by someone else and that's not relevant here."

"But it sounds interesting."

"Kyle, stick with watching your soap operas for drama. We'll never finish if you want details." Sara glared into her screen and Kyle looked chastised. She continued, "The relatives accessed the accounts offshore because they figured out how or found the passwords and began withdrawing small sums. I think they were doing it to help the family business stay afloat during lockdown." Another forehead rub. "The relatives decided to close down the accounts for some reason. At the same time, Quinn's brother-in-law may have been watching the accounts for his own reasons and followed the family's signal back to the brewery. He appears to have been in some sort of partnership with several men who all died by various means. Except Mahaffey who withdrew his money to fund his defense."

"So your criminal brother-in-law who was stealing from David came to River Bend to reclaim his money?"

"I think that's close enough to the scenario." Sara hung her head as fatigue set in.

"How much money are we talking about? And how much did that family take?" Kyle asked.

"Twenty or thirty million of which the family may have gotten five to seven over time since the death of their cousin." She stared at her computer again. "I can't account for any of the money except what came to River Bend folks."

"What do you mean?" Kyle rubbed his eyes.

"There's about twenty-five million that has vanished. Someone with more skill than CJ or the local family here in town has taken the money."

Kyle thought that over and chuckled. "That's Claire's problem. What's with the money we do know about?"

Sara gave Kyle what he always thought of as her virgin bride look. She smiled innocently. "I should tell you that the family in question owns a brewery that was established by three disabled veterans, Marines, who were all injured in an explosion in Afghanistan."

Bam! He hadn't seen that coming. "Disabled?" She nodded. "Marines?" She nodded again. Kyle stared off into space. Sara held her breath. Finally, "I've got some ideas."

"Claire?" FBI?"

"Not your affair. She and I will work things out. We may have a line on someone she's hunting. I'll get my team looking into the rest of the money. Maybe I can surprise her with a clue."

"What about the Marines?"

"My guys will erase the brewery signal." He chuckled. "Let me solve the problem, then I'll send Janet out to have a little talk with them."

She nodded her thanks.

They signed off.

* * *

Walter Varney read the story in the River Bend Chronicle about that jackass CJ Kirtley and his attempted break-in at that brewery. The garbled story suggested that Kirtley was following an internet thief to Portage. The whole story got Varney thinking. He recalled that when he closed out all the Cayman accounts he had left a teaser. Some internet cowboy had taken the money and Varney had followed his trail back toward River Bend. He had chuckled at the time and allowed the thief to keep the two million. He had been entertained with the challenge of following his signal.

Kirtley must have better computer skills or a better hacker to have followed the signal to Portage. Varney had only been able to get to somewhere in western North Carolina with his tracking. Portage, hmmm? He made a call and learned that a fellow named Darwin Masterson was the internet guru in that small burg. He had the whole town wired with an emphasis on security. Varney chuckled, that's why Kirtley got caught. Masterson had the town tied up.

All this thinking suggested that he might be looking at a solution for a problem he had been trying to solve. Well, not solve, but be prepared just in case. Walter Varney was a family man. That is, he had a divorced sister who had two teenaged children. Over the years she had helped him, especially during his divorce and he had helped her, usually with extra money because her ex was an idiot. During his divorce she had allowed him to shelter assets in her name in a shell corporation. He never dissolved the corporation and had been putting aside some investments for his old age to be safe from all his criminal partners. But what should he do with the Cayman accounts? And he decided that Darwin Masterson was his man.

As he sat alone in his cluttered, dusty, warehouse office, he listed his accounts and passwords. He wrote a note to his sister telling her that if she found this letter, he was dead and he was leaving her his offshore accounts. She should contact this fellow and he would understand what to do with all the codes. He added Darwin's name and contact information to the letter and sealed it. He would place it in his desk drawer at home this evening.

CHAPTER TWENTY-NINE

"We're closed until four," a fellow shouted from the shadows of River Dog Brewery.

"I know," came a timid reply. "I'm here to talk with Mr. Masterson." A woman holding a baby at her shoulder walked out of shadows and into a sunlit square highlighting the barroom floor.

"JAN-ET?" came an excited squeal from another shadowed corner. "It that you?" A woman came rushing into the sunlight.

"BAR-BA-RA?" came an answering squeal. Janet juggling the baby in her arms rushed to embrace the woman. They were soon chattering, crying, laughing and clinging to one another. Barbara and Janet had both been victims of a serial rapist several years ago. Barbara had been raped but Janet, being groomed as the next victim, had escaped because the rapist had been murdered by one of his victims. They had spent time together in group therapy with Lee Hennessey.

"Ahem." A man had followed Janet into the bar pushing a stroller with two youngsters strapped in. He tried to rescue the baby Janet had squeezed in her arms.

From behind Barbara came a voice of equal concern. "I'm Mr. Masterson." The bearded man limped to stand beside his wife, his prosthetic leg exposed beneath his Bermuda shorts.

The women separated. Laughed, hugged one more time. "This is my husband Zeke," said Barbara, acknowledging the man at her side.

Janet checked the baby for crushed ribs, passed him to Barbara and shook Zeke's hand. "I'm Janet Bergman. And this is Tim and our kids." Tim waved a hand and the stroller duet watched the man with the funny leg. Janet, unskilled in social situations, replied to Barbara's husband "No, you're not the correct Masterson. I need Darwin Masterson."

"He's my cousin," said Zeke. He turned to a CCTV camera and waved. "He'll be here in a minute." He studied his guests. "Bergman?"

"Yes, I'm the old sheriff's daughter."

Zeke squinted at Tim. "And you're retired military."

"Navy." Tim grinned.

"Marines," came another voice from the shadows. Kane Solomon, another brewery partner and retired Marine, walked into the sun and held out a hand to Tim.

"Barbara?" shouted another man from the shadows, "I got this supplier on the phone. Can you talk to him?"

Barbara passed the baby to Zeke. "Be right there." She turned to Janet. "That's our brewmaster, Lonny. Don't you leave." She rushed out of the bar.

"Here's Darwin," said Zeke as he handed the baby to Janet and hustled over to chat with Tim and Kane as they stood in front of the Memorial Wall, a solemn, heartfelt, yet sometimes playful, tribute to military service. Several young boys had appeared and were helping the toddlers escape from the stroller to play in the designated child safe area.

Janet looked over the brewery IT director as he approached. He seemed to be what the general had suggested, a self-taught computer hacker. She just had to make certain he understood that hacking was no longer in his future. "Can we talk?"

After the events of the other night, Darwin had been expecting a visit from someone. Was this lady it? "Am I in trouble?"

Janet kissed the baby's head and smiled, "No. But you can't hack anymore."

He nodded. "We just took a little money in case the bar had trouble."

"We?"

Granny Masterson appeared at his side. "My boys built this place and we had to protect them."

Janet had stopped to get some background from her father before coming to Portage to meet the Mastersons. This must be Miz Masterson. Her father had a lot of respect for the woman. She held out a hand. "I'm Janet Bergman. My father sends his regards."

Granny shook the hand then took the baby. "He's a good fellow. Much obliged." She rested the baby on her shoulder. "We ain't in trouble?" The baby gave a little burp.

"No, ma'am." Janet moved into the shadows and nodded for Darwin and Granny to follow. "You almost got caught in a dangerous game. The money you took belongs to some drug dealers. The general sent me to warn you to stay away. He had his staff erase your signal. He also fixed it so the money is yours. He learned about the men who built the brewery and their bravery. He said to tell them he appreciated their service."

Granny sniffed and kissed the baby's head. "That would be my grandson Zeke, that there fellow Kane talking to your man and our Eddie. We lost him about a year ago to this here virus."

"Darwin, honey?" A whirlwind of energy in an iridescent pink smock rushed into the bar. "Darwin, honey, Barbara says we should order lunch and don't let her friends leave." She kissed Darwin, kissed Granny, kissed the baby's head, and turned to Janet. "I'm Shonda and Darwin here is my sweet, lovin' man." She held out her hand. Darwin's face flamed.

Janet took the hand as Shonda inspected it. "I'm Janet a friend of Barbara's."

Shonda turned the hand over and commented in her thick Southern charm style, "Janet, honey, you come see me. I do mani-pedis at Bernice's Beauty Boutique next door. You need some attention. I have a special family rate." She returned Janet's hand. "What should we order? You nursing? We'll make it not too spicy. How about Asian?" Janet opened her mouth to reply but Shonda had moved on to Tim and the other men. "Kane, honey, let's call Han to feed everyone. Zeke, honey, Barbara said steamed dumplings for the little kids." She looked around. "There they are." She ran over to the play area and kissed all the children including Janet's toddlers. She returned to Tim who was still attached to the empty stroller. "You must be the baby daddy."

"I'm Tim."

But he couldn't say more because Shonda drawled on, "Tim, honey, we're getting lunch. You and Zeke and Kane order. The boys will collect it." She rushed over to Granny, took the baby, nuzzled her, kissed her head and handed her back to Granny. "I'll be right back. I left Mrs. Harrington drying. We tried a new color. That woman is becoming a real vamp." Shonda vanished into the shadows.

Kane slapped Tim on the back. "Well, Navy, I guess you're having lunch with us. I'll call the Asian Market." When he got off the phone he said, "I told him to send whatever he had. He said ten minutes." Kane looked at the three boys close by. They took off.

Zeke signaled to Tim, "Take the big table we'll all join you in a minute." Tim pulled out his wallet. Zeke pushed it away. "We got lunch. But you owe each of those boys five bucks for pick-up and delivery." He limped over to Janet and Darwin. "I see you found the other Masterson. What did you need?"

Granny and Darwin held their breath. Janet said, "I do a little IT work and heard that Darwin can sometimes be helpful if I get stuck." In the shadows Tim rolled his eyes—a little IT work? But they were getting lunch and he hoped it included a beer!

Zeke beamed with pride. "My cousin here is the best I've seen. He keeps up our IT and security. Why, the other night someone tried to break in." Janet nodded and Zeke told the whole story. The food came. Barbara and the rest of the family turned up for lunch. It was a great afternoon. And Tim got a beer.

* * *

"Thank you for setting up this meeting," David told Lynn as they arranged the chairs around her small office table. He had come into town with a plan that Rory had encouraged. "I didn't know how to approach Audrey."

Lynn felt tears come to her eyes. David took her hand. She said, "It's been a very difficult time for her and the children. She resigned her job and is planning to find a job away from all the drama."

"I want her to work with me on developmental issues." David had invested years and millions of dollars in research and support for people with Jimmy's mental disabilities. "She has done so much with the program here. I think she can become a national leader in the area speaking from a platform that could be funded by my foundation."

There was a light tap on the office door. Audrey walked in. "Good morning, Lynn. What did -? Mr. Templeton? I'm sorry. Am I interrupting a meeting?"

"Please take a seat, Mrs. Decker," David invited the woman. "I asked Lynn to bring us together." He winked at Lynn. "She can always find time to help me."

"Do you want me to leave, David?" asked Lynn.

"Please stay," he replied. "I think Mrs. Decker will be more comfortable."

Audrey took a seat. She sniffed and tapped a tissue at the edge of her eye. "I'm having a difficult time acting as a professional these days. I feel that I am, in part, responsible for all that has happened."

David said, "This is certainly a tragedy for all concerned. I'm sorry for the loss of your husband. And, I'm sorry to say, I'm here to take advantage of the situation." He smiled at Audrey. "I have funded a lot of work in the area of developmentally delayed adults. I want you to come and work with me. I want to build on the program you started here in River Bend. I want to bring it together with other best practice models and see what we can accomplish."

"Who would believe me after this disaster?" Audrey sobbed.

"In a year or two, no one will remember," replied David. "I've seen people reinvent themselves after far more, shall we say, interesting episodes. It's your work that will be your focus."

Lynn brought some coffee to the table. "I think David's offer is just what you need. You and the children can leave River Bend and have a job that's perfect for you." Audrey started to speak, but Lynn continued, "You don't have to punish yourself and your children. I know you claim some of the responsibility for Mr. Thurman's death. And Bart's death. But no matter what blame you claim as yours, you still must continue your life and support your children."

"I'm ready to leave town," Audrey admitted, "But I can't leave James's brother. There is no one else."

"Who has guardianship?" asked David.

"I do."

"Then that problem is solved. We can move him to live with my son, Jimmy. If you move to Raleigh, you and your children can help me care for both of them." David sipped his coffee but kept his eyes on Audrey.

"You certainly have thought of everything," said Audrey. "I'm not certain how I feel about that. Things shouldn't work out so easily for me. I did a horrible thing. I was an unfaithful wife."

"I don't see easy," said Lynn. "You lost a man for whom you cared deeply. You lost your husband in a horrible manner. Your children are caught in a media storm that they may not understand fully, but they still know something bad happened. Your family will never be the same. One young man lost his only relative and advocate. And you still have to get up every morning and be a full-time single parent and find a job to keep you and your children together. I don't see anything easy."

They sat quietly while Audrey thought about Lynn's little speech. Finally she said, "Mr. Templeton, I want to work with you. But I want to take some time to settle my children in a new home and new school."

"Why don't you begin by working for me part time? My staff can help you resettle. I'm certain Lynn and your friends here in River Bend can help you close out your life here." He stood. "I'm taking this as a 'yes' and hope in the coming months to have you ready to meet the challenge I've laid out." David shook her hand, gave Lynn a quick hug and left the office.

The two women sat for some minutes while Audrey tried to contain her tears. "It's too good. I don't deserve anything. But I must do this for my kids."

Lynn moved closer and put an arm around the woman. "Take everything David has to offer. You will do great work. I know it."

"Maybe I can work for him as part of my redemption." Audrey gathered her things, gave Lynn a hug and left the office, guilt like a cloud around her.

Lynn thought about the meeting. David was a very practical man and very committed to serving his son and others like him. Audrey had the skills he needed. Maybe this *would* be her redemption. Maybe she would find a new and rewarding life with her work and her children. Maybe one day she would finally be happy again.

* * *

The proliferation of breweries around the region made it easy for two men to meet quietly at a small brewery without drawing attention. Walter Varney and Ralph Ebetts sampled the in-house brew along a popular trail as they watched hikers drift into the parking lot, tired and thirsty. "What happened in that cabin?" Ebetts asked.

"Fish and I were inspecting that new line of guns the guys got from Cuba." Varney was clearly disgusted with events. "No one had been at that cabin since they raided Mahaffey. Two months! My contact said the heat was off, and then that asshole Decker barges in. He recognized me because we played together in some charity golf tournament."

"I only saw the report in the Chronicle online story. Fill me in."

"He sort of applied for the job to replace Mahaffey and keep the operation going." Varney sipped his brew and rolled his eyes. "I gave him some pills. Told him I needed someone to try them before I ordered more. Once he was unconscious, we cleared out. Fish set it up to look like the guy was heating something on the stove and fell asleep."

"What's your dirty cop say?"

Varney nodded. "Yeah, I didn't trust the newspaper story either. So I had him nose around. The River Bend cops say accidental fire and death by smoke inhalation. Some hikers saw the fire before the body could burn. Damn, it would have been easier that way." He shrugged. "But I still got my results."

Ebetts pulled his baseball cap lower. The sun was moving and there was a glare. "You don't expect anyone to look deeper?"

"Nah," he shook his head, "My guy says the River Bend cops got enough other crime to worry about. Some gunman tried to hold some kids hostage, then tried to rob a brewery."

Ebetts knew that story, too. That fool CJ Kirtley! Ebetts was just glad the consortium had ignored Kirtley when he hinted at his interest in drug money. Another asshole just like Mahaffey, guys with money and never satisfied. They shoudda been born poor then they would appreciate what they got. They wouldn't need crime to make more. But he got back to his conversation with Varney. "Does this leave a hole in your operation? Where do you stash merchandise?"

"Fish has been working on a guy at the botanical gardens." Varney sipped his beer. "Another guy who wants more than he has. My barge takes plants from the gardens and delivers them across the river to some organic greenhouses. He has a shed near the dock and lets us slide crates in there. When the gardens shut down my guys go in and move the merchandise."

"No one sees you?"

"It's a work area near the river filled with crates, barrels and old equipment. We don't go near the gardens, just enter a back way along an old farm track."

That got Ebetts thinking. "How reliable is your guy?"

"As long as we pay him, he doesn't care what we do."

"Has he met you?"

"Nah, he talks to the bargemen and meets Fish for payment." He scowled. "Only that asshole Decker ever saw me. And he can't tell anyone."

* * *

Audrey looked at her children and knew they didn't understand any of this. How would she explain? "Daddy has gone to heaven." The two older children looked at her for more information. The baby, only four, just sat on her lap burying her face in Audrey's shoulder.

"What will happen to us?" asked her son, Logan.

"I have a new job in Raleigh. We'll move there and have a new house and a new school."

"My house?" cried Maya, the baby.

"I don't want to leave our house," argued Alex, the middle child.

"We have to, honey," said Audrey, "we have to go where Mommy can get a new job." She pulled the other two children into her arms. "We'll have to be brave."

"We move to Daddy?" Maya didn't understand death.

"No, sweetheart, Daddy moved to heaven." Audrey knew what she would be doing for years to come—manufacturing memories that helped her children remember their loving father. She would ignore the flaws. She would ignore her flaws, too.

Her first job was to take advantage of Templeton, Inc. assistance for new employees. They were ready to help her find a house and find a school and daycare. She would move into her new job in a few weeks and looked forward to being with her friend, Rory Prentiss as they both tried to turn the Lela Templeton Foundation into the granting vehicle that the family would be proud of.

* * *

Quinn listened. Chop. Chop. The sounds of Mouse preparing dinner. How had he never noticed those great sounds in his previous life? He was even learning how to do a few things, like set the table and empty the dishwasher. He started toward the kitchen, certain she would find things for him to do. Mouse never disappointed.

Before he could enter the room, Colt charged into the kitchen with some shopping bags. He came in through the back door all sweaty and out of breath. "I didn't want to be late for dinner." He flopped his bags on the kitchen table.

"You went shopping?" Mouse asked as she continued to chop peppers. Quinn was certain it would be a fajita night. Yum!

"I took my bike and rode on the greenway. I was safe," said Colt, and Mouse nodded her understanding. "I got some soccer shoes."

Mouse put down her knife a little hard, Quinn froze in the doorway. His wife's attitude signaled some sort of confrontation with Colt. He thought he would listen before he leaped.

"Colt, we bought you new shoes when you made the team. We even got you two pair because you said you needed a practice pair and a game pair." Mouse sighed. Quinn knew why. She always had trouble with this money thing and kids having too much. He reminded himself he was listening, not leaping, as he hunched in the shadows out of sight, making certain his ears were focused.

"I gave my practice shoes away."

"What?" Mouse was trying to stay calm. Quinn could almost hear her thinking about having to buy shoes for the whole team. He could afford to do that, but Mouse still had money issues.

Colt rattled the bag and pulled out a shoe box. "The goalie didn't have any shoes. I gave him mine." He sounded as though he were admitting to murder.

Mouse wiped her hands on a towel and walked toward the boy. "You gave your shoes to a boy who had none?"

Colt hung his head. "His dad's in jail for hitting his mom and they couldn't buy him school supplies and stuff. We all gave him things."

Mouse threw her arms around him. "You're one of the best deals that I got in this marriage." She kissed her new son.

"Hey, hey," called Quinn as he came into the kitchen. "What's all this kissing?

"Our son," Mouse dashed a tear from her eye, "is perfect."

Colt grinned.

* * *

Lynn flopped into bed. Dusty walked out of the bathroom, water glistening in his hair from a quick shower. They had just returned to town after helping Jason move into his apartment at law school. "He won't starve," said Dusty. "You left his place with enough ramen noodles."

She moaned. "I hope he buys some fruit and vegetables."

Dusty laughed. "We can always join one of those mail order food services."

"Let's see if he figures it out first. Besides I have too much work at the office without Rory. Jason will have to find his own food."

"Things should be quiet for a while." He tossed his towel in the direction of the hamper.

"After the summer of drama, I hope so." She started to list names. "Who would have thought Sara and Quinn? And Audrey losing both men in her life."

Dusty crawled under the covers beside her. "What's your analysis? Is everyone on the right track?" He nibbled her ear.

"Sara and Quinn are." She sighed into his arms. "I hope Audrey finds some peace. Rory will stay in Raleigh another month to help her and to wrap up his commitment to the Templeton Foundation."

"That Quinn sure took up a lot of my staff's time."

Lynn struggled to raise on her elbow. "What do you mean? He didn't kidnap Sara's kids. He didn't rob the brewery. He didn't cause another FBI raid!"

Dusty pulled her back to his arms. "I know. But he was related to it all. I just hope Sara keeps him out of my hair."

Lynn laughed. "I'm sure she'll think of something." And she showed Dusty what she was thinking.

THE END

Love Returns

The River Bend Chronicles - Book 23

Moving into Autumn Lynn and her family are wrapped up in Rachel Teague's mayor election. It reminds Lynn of the days she worked on her father's campaigns. But the days up to the election hold drama: the old Sheriff dies and politicians jockey for appointment to the post; murders occur at the botanical gardens; and an old love returns.

By the time Rachel's election is secure, the gang has moved on to preparations for the appointment of the new sheriff. At the same time the friends of the botanical gardens are soliciting a donation of additional land for expansion. Lynn orchestrates several donor opportunities and, in spite of the murder of the retiring director, the botanical gardens gains more property and supporting funds for needed improvements.

Introducing A New Series
by Renee Kumor (2025)
Annabella

Book 1: "Cloaked in Loneliness"
Wyoming 1890. Annabella Chase was sent out west to teach
by a brother who didn't want his sister intruding on his marriage.
She spent almost ten years as a lonely spinster teacher moving from
one school to another each time moving further west. One day
having lost her enthusiasm for teaching she answered an ad for a
wife, marrying a widower with a young son, becoming Annabella
Chase Winters. An accident claimed her husband and stepson
within a year of marriage. The father-in-law she had never met
invited her to live with him in remote Wyoming. Accepting the
invitation she arrived in Deep Wells, Wyoming, and her life was
never dull and lonely again.

Book 2 "A Growing Business"
Five years ago Annabella Chase Winters came to Deep Wells,
Wyoming. Five years later she is married to a prosperous rancher,
the mother of nine children, waiting to meet the young woman her
oldest son, Patrick plans to marry. A natural disaster and a
terminated engagement begin a year of her older children trying to
define their roles in the world. As the youngsters find their way,
Dell, Annabella's husband, begins to organize his land and related
businesses into a functioning operation that will serve his family
into the next generation, much like the corporations beginning to
function throughout the country.

About The Author

RENEE KUMOR was a stay-at-home mom for several years developing a personal ethic of community service. She began writing a political opinion column for the local newspaper, but retired from writing when she announced her candidacy for local political office. After eight years as a county commissioner, she returned to non-profit service and began writing a monthly column for the newspaper on non-profit management and service issues. The setting for the *River Bend Chronicles* series reflects her early life in Ohio and her later years in western North Carolina.

For sales, editorial information, subsidiary rights information
or a catalog, please write or phone or e-mail

AbsolutelyAmazingEbooks
Manhanset House
Shelter Island Hts., New York 11965, US
Tel: 212-427-7139
www.AbsolutelyAmazingEbooks.com
bricktower@aol.com
www.IngramContent.com

For sales in the UK and Europe please contact our distributor,
Gazelle Book Services
White Cross Mills
Lancaster, LA1 4XS, UK
Tel: (01524) 68765 Fax: (01524) 63232
email: jacky@gazellebooks.co.uk

www.ingramcontent.com/pod-product-compliance
Lightning Source LLC
Chambersburg PA
CBHW051149030726
47504CB00004B/1108